For my friend Rose,

who came to Elba and fell in love

"What's past is prologue."

—*The Tempest*

Lizzie & Dante

Chapter One

JULY 13, 2019

Water sliced past the boat in a froth of deep blue and grey, the kind of froth that made you think about pollutants. Off in the distance, the island of Elba was a dim green mound.

Elba isn't known for much. It produces a perfume called Acqua dell'Elba that smells of white flowers and the sea. It's regularly visited by yachts the size of the *Titanic*. But mostly, it's the island where Napoleon was exiled with a throwaway title, Emperor of Elba.

Lizzie Rose Delford was headed to Elba because of Napoleon's whining comment, *Able was I, ere I saw Elba.*

It had a dark humor that worked for Lizzie. A stupid little sentence, although the English professor in her noted that "Able was I" was an aphorism and a factoid, as well as a palindrome. Symmetrical, beautiful, and meaningful in its own dark way. To Lizzie: perfect.

Not that any woman with Stage Three cancer could call herself "able."

An arm abruptly wrapped around her shoulders. "Rohan sent me up to see if we're about to capsize."

The boat was pitching in a strong wind. Lizzie rubbed her head against Grey's chest. "We're fine."

"Is that Elba?"

Lizzie nodded. "Should Rohan know? Would he want to come up?"

"No. He's down in the cabin pretending to be nauseated so he can do the *Times* crossword in peace." Grey drew her closer, tucked her into the crook of his arm. "Remember that time when we almost capsized on the way to Lesvos?"

Lizzie leaned against him, loving the lean strength of his body and the Georgia drawl he'd never managed to get rid of, though he complained that there was nothing more out of place than a southern man living in L.A. "I dreamed about it for years after," she admitted.

He opened his mouth and shut it. Probably about to tell her, again, that she should confront her demons, before he thought better of it. Screw her demons.

Elba grew larger in a lumpy sort of way, and German tourists standing in the helm took numerous pictures with their cellphones. The water turned clear turquoise closer to the shore, little white-caps glinting like sparklers.

Stores lined the harbor, and above them, smoky pink and saffron buildings sprawled on rounded hills.

"The town looks so accidental," Lizzie said, liking the way the houses piled on top of each other and spilled down narrow streets.

"Italians don't do city planners," Grey said.

A half hour later, Lizzie humped her suitcase down the narrow metal stairs and got herself out of the belly of their ferry, the *Moby-Dick*. Once on shore, she stopped.

The pitted cement at her feet was so hot that it seemed to undulate. The air even smelled hot, like brilliant sunlight turned corporeal. Close up, the saffron buildings were cheerfully yellow and orange, and looked even more disordered.

Italians streamed by her, chattering loudly, their tickets littering the ground like confetti. Perhaps they had come over for the day, since they had no luggage.

Someone recognized Rohan. No, a whole group of someones.

He was smiling, likely telling them how much he enjoyed being an Avenger, or an ER doctor, or, since they were middle-aged, lauding the days when he played a feisty kid in a well-meaning gang, he and his buddies roaming around, airing their tats, and accidentally doing good deeds.

Lizzie had watched a few episodes three years ago, after Grey told her he'd met Rohan.

Not, I met a famous actor, or one of *People*'s most beautiful people, but: "I met a man named Rohan." That was enough to get her to watch a couple of Marvel movies, a lot of *Diagnosis: Unknown*, and a bit of *In the Hood*.

Grey was striding toward her, brown satchel over one shoulder. It looked like the same satchel he'd had when they wandered around Europe before she went to grad school.

"A coven of fans," he said unnecessarily.

"You can't fall in love with Rohan Das and expect to avoid his fans," Lizzie pointed out.

"I could have fallen in love with an unsuccessful actor."

"True. All those gorgeous failures in L.A. to choose from, and you somehow decided on the 'most beautiful.'"

"Don't bring it up," Grey said, elbowing her. "He really thought he might get the cover this year."

"Oh, for Christ's sake," Lizzie said, sitting down on her suitcase.

"He's not bad for a Hollywood type."

"I like him," Lizzie said. "I really do."

Grey reached over and tousled her hair. "I really like your curls."

"Here he comes," Lizzie said.

Rohan was striding down the cement toward them. Narrow-hipped and broad-shouldered, he looked taller as a Marvel hero than he did in real life. In the Italian sunshine, his skin was a shade darker and warmer than the tea-dyed linen he wore. Grey turned and they watched together as Rohan slipped on sunglasses, jacket slung over one shoulder.

"Why no luggage?" Lizzie asked.

"His assistant sent his stuff to the hotel last week."

Lizzie tried and failed to imagine having so many clothes that she could mail them ahead. "He's even more handsome than the billboard."

"Weird, right?" Grey said, one side of his mouth quirking up.

She got it. Whenever she caught sight of Rohan's underwear ad in Times Square—a gorgeous forty-year-old sprawled on a couch in boxers—she had to wrestle with the fact that he was a real person, let alone that she knew him, and was going on vacation with him.

"Because he's a regular guy?" she asked.

"Because he's mine," Grey said. His happiness was usually unspoken, so Lizzie stood up and kissed his cheek.

"What's that for?" he asked, squinting at her.

"A salute to certainty, which isn't your forte, you have to admit."

Once Rohan joined them, two men appeared out of nowhere, picked up Lizzie's suitcase, and drove them halfway around the island to a village made up of a few hotels and a handful of houses. Their hotel was low and white, with lavender shutters closed against the sun.

The hotel manager rushed to meet them, not to ask for passports and credit cards, but to offer prosecco in a shady courtyard. They sat down under a huge oak tree, at a table that had faded from violet to a gentler hue.

Lizzie couldn't stop grinning. The hotel was way above her pay grade, but Grey had asked her to join them with the excuse that

Rohan had wrangled his first deal as director—a new film version of *Romeo and Juliet*—and she was a Shakespeare professor. Time was, Lizzie might have been affronted by such obvious charity.

She thought about it. No, she'd still have taken the vacation, but she would have insisted on Paris instead of Elba.

After they were escorted to their rooms—whitewashed walls, lavender windowsills, fresh flowers—Lizzie had a shower and unpacked, pulling on a short raspberry-colored linen dress that almost felt equal to the hotel before she went back to the courtyard.

Grey and Rohan were there already. Rohan had a copy of *Romeo and Juliet* tucked in the fold of the *Times*. "I've always wanted to direct Shakespeare," he told her. "I plan to make Romeo relevant, you know? I played Mercutio in high school and most of the cast didn't get it. I knew right then that someday I would make the play everything it could be."

When they were together, Lizzie tended to forget that Rohan was a movie star. He never flaunted it. But when he focused his attention on her, the contours of his face came into focus and she found herself nodding every time he paused.

"Roh's not just directing," Grey said, squinting across at Lizzie. "He's writing a new script."

"I have to, don't I, to make it relevant," Rohan said. "No offense, Lizzie." He flipped the book over on the table and spread his hand on top, as if he was pinning it to the wood. "Great writer, but this language doesn't work. Grey thinks I might have trouble writing the script."

"There's an art to writing," Grey said.

That was the weary response he gave to random readers who told him that they too planned to write a bestseller, just as soon as they had time.

"I sleep with a bestselling author," Rohan pointed out, grinning. "I've got a leg up on those poor sods at your book signings."

"Sleeping with Hitchcock wouldn't make me a better horror writer," Grey retorted, but he reached out and squeezed Rohan's knee.

"There's your next plot," Lizzie said, feeling third-wheel-ish. "The ghost of Hitchcock seduces would-be screenwriters and improves their scripts while they sleep."

"My point is that I have Grey to help," Rohan said. "And I have you, Lizzie, a real Shakespeare professor. I've been jonesing for this project my whole life. It's my chance to sink my teeth into something deep, with *substance*."

"Have you read any other Shakespeare plays?" Lizzie inquired.

"Sure. I was actually taking an elocution class, working on *Othello,* when O.J. started driving down that highway in L.A. My teacher loved it."

Loved it?

"I haven't had time to reread *Othello* since, but the play stuck with me. Iago came along, a sweet-talking white guy, and drove Othello crazy, talked him into killing his wife."

"You remember the play as being about Iago?"

"Yeah. He made Othello do it. He drove him crazy."

As Lizzie saw it, every Shakespeare play was like a kaleidoscope: You could shake it and come out with an entirely different script every time. "How about if we discuss *Romeo and Juliet* after you finish rereading it?"

Rohan nodded. "I just have to take a call from my agent."

"Don't be too long," Grey said, bumping Rohan's shoulder with his own. Not a kiss, because they were in public, but still sweet, she decided, watching Rohan's face ease.

"I've figured out this hotel," she told Grey in the early evening, as they waited for Rohan to stop talking to strangers. "Yacht people empty out here." They were seated in the parlor, which was frescoed up the wazoo and dotted with clusters of low sofas and bronze statues of lean ancient Etruscans.

Grey looked around, owlish and disinterested. "There does seem to be a preponderance of good bloodlines here. Likely the effect of generations of powerful men marrying the most beautiful women they could find."

"I count four teenagers and not one has acne," Lizzie said. "Let alone lumpy hips and a hangdog look."

Grey shrugged. "Acne wasn't my biggest problem growing up. I don't remember you breaking out."

"I must have a drop of yacht blood in me." Since she had no idea who her father was—neither had her mother—she had always felt free to speculate about her ancestry.

"The hotel made a lot of promises about Roh having room to breathe, and people not bothering him," Grey said.

Rohan returned with the news that he'd run into an old friend. "We were at school together when I was a kid, in Bournemouth. Her name's Ruby. And get this, she's a makeup artist now."

Lizzie looked over. A pretty woman with twisted curls and a pointed chin waved, so she waved back. "Film or fashion?"

"Normally films, but she's working on a yacht right now," Rohan said, jerking his head at a corner crammed with more beautiful people than the Oscars. He picked up the *acqua frizzante* that Grey had ordered for him. "Cheers."

"How'd you do with *Romeo and Juliet* this afternoon?" Lizzie asked.

"I didn't get to it," Rohan said. "I was trapped for hours trying to sort out the bloody script for my next Marvel movie. I'll be damned if Captain Britain has to kiss Captain America's ass again. They're promising to give me my own arc."

"Didn't you tell me that Marvel could kiss *your* ass?" The waiter had brought them a plate of hors d'oeuvres: olives, tiny pizzas, and curls of prosciutto balanced on melon medallions. Lizzie picked up a pizza that smelled like fresh rosemary.

"Yeah." Rohan downed his sparkling water. "I had to give in to get *Romeo*. Loads of CGI, boring as hell, six months on set, but worth it because after that, I'll finally be doing a project that could make a difference. They wouldn't give me a go-ahead on *Romeo* unless I committed to the Avengers."

"I still have nightmares about failing the *Hamlet* quiz sophomore year," Grey said. He had eaten through a pile of olives, putting the pits neatly to the side, and was starting on the pizzas.

"I'm not worried about understanding the language. The play is in my bones. I know all about men," Rohan said, "and that's what interested Shakespeare, obviously. How's your room, Lizzie?"

"Marvelous," she said, snatching a pizza before Grey could finish them.

"The hotel has a private beach," Rohan said, eyes happy. "I'm going to do yoga every morning, early. Be alone, in a way I haven't been in years. Spend the rest of the day writing the screenplay I've dreamed of doing my whole life."

"Sounds like bliss," Grey said, irony leaking into his voice.

Rohan squinted at him. "Mind the negativity. Stop worrying about me. I can see the screenplay in my head." He sprang to his feet. "I'm not hungry. You guys eat. I'm going for a run on the beach."

They watched him leave, stopping to exchange greetings with yet another yachtful.

"What did he mean that he knows men?" Lizzie said. "Is his Romeo gay?"

"You think I got him to bring you because I want you to come with us on vacation," Grey said. "That wasn't it. This production might be a phenomenal failure. Marvel ventures into Shakespeare: A disaster couldn't get more public, right?"

Lizzie eyed him. "You need to up your supportive spouse game."

"I'm not his spouse. And you know how I feel about people who think that writing is an easy gig."

"Is Marvel making him set the production in outer space?"

Grey shook his head. "Stan Lee, Marvel's overlord, loved *Romeo*. One of the last things he did before he died was adapt the play into a graphic novel. They're proposing Roh's version as a tribute to Stan. Which doesn't mean that the critics won't savage it, even without CGI and spandex."

"Probably more so," Lizzie agreed.

"How are you feeling?" Grey asked.

"Fine," Lizzie said. "How's the new book coming along? We haven't talked in ages."

"Are you really fine?" Grey frowned at her, managing to look like Gregory Peck's Atticus, in the trial scene. Big question to him, in other words.

Not a question she wanted to delve into.

"Yes," she said. "Book?"

"It's going. Remember when we moved into that first apartment in New Haven, and I wrote all day long?"

"Stained carpet," Lizzie said, wrinkling her nose. "We didn't have any furniture."

"Not to mention the murder next door. But what I mean is that back then my mind was boiling with ideas. I could scarcely breathe because so many plots wanted to be written."

"I mostly remember trying to fit in with Ivy Leaguers, while you only wanted to talk about the fungus in the bathroom."

"Fungus got me my first contract. Horror is all about the little stuff. This book isn't boiling out of me, the way they used to."

"Maybe you should set a novel on a yacht." Lizzie waved her

hand. "You're always writing about normal people; how about ter-rifying the one percent for a change?"

"On the plane, I got the idea that I could do something with mold spores," he said. "But it isn't working."

The waiter went by, so Lizzie asked for more pizza.

"Returning to the question of spouses," she said, putting her elbow on the table and propping her chin on her hand. "Are you two going to get married one of these days? Big Hollywood wed-ding with helicopters overhead?"

Grey shook his head.

"Why not? You've lived together for, what, two years now?"

"As his friend, the bestselling author, who is supposedly writing a script."

"That's kind of shitty," Lizzie said, trying to keep indignation out of her voice.

"It's not Roh. He wants to marry me, come out, the whole thing. He's sick of being a superhero, and he wants to be an artist."

"And love publicly," Lizzie said, nodding. She chose her words carefully. "So you're the one saying no to that, why?"

"He's not looking ahead. His career will die. Captain Britain can't be gay. No more jobs, no more *People,* no more underwear ads, that's for damn sure."

Exhaustion was making the skin around Lizzie's eyes feel tight. She couldn't ask, *Isn't that up to Rohan to decide?* She liked Rohan, liked him even more knowing that he wanted to marry her best friend.

"Roh is dramatic and emotional, and I'm not," Grey said, an-swering the question she didn't ask. "You and I, we run away from the tough stuff. Roh falls into it. No, he runs toward it."

"Runs toward emotion?" Lizzie had no idea what Grey was talk-ing about, maybe because she was so tired.

"He's eager. Permeable. He's—and this is ridiculous—he lets himself be unknowing. Over and over."

Lizzie couldn't make head or tail of that.

"Innocent," Grey said. "Choosing *Romeo and Juliet,* for Christ's sake. I'm terrified for him, but he isn't. He's excited."

"You're a worrier," Lizzie said. "Maybe not worrying is the actor thing?"

He shook his head. "I've met lots of them in the last few years. They're a hardened breed, overall. Rohan is . . . I'm lucky to love Roh. But marriage is a big step." He was on his feet. "I want to have dinner in my room."

She didn't believe that, but old friends should accept obvious fibs.

"I'll order some pasta and have it sent to your room too."

"What kind?" she asked.

He shrugged. "Something simple that you'll like. I'm sure it's all good here."

They walked up the stairs together as if they were going to the same room, but she turned at the end of the hall and opened the door to her own. A lovely pool of silence greeted her. After a shower, she sat in her pajamas on the balcony, overlooking the Mediterranean. Room service had brought her pasta with a sauce apparently made from a lemon and a sprig of rosemary, which managed to be incredible.

She found herself asking unanswerable questions rather than avoiding them.

How did she feel?

She felt curious.

Were there ever dinosaurs on Elba? Had they looked up at the stars, or out at the darkening sea?

At breakfast the next day, Rohan informed them that he had done yoga on the beach at dawn. "You should join me tomorrow morning," he told Lizzie, having long ago decided Grey was a lost cause.

"Do you see the horror in my eyes?" she demanded.

He peered at her. "No."

"I have a free pass from exercise," she said patiently. It wasn't the first time she'd explained this. Cancer would never stop Rohan: He would topple over and die in the tree pose, so her explanation never seemed to sink in.

They talked superheroes over crusty bread and jam made from wild blueberries. Then Grey went back to his writing, Rohan pulled out *Romeo and Juliet,* and Lizzie took a last slice of bread and wandered down to the public beach, not the hotel's exclusive patch of sand. The path to the beach was built from weathered boards and lined with lazily commercial stores full of shells painted to look like ferrets, and handbags woven out of seagrass. They weren't doing much business.

She rented an umbrella that came with a flat sunbed and a chair, which she folded up. She had neighbors, but they carefully circled around her patch when going to swim.

Italians were very polite.

Dogs? Not so much.

The dog that trotted over to greet her had the kind of hair that bristled in some places and lay down in others. She was scruffy and ugly and very fond of licking.

She could have been homeless, a wandering dog, given the way she gave so many kisses and wagged her small bony behind. She put on a good display of ecstasy after being given a bite of Lizzie's jam toast.

"But homeless dogs," Lizzie said to her severely, "don't wear velvet collars with the name Lulu embroidered on them."

Lulu flopped down and rolled over, showing a scruffy stomach with sagging nipples that had seen better days.

"I'm not a dog person," Lizzie told her.

Lulu was too busy wagging her tail in the sand to be insulted. Lizzie ended up scratching the dog's belly, because it seemed the polite thing to do. Later, when the sun moved, Lizzie dragged her bed around to stay under the umbrella. Lulu wanted to be in the shade too, so she crowded Lizzie over, and they went to sleep.

Like that. With Lulu's back against Lizzie's stomach, the way that lovers sleep in films. Except that Lulu was moonlighting and presumably belonged to someone else's umbrella, and Lizzie didn't do lovers anymore.

Lulu snored, which was par for the course. Lizzie's previous lovers had always snored. She knew because she couldn't sleep with someone in her bed, so during those years when she had entertained men, she generally didn't sleep much. Or at all.

A hangover from foster care.

Not that Lizzie had had an unpleasant experience in foster care, because she hadn't. She was one of the lucky ones, whose various foster mothers had cared about the job. But she had learned quickly that one's bed was never really one's own, because at any moment a fraught social worker might drive up in a battered car with three kids who'd end up in "your" bed, while you moved to the couch.

It was so obvious that Lulu wasn't someone to worry about that even Lizzie's absurd subconscious finally accepted it.

An hour after she fell asleep, she woke up with the panicky feeling that she had gotten behind on her meds. Could she have? No. Sometimes just remembering that she had taken the pills helped. Before her nap, she had washed one down with sparkling water.

There was a man sitting between her umbrella and the sea, where the children usually played, reading. Lizzie sat up, spilling Lulu onto the ground.

"Excuse me," she said, not quietly. "That's my book."

"That's my dog," he said, looking up. He was as scruffy as Lulu, and his nose had a distinct bend, as if he'd been in a fight. Dark hair tousled in a sandy, windy way. Facial hair. It was short, but still a beard.

Lulu was licking his ear, so she guessed he had a point.

"*Romeo and Juliet,* huh?"

Lizzie always woke up irritable, even more so since she was on so many meds. Sleep dragged at her cheekbones and made it impossible to smile. "Yeah," she said flatly. Now he would either reel off a verse or two, or confess that he never understood the Bard. Or that his fourth-grade teacher saved his life.

He quoted from *Macbeth.*

At least it wasn't tomorrow and tomorrow and the whole petty pace thing. Now that she didn't have many tomorrows left, she'd lost all patience for Macbeth's self-centered response to his wife's suicide.

"Live you?" he asked with a grin. "Or are you aught that man may question?"

"Questions are out," she said, pulling her sunglasses back down over her eyes. "Do I look like a witch to you?" Stupid question. "Don't answer that," she added. "Are you sitting on my hat?"

"No." He stopped staring at her and looked around. "Is it a pointy black hat? Didn't the *Macbeth* witches wear wild clothing?"

Lizzie was wearing her favorite new bikini: white eyelet embroidered with yellow flowers and crochet trim. The queen of England might consider it wild, but no one else. He must be trying to pick her up. He must be desperate.

She got herself to her feet. So what if she'd paid twenty euros for the umbrella? She could give it up for the pleasure of getting herself away from the amateur Shakespearean reading her book.

She gave him a smile, one without any joy. "I'm so sorry, but I'm going to my hotel now. May I have the play back?"

"Where are you staying?"

Oh, great. This was like those stories about countries where you were pestered to go stay in somebody's cousin's hotel, and the only way they could identify you later was by your fillings. "I'm not interested in meeting an Italian man, and I don't need a recommendation for a hotel," she told him.

"I live in America most of the year," he said.

"America is a big place."

"Do you live in New York?"

"Absolutely not." It was a lie.

Lulu pranced up to her, an orange straw hat in her mouth. "Bad dog," Lizzie said, but she couldn't help laughing. Lulu wagged her tail and danced backward.

Lizzie dropped to her knees, holding out her hand. "Please give me my hat."

He intervened. "Lulu."

Lulu looked at him sideways and shook the hat.

"*Lulu.*"

She pranced over to Lizzie and dropped it at her feet.

"Sweet dog," Lizzie said, rubbing her ears. "You're a good dog, aren't you?"

"Do you ever—"

Lizzie had found that honesty could be devastatingly effective. "Please," she said, standing up again and letting the smile fall off her face. "I want to be alone."

He stood up and handed over the play, and didn't even look sulky, which was a miracle. Or perhaps it meant that he shambled around the beach all the time, getting turned down. He had to be in his forties, after all. He had nice muscular legs, but he was no youngster, like the Italians strutting up and down in their miniature Speedos.

"You should go to Fabrizio's for lunch," he said. "It's the pink one, down that way. Just tell me one thing. Why are you reading *Romeo*? Isn't that high school fare?"

"And college. I teach Shakespeare in a university."

"That's even less of an answer. A busman's honeymoon."

"What?"

"Haven't you read Dorothy Sayers's mysteries?"

Lizzie shook her head. Violence was all very well couched in sixteenth-century language, but otherwise—no. She didn't go anywhere near Grey's novels, for example.

"A busman's honeymoon is a phrase from the 1940s referring to a man who drives a bus for honeymooners, so he's bored to death when it's his turn. Why *Romeo*?"

Lizzie shrugged and tugged her hat over her eyes. "I guess I like the smell of petrol and the squawking of honeymooners."

He nodded and snapped his fingers at Lulu. They wandered off down the beach as Lizzie watched to make sure that he went.

He had a nice ass. Worth watching. He didn't look back.

Fabrizio's was painted the faint pink color of the inside of a seashell. It was weather-beaten and old, and no one from a yacht would consider eating there. The dining room smelled like salt and tomato sauce, though the windows were open to sea air and screaming gulls.

A teenage waitress, sullen and pierced, served Lizzie a dish of polenta with wild mushroom sauce. It was crispy and savory, and came with a little pitcher of Elba wine, which looked milky white and bubbled slightly, like flat champagne.

She wasn't supposed to drink, not with her meds. The Elba wine slid down her throat with guilty pleasure, like a cigarette smoked in a middle school bathroom.

After lunch she waded into the sea. She had made brownies once that tasted as salty as seawater. She had measured salt instead of sugar, and her foster mother had laughed and thrown them out.

After reclaiming her umbrella, she watched children killing jellyfish. The jellyfish were transparent pink, a clearer color than Fabrizio's walls. The children were scooping them out of the water in little pails and digging holes to bury them.

After a while she couldn't watch anymore because she started to wonder if jellyfish had central nervous systems. And if they did, what did they experience when they were pulled out of the salty water in which they bobbled and swayed, and found themselves buried in—

It wasn't a line of thought worth pursuing.

When she woke, the Italian mothers were tidying up their children, screaming at them in cheerful voices. The sun was low over the ocean, a fiery ball surrounded by layers of red and orange. The shadows of umbrellas stretched out like the ghosts of long, lean Etruscans.

She watched as the sun slid down, lower and lower. The change between there and gone was so fast . . . a slow dip and then a plunge.

Back in the hotel, Rohan was in the courtyard, but he didn't want to talk about Shakespeare.

"I still haven't got past the first act." He was wearing such dark glasses that she couldn't see his eyes. "I need to ease into it."

"Why?"

"I didn't remember that Romeo was such a dunce. I want the film to be about manhood, and Romeo prances over the stage whining about being in love."

That was true.

"I often teach it as comedy," Lizzie offered. "At least until the end when the tomb gets crowded. From that point of view, it's very modern. The Coen brothers would love it."

Rohan frowned at her. "Are you saying I should get RuPaul to play Romeo? *Oh me, what fray was here!* I'm being backed by Marvel, aka Disney, so I'm seeing some problems with a drag queen playing the hero."

"It would be fun," Lizzie said, starting to get into it. "The first scene could be hysterical. All the swords and blood—and Romeo wants to have lunch?"

"Yeah, he's hungry. And then he throws himself on the ground. At least, I think that's what he does. He clearly doesn't give a damn

about Rosaline rejecting him. He doesn't really want her. No testosterone."

"He's very young."

"I told Marvel that Romeo was at the heart of the modern male
consciousness—and I didn't mean queer preteen consciousness."

Lizzie grinned and patted Rohan on the shoulder. "You could
switch to the Public Theater in New York. They staged Constable
Elbow from *Measure for Measure* in a diaper. They won't care
what you do."

He looked at her incredulously. "This is a film, Lizzie. A major
film." He dropped the play on the ground. "I'm thinking of setting
it in an American public school, maybe in Minnesota. The important thing is that Romeo has all these dudes around him, his wing-
men."

"Rival gangs have been done. *West Side Story*."

"I can't go anywhere near gangs, or all I'll hear about is what a
wanking terrible actor I was at fifteen. No, my *Romeo* is about men
who are friends, real friends, who'd die for each other. I'll put race
in there too, make Romeo Indian and Mercutio white."

"Interesting," Lizzie said, pulling on her hat and thinking that
his characters sounded like Rohan and Grey, not Romeo and Mercutio. "You're going to have to cut a lot of the play. Where does
Juliet fit in?"

"Obviously I have to write some extra scenes," Rohan said, nar-
rowing his eyes. "It won't be too hard because I can *see* what this
play needs."

Jesus.

Time to go.

Chapter Two

The next day, Lizzie rented an umbrella in sight of the seashore and the children's jellyfish massacres. She paid for a month, and then pulled out *Romeo*.

If Rohan turned the play into a celebration of dudes, what would happen to the balcony scene? She got up to fold away the extra chair and tilt the umbrella just so. Reluctantly, she returned to the sunbed and opened the play again.

What was a Minnesota teenager like, anyway? As opposed to one from the Bronx?

She put the book down and adjusted her sunglasses. The two kids closest to her umbrella were building something with rocks and sand. Their mother was sprawled in a seat, talking on her cellphone. Her hair was streaked the color of . . .

The weathered seat of an outdoor toilet.

That Norwegian goat cheese that smelled terrible.

The cork top of her old desk.

Not bad. She was out of practice. She used to do metaphor trios all the time, back when life was long, and she was going to write a novel.

Not true.

She found it remarkably easy to be honest to other people, which probably explained why she didn't have a special someone. That didn't mean that she was honest with herself.

She had never really meant to write a novel. She had planned to write a book about her childhood. A memoir, brisker and funnier than *Mommie Dearest,* not that she'd ever read it.

Some book that would be. Around three pages, since she could scarcely remember her mother, and she had no harrowing stories from foster care. Her water bottle was baking in the sun, and it scattered sand all over her medicine bag when she picked it up.

She snapped the play open, skimmed scene two. One problem was that there wasn't anyone evil in *Romeo and Juliet,* ready to take out Manhattan, a baddie like Voldemort. The three witches in *Macbeth* were theatrical gold, with the way they babbled about killing swine and tormenting sailors. Even when they awkwardly circled a pot, hand in hand.

How hokey was that? If only evil could always be visible. You could fight it then. You could do something about it. If only evil wore wild clothing and spoke in rhymes.

The worst evil snuck up, like a nasty compliment. It didn't announce itself the way Voldemort did, with shining signs filling the sky at night. You can't pretend to be good when your face is pasted on the back of someone else's body. Or if your only friend is a big snake.

Evil snuck into your blood at night, hiding, showing up under a microscope.

Of course, death was everywhere in *Romeo and Juliet.* The tomb was crammed with young dead people at the end. Death—

Lulu was on top of her, scrabbling up and licking her ear before Lizzie knew what was happening. Lizzie shoved her hard, and Lulu flopped backward off the sunbed onto the sand, still wiggling, and had to be scooped back up in a burst of regret after Lizzie took a quick look around and confirmed that Lulu was on her own.

"I'm sorry," she said, pulling Lulu's furry body back up next to hers. "I didn't know it was you. I didn't mean to throw you off."

Lulu lay down and panted. She was too hot, the poor dog. She should be at home, in one of those deeply shadowed Italian houses, built with walls so thick that heat never intruded. That man should be giving a damn about her.

"If you were mine, we'd be in the air-conditioning right now," Lizzie told her.

Lulu panted some more and wagged her tail. It wasn't much of a tail. Some of the hair on one side was missing. Lizzie picked it up for a closer look. "What happened to you, Lucy-Lu?" she asked. "It looks as if a rabid cat munched on you for breakfast." That wasn't a very good one. "Like a child came along and stripped your bark like a beech tree." The jellyfish killers must be getting to her. "Like . . ."

Of course, children were cruel. Her foster mothers had been nice, but the kids at school always knew. She would have had to relive middle school in order to write a memoir.

Embrace the suck, cancer patients say to each other. The upside of her diagnosis? Not thinking about eighth grade, ever again.

They managed to stay relatively cool for another hour. When Lulu panted hard, Lizzie poured water over her head. She put Shakespeare to the side and started reading a book about Georgian courtesans.

"I would have made a terrible courtesan," she told Lulu a while later. Lulu opened one eye. "I am very hardheaded when it comes to money, and these women seem to live for the moment. Plus . . . all those penises."

Lulu looked bored.

So far the book hadn't answered the questions she'd wanted to ask. One had to suppose that a courtesan didn't have the right to get a headache, as it were. But her period? What about that? Maybe men back in the 1800s were less squeamish than they are now.

She adjusted her hat so that it cast an orange glow over the pages and spared a moment for her first boyfriend, Jake, who'd been fussy when it came to bodily fluids. Sweet, but fussy.

She was still thinking about Jake, and whether it would be fair to blame her imperfect relationships on him (answer: no), when a shadow fell over her legs.

Lulu's owner brought a towel this time and threw himself down at Lizzie's feet as if they were old friends. Lulu went into transports of ecstasy, leaping off the sunbed, wagging her whole body.

"Ciao," he said, twisting away from Lulu's mouthy kisses enough to speak.

He was looking at her and smiling, so Lizzie said "Ciao" back. He was obviously not from the yachting contingent, which was a point in his favor. His hair was black with silver streaks, but his brows were still black. Most of the men in the hotel had hair that was resolutely dark, no matter their age.

"How's *Romeo* coming along?"

"Boring as a busman's honeymoon," she confessed.

"Why are you reading it, then? I can lend you a Terry Pratchett."

He liked satirical British fantasy? Another point in his favor.

"A friend of mine is directing a film version of *Romeo*. I've never read it with an actual performance in mind, let alone a movie."

"Are they doing it in iambic pentameter?" He looked vaguely alarmed. "I failed that test."

"Your professor made you accent a speech?" She only hammered on iambic pentameter if she disliked a class. Mostly, her students were lovable. Mostly.

"No, it was *scuola media*. Middle school to you." He shivered. "*Interrogazione,* otherwise known as ritual humiliation. Stand up next to your desk and read Shakespeare in iambic pentameter until you miss an accented syllable. We'd all been taking English for years, but no one could understand a word we were reading."

"Sounds tough."

"When you messed up, Mr. Baldini would hoot with laughter and make everyone clap for the dunce."

"Brutal," Lizzie said, impressed. "My students think that I'm being mean if I call on them."

"Americans like to complain. I have a restaurant, so I see it all the time."

"Aren't they allowed to offer an opinion about your cooking?" Lizzie asked, feeling defensive. It was sometimes hard to defend her countrymen, but she always did it, even if she had to fib.

"They think I'm mean because I won't give them exactly what they want."

"French fries? Hamburgers? What kind of food—" She broke off because that was a stupid question.

"Italian," he said, not bothered. "We love French fries; we just shape them differently. But I serve one dish every night with no substitutions."

Lizzie thought that over. "What about vegetarians?"

"I do vegetarians, nut allergies, and gluten. But I won't do vegans, and I won't make French fries on command."

She thought about pointing out that his restaurant might not thrive under those circs, but he likely didn't care.

He was flat on the sand now, only his head under the shade of the umbrella. He was wearing long swimming trunks covered with poppies. Lulu jumped back up onto the sunbed. He had his eyes closed, so Lizzie examined his body under the shade of her sun hat. It was a beautiful brown color. For someone who had a beard—albeit clipped short—he wasn't very hairy.

"My name is Lizzie," she said, after a while.

"You're going to love this, English professor," he said, sounding drowsy. "Dante."

She *did* love it. "If I ever had a son, I meant to name him Dante, Prospero, or Lucio."

He raised his head and peered at her. "Thirty?"

"Thirty-two, but not for long."

"Even if your birthday is tomorrow, you have time to have Dante, Prospero, and Lucio. Could I persuade you to avoid Dante? No one can spell it in the U.S. It's a pain in the ass."

His casual comment felt like a punch in the gut, the kind that sent Lizzie's mind racing down a familiar path: How could a thirty-year-old have been diagnosed with cancer? How— She pulled her mind away. If two years of cancer treatment had taught her anything, it was that there was no point in comparisons, or grieving for time (and children) she wouldn't have.

"I won't have a son named Dante," she said. She took a swig of water.

He sat up and looked at her. "Something's wrong."

He had beautiful eyes. They weren't unlike Lulu's, actually. Dark and sweet. Lizzie turned back to her book and read a couple of lines of the play. "Here and there," she said, not looking up. "A few little things, nothing much."

"Ah." He lay down again. "I have a twelve-year-old daughter."

Did his phrasing imply he didn't have a wife? He'd better not have a wife, the way he was ambling around the beach being friendly to strange women.

"What's your daughter's name?"

"Etta. So are you teaching the director iambic pentameter?"

She shook her head. "The film isn't going to have tights or long speeches. Last night he was talking about adding scenes he means to write. I thought I was supposed to make sense of the play for him, but apparently he learned everything he needed while playing a stoned Mercutio in high school."

Dante put his hands behind his head, staring up at her umbrella. Lizzie discreetly ogled his biceps. "I don't see what there is to make sense of," he said a while later. "They fall in love, and then they die because they're teenagers. I hope Etta is never that stupid. I'd rather she was Lady Macbeth, without the homicides."

"Are all chefs as well read as you?"

"Italian high schools split between science and literature. I took literature because I was already working in a restaurant, and there was less homework to worry about."

"Desdemona wouldn't be a bad role model," Lizzie said. "She was awfully softhearted, though. She loved Othello for the dangers he'd gone through as a soldier and a slave. Pitied him, in fact."

"Not a good reason to date, let alone marry someone," Dante said. "I get it, though. I pitied Etta's mum because she seemed lost, island-hopping, looking for something it turned out I couldn't give her."

"Pity is a terrible reason to start a relationship," Lizzie said, registering his lack of a spouse. She had learned in the last two years that cancer had a golden glitter that drew strangers who radiated sympathy. Her old friends were busy with babies and tenure, and the new ones she'd made in treatment weren't sustainable. Cancer wasn't a good glue, or perhaps it attracted people for the wrong reasons.

"It wasn't much of a relationship; pregnancy kept her with me for nine months, and then she took off." He stood, shaking off sand. "I'd better get back. I left one of my sous-chefs in charge of the second course, *cacciucco*. Fish stew that's trickier than it might be."

She looked up, brushing curls out of her eyes—white-blond curls, the gift of chemo—and smiled because, willy-nilly, she'd made a friend. "Taking Lulu with you?"

"She knows her way home." He nodded up the beach. "You should come to dinner. Where are you staying?"

"The Bonaparte."

He raised an eyebrow. "Fancy."

"Full of yacht lice."

His shoulders were broad enough that they blocked the sun and made it hard to see his eyes, but he gave a crack of laughter. "Like gate lice? The people who jump up and try to get on a plane first?"

She nodded, liking the way his laughter came from the belly. "I could come, but I have two friends with me."

"Three people for Lizzie at eight-thirty. My treat."

He took off as she was about to ask the name of his restaurant, which likely meant it was called Dante's. She had tried to wring every bit of beauty out of last night's sunset and failed. His ass was better.

Damn it.

It was like her failure to reread *Romeo*. She was as trivial at the end of her life as she had been in the middle. She didn't want to read great literature, even though Shakespeare had been her bread and butter. She wanted to read Terry Pratchett, eat fish stew, and ogle Italian asses.

Back in the Bonaparte, she read about courtesans for a few hours before wandering down to the courtyard in the late afternoon. Grey was sitting at a little table, doing the *Times* crossword puzzle.

He pulled out a chair and offered her a glass of water. She poured herself a glass of Elba wine instead.

"How long do you think it takes to become an alcoholic?" she asked. "Or rather, a wino. Would six weeks in Elba do it?"

"Took my father most of his life," Grey said. Then: "Vodka. *Lemon*." He glanced up. "Sorry, that didn't make sense. 'A car that's not a peach' is a lemon. You're turning a lovely color."

"Brown as a berry," she said, wiggling her toes. "I think it suits my new hair." Her curls stood out around her head like a halo, far more chic than anything she'd aspired to before. "Have you even walked down to the beach?"

"I'm not a social animal," Grey said, which was no news to her. "In L.A., no one cares if I spend all my time inside, but here the maid insisted on opening the curtains, so I came down."

"How is it going with the mold spores?"

"Didn't work. Now I'm thinking about swamps, but I can't focus."

Lizzie took another swig of wine, because she knew the sound of trouble coming down the tracks like a steam engine. Like the arrow from a loaded crossbow. Like—

"Where are you with your treatment? When's the next scan?"

"I'm still taking the pills," she said. "The new chemo. Maybe it's working. I can't tell."

"It's working." He gave a sharp nod.

"It doesn't make my hair fall out, or my teeth ache, but I feel as if it's put me in stasis," she said, trying to explain. "Like not dying any more, but not living either. Waiting. It's not a cure, Grey."

She couldn't bear the look in his eyes, so she looked off into the thick leaves over her head.

They sat there silently while a couple of people drifted past them and out of the courtyard. "I wish I was in charge of sorrow," she said, finally.

"You'd make it so that I wouldn't grieve for you?"

He sounded wryly amused rather than grief-stricken or angry. That was pure Grey. Even when she was first diagnosed and raged at the unfairness, he never let himself get angry. He just worried.

"Maybe?"

"No wonder it's so hard to write this fucking book." He gave her one of his lopsided smiles. "I'm sitting up there wondering if a swarm of flies is horrific, and you're casually suggesting excising you from my memory. Horrific by definition."

"I didn't mean it that way. Flies are gross but not scary." She gave him a little kick under the table because she'd done enough sympathetic squeezing of hands for one lifetime.

"You may have soured me on the whole genre. My agent will kill you."

"I'm not taking that on," she said, smiling even so, because the one person in the world she didn't want to let go of was him. He knew it.

So yeah, she got it.

Rohan came from behind her and tossed *Romeo* onto the table as he sat down.

"Did you finish reading the play?"

He looked pained. "I don't like Romeo. I went down to the beach, but I couldn't find you."

"I rented an umbrella on the public beach," Lizzie said. "Which was fun, because I met a chef and made a reservation at his restaurant tonight."

Rohan was clearly in a temper. "That's another thing. I came to this island because of Nicola Moretti's food, and these fools have only managed to get us a single night's reservation." He jerked his head toward the hotel. "I can go to any bloody restaurant in L.A., any night."

Lizzie had thought it was odd when Grey reported that Rohan wanted to go to Elba. She would have imagined the two of them in Capri.

"We have a reservation tonight for eight-thirty," Lizzie said, making an effort not to sound as if she thought Rohan was acting like an irritable prick, and failing. "His name isn't Nicola, though."

Rohan wrinkled his nose at her. "Sorry. Where are we going?"

"Huh. He never said. I guess I'll ask at the front desk where a guy named Dante cooks." She finished her wine, feeling a little dizzy. "Nap first."

Grey stood up. He would be thirty-four in exactly a month and to Lizzie's mind he had never looked better. Some men grew into their beauty, and Grey was all cheekbones and navy-blue eyes, with a body that looked—

She wrenched her mind away.

Rohan got up lazily, put a hand around the back of Grey's neck, pulled him closer, and kissed him. Even though they were in public.

Of course he wanted to marry Grey. Publicly. The way she had, years ago.

Lizzie looked down at the table.

"We should all nap," Rohan said. His voice was velvet dark with anticipation.

Lizzie swung her feet to the stones and sat for a moment, gathering strength to stand up. Rohan was already walking into the shaded doorway of the hotel. Grey's big hand came under her elbow and got her to her feet. "Let's go, Buttercup."

"I'm no buttercup." Her throat felt tight and sad. She couldn't shake off emotion as quickly as he did.

"Your hair looks like one."

Grey's sudden bellow of laughter echoed in the courtyard, and Lizzie fastened onto it. He had the most annoying laughter she'd ever heard. Who would want to live with that for a lifetime? Be married to that laugh? His hand slid down her arm, and his fingers curled through hers and gave her a tug. "I don't think wine is good for you."

Lizzie lifted her sunglasses and gave him a look. "We discussed this."

Rohan was lounging in the doorway, looking like somebody in a magazine.

"He's too famous," Lizzie said meanly. And then, after a beat: "Sorry, that was jealousy talking. He's great. You're great together. You really have to marry him. Do you mind if we just stand here for a moment?" She leaned her head against Grey's shoulder. Rohan disappeared, probably lured inside by some fans.

"What show is the chef on, the one Rohan's excited about?"

Grey's arm tightened around her. "Show?"

"Obviously not *Hell's Kitchen,* but *Top Chef? MasterChef? Chopped?*"

Lizzie used to have Grey's deer-in-the-headlights look when people talked pop culture. Now she could name a romance author and cap it with two more. She had become a space opera expert, from *Firefly* to Blue Aliens (bananas but great). Reality shows got her through the first round of chemo.

"You mean Nicola Moretti," Grey said, catching on. "No idea. His restaurant is a block from our New York apartment, so Roh skips breakfast and lunch and eats there every night when he's in New York. The thing is, Moretti won't come out and chat in the dining room, the way other chefs do. Roh is hoping that he'll actually get to meet him here."

Rohan rationed meals like a person in the Blitz, because being in one's forties and the sexiest man alive were incompatible.

"I wondered why he wanted to come to Elba."

"I think the Pancetta Blu has two stars," Grey said.

"Blue ham? This guy Moretti named his restaurant after blue ham?"

"No, let me think. It's Blue Prince in English."

"Principe Blu," Lizzie guessed.

"Did you learn Italian while I wasn't looking?"

She shrugged. "Some. I've had a lot of time to sit around."

"I'm sure the chef you met will be just as good as Moretti."

"Sure." Lizzie took a deep breath. She felt like the flush of a toilet. Like a flea that was going down the drain. Like a cat trying to cross a stream.

OK, those sucked.

"Time to get you to bed," said Grey, who always seemed to know when she hit bottom. "I'll send up some toast."

"I didn't eat lunch."

"Jesus."

Chapter Three

Another nap followed by a judicious mix of meds got Lizzie back on her feet. The ubiquitous trays of prosecco were going around when she walked down the stairs at 8:15. Rohan and Grey were in the corner they'd claimed as their own, having a lively discussion about chamber pots.

"If Rohan gets up to go to the bathroom, he's inevitably flagged down before he can get to the other side of the room. I suggested we get him a chamber pot," Grey explained. "In the nineteenth century, people peed straight into a pot without moving from their chairs."

"No, they did it behind a screen in the corner of the room," Lizzie said. "Or against the wall."

"How do you know?"

"Historical romances," she said smugly. "Also a book about courtesans that keeps sending me to sleep but is full of interesting details."

"I have great news," Rohan told Lizzie. "We're booked into Moretti's restaurant day after tomorrow *and* once next week. He's very uptight in New York, no photos of the food, no getting to know the customers. I'm sure it's more informal here. I'm going to tell Moretti that I eat his food every night in New York, and then wrangle at least three or four more reservations."

"Do many chefs have restaurants in two countries?" Lizzie asked.

"It's pretty common with Italian chefs. You either have your own restaurant, or you work as a sous-chef in New York during the winter, and then you go home in the summer and run your own restaurant and cook whatever you want. That's one reason why I'm so excited to try his food here."

"The chef I met only cooks one dinner a night."

"One table?"

"No, just one dish. No choices."

"I suppose he doesn't have enough customers to justify making lots of plates. According to the manager, most of the yachts stop in this harbor only to eat at Moretti's restaurant. They reserve months in advance, which is why they can't get us in there tonight."

"Did you find out where your mystery chef works?" Grey asked Lizzie.

Rohan gave her a squinty look. "We don't know where it is or what he's serving. It might be better to stay here."

"If you hate the menu, the two of you can come back. I'll eat whatever and join you later." She got up before he could answer and walked over to the counter.

"*Buona sera, Signora,*" chirped a twenty-something-year-old named Giordana. "How can I help you?"

"This morning on the beach, I met a chef who was kind enough to give me reservations at his restaurant for tonight, but I didn't ask what it was called."

"Do you remember anything about him?" She smiled encouragingly. "We are a small village. Did he have a long mustache?"

"No. His name was Dante. I think his restaurant might be only for locals." Lizzie lowered her voice. "He told me that he doesn't bother to prepare more than one dish a night. Do you think I should go on my own and leave my friends behind? I just need to know how to find it."

"No, no, they will like it," Giordana said, beaming at her. "The restaurant is just a short walk to the left down the road. It doesn't have a name, and it's somewhat dilapidated—the mayor keeps threatening to fine Dante if he doesn't renovate—but you can't miss it."

She and Grey walked out into the courtyard and waited for Rohan to disentangle himself from strangers. Then they set out under the arch leading from the courtyard and ambled down the street.

The road dead-ended in a low building with a courtyard shaded by swaths of white canvas strung with little lights. Five or six tables were sprinkled around a space demarcated by faded boards that had once been painted blue. As they came closer, she saw that the building was a big kitchen, light spilling from a long window into the yard.

"I remember a place like this in Mexico when I was filming *Hotheaded*," Rohan said. "Fantastic tacos." He sounded more cheerful.

They were greeted at the door into the courtyard by a middle-aged Italian woman with the figure of a hard-boiled egg. She looked all three of them from top to bottom before she said, "Signora Lizzie?"

"Yes, I am, thank you," Lizzie said. "I have a reservation for three at eight-thirty."

"It's eight-fifty."

"You gave away our table?"

Her eyes narrowed. "We never give away a table."

"Signora, please forgive us for being tardy," Rohan said. "The smell is making me faint with hunger."

She didn't seem to recognize him. "No cellphones, and no photos," she stated. "Under any circumstances. The food is to be eaten, not shared, and you can talk to the people at your table but not in your phone."

They were led to a table just outside the window looking into the kitchen.

"Best table in the house," Grey said, waggling his eyebrows at Lizzie. "You must have made quite an impression on the chef. You do look great in that crocheted bathing suit. How old is Dante, anyway?" He twisted about and looked in the window.

"He's the one in the middle," Lizzie said. The kitchen was manned by three people who had their backs to the window at the moment. It looked like a peaceful workplace.

"They're playing the soundtrack from *Midnight in Paris*," Rohan said.

"Sidney Bechet," Grey said.

Lizzie chimed in, *"Si tu vois ma mère!"*

"God, I hate it when the two of you do that," Rohan said. But he was smiling, so it was all good.

A waiter approached with sheets of paper and put them down with a flourish.

Lizzie was watching the kitchen, trying to catch Dante's eye so she could wave at him, but she looked back when Rohan said, "What the fuck!"

"I'm sorry," she said hastily. "I can stay and you—"

Rohan's eyes were shining.

"Look at your menu," Grey said, laughing.

Principe Blu was typed at the top.

"Met *a* chef," Rohan said. "You met *the* chef! Like if you had one of those half-assed conversations at a party where someone promises you a part, but later you found out you'd been talking to Martin Scorsese."

Lizzie grinned at him. "You know how you invited me to Elba, and we haven't really discussed *Romeo and Juliet* so far?"

"Tomorrow," Rohan said unconvincingly.

"This evening can be my thank-you present."

Lizzie felt a prickling in her shoulders and looked over at the window. Dante was staring at them. She smiled and waved. "Hi, famous chef!" she called.

"Jesus," Rohan said. His head swiveled, which meant Lizzie had a good view of the moment when Dante caught sight of the (almost) sexiest man of the year. His eyes went from Rohan to Grey to her.

Work that one out, she thought, and smiled at him again. He waved, then put his head down, his hands moving fluidly between three or four plates.

Their waiter put down two large pitchers. He was somewhere around thirty, with rimless spectacles, many tattoos, and the air of a judge. "My name is Augusto," he said. "The chef designs the menu to go with Elba wine, but water is an option as well."

"Not Scotch?" Lizzie asked.

"No," Augusto replied, looking even more severe.

"She doesn't drink Scotch," Rohan told him hastily.

"Do any of you have requests for amendments to the menu? The kitchen can offer gluten-free pasta, homemade, of course, but the chef does not recommend it. There is also a vegetarian *primi piatti,* if desired."

At breakfast Rohan had opted for gluten-free crackers, explaining that if gluten made so many people sick, there must be something wrong with it. "Absolutely not," he said.

"I'm fine," Grey said.

"I'd like French fries," Lizzie said, thinking of Dante's complaints about Americans. "With a hamburger."

"Madame, we do not make substitutions."

She squinted at the first course. "*Polpo?* That's octopus, isn't it?" She treated Augusto to both of her dimples. "Please won't you ask the chef, just for me?"

"I'm surprised you didn't wear that bikini to dinner," Grey observed, after Augusto stomped off in a huff. "What was that about? Feeling bloody-minded, are you?"

"Private joke," Lizzie said, pouring the wine. "Cheers."

"I bought my flat in New York because it was so close to Principe," Rohan said.

"No, because you're cracked," Grey said. "What are you going to do when you stop caring about *People*? Gain fifty pounds and turn into Marlon Brando?"

"A superhero with a gut," Rohan said. "That might be interesting."

They were discussing how few roles existed for heavy actors when a plate was plunked down before Lizzie.

Chapter Four

Etta Moretti's bedroom door,
from *The Breakfast Club:*

Why?
'Cause I'm telling the truth?
That makes me a bitch?

"You want me to bring out the antipasti?" Etta was watching her babbo plate. She'd come to the conclusion years ago that he was delusional. Why would he care so much about the placement of two violet petals on top of a smear of black sauce, topped with a skinny carrot and three pomegranate seeds?

"Yes. Tell that crazy woman that she cannot have a hamburger."

Oddly enough, he was grinning. He hated infidels who asked for substitutions.

She looked out the window and gave a little squeak. "Babbo! That's Rohan Das."

"I know. Lizzie is sitting across from him."

"Are they together? She must be spoiled to death, living with a famous actor," Etta said. "You know what those people are like. He's even prettier in real life. Do you think I could ask him for a selfie?"

"You know the rules about photos, Etta, and they apply to you too."

"They shouldn't. Besides that German couple over in the corner are taking— No, Signora Pietra is descending on them like the hand of God. She deleted their photo."

"Good," her babbo said, but he wasn't listening. He was plating, but under his lashes, he was staring out the window, so Etta looked too.

This Lizzie was young but not too young, which was surprising, because generally movie people showed up with teenagers. Plus, she wasn't rail thin. She had curves. And she was pretty rather than gorgeous, with normal cheekbones and eyes that tipped up at the corners.

"I like her sundress," Etta said.

Babbo just grunted and went back to plating.

The woman's breasts were designed for somebody considerably taller. Whether that was cool or not depended on whether those breasts were bought and paid for, or just grew in place.

At twelve years old, Etta was interested in the question of breast growth. Hers didn't show any sign of it, though there were some hard nubbly bits under the skin. She might ask her pediatrician about them when they were back in New York.

Or her best friend, Anna, except that Anna would roll her eyes and say to google it. She was pretty sure that disgusting things would come back in response to a Google search like that. She'd been burned a couple of times and still thought she might have been put off sex for life.

Her babbo was using tweezers to place red peppercorns on a diagonal.

"You're not going to make her a hamburger?"

"She's having me on."

"You can't just send her the same old food that everyone else is getting."

"Same old food?"

"You know what I mean." Etta straightened. "I'll go see the lay of the land. What's the antipasti tonight?"

"*Rombo arrosto su coulis di cachi, salsa alla liquirizia e pinoli tostati.*"

"Roasted turbot, persimmon coulis, licorice sauce—ugh, that's the black stuff? What were you thinking?"

"Wild licorice herb at the market this morning," Babbo said. "Don't forget the toasted pine nuts. Get out there, Etta."

"No wonder she wants a hamburger," Etta muttered, making sure she had two plates balanced before she grabbed the third.

She threaded her way through the kitchen, nodding at Augusto. He smirked, glad to get rid of the hamburger lady. *He* might have fallen for that, but she wasn't stupid. This Lizzie didn't want a hamburger.

It remained to be seen what she did want. She had Rohan Das at her table, after all.

He was even more beautiful up close, so much so that Etta had an irritating spasm of shyness. She put down the plates, whisked an unused chair from the table next door, and sat down.

"Hello!"

Chapter Five

Dante's daughter was the age when girls are rail thin and affect a skeptical air that covers up how much they are learning about the world. Her face wasn't quite working yet: Her nose was too big, though her bottom lip might balance it out in a few years.

"Hello," Grey said, his voice sliding into the Deep South, because he never knew how to handle himself around very young women. "I'm Grey, this is Lizzie, and I suspect you know who Rohan is."

"I do," she said, beaming at Rohan. "Not that I've seen your doctor show because Babbo won't let me watch shows that have a body count over two per hour."

Rohan grimaced. "Cost of doing business."

"You must be Etta," Lizzie said, smiling. Dante's daughter looked a lot like her father, especially all the unruly hair.

Squinty look. "What did he say about me?"

"You are beautiful, exquisitely mannered, a great help to him in the restaurant, with a superb palate."

Etta giggled, and suddenly looked much younger. "My palate is a disaster! He's always telling me to close my eyes and putting different foods in my mouth. I never have the faintest idea what they are."

"That's my favorite challenge in *Hell's Kitchen*," Lizzie said.

"Did you see the episode that my babbo judged?"

Rohan intervened, "Darling, would you mind telling us what we have there?" He had his eyes fixed on his plate. Unappetizing, to Lizzie's mind, but pretty.

Etta reeled it off in Italian and then said, "Fish with persimmon and licorice. Oh, and pine nuts."

Rohan made a happy sound and picked up his fork.

"Did you know about the licorice when you ordered a hamburger?" Etta asked Lizzie. She had green eyes that sparked happy and smart. Dante was a good dad.

Lizzie shook her head and poked her fork at the viscous black sauce. Rohan was eating faster than he had since they arrived on the island, and Grey was doing what he always did: methodically putting calories sufficient for life into his mouth.

Etta put an elbow on the table and propped her chin on her hand. "So, Rohan, what's it like being famous, like being in *People* magazine and stuff?"

"It means I get to eat your father's food."

"Good answer. I'll tell him that. But what's it really like?"

Rohan looked at her. "You're never private. Someone always wants to come and sit with you."

"Burn!" Etta said, delightedly raising a finger. "Sizzle!"

Grey gave a bark of laughter.

"My babbo told me to entertain you all, but especially Lizzie because she broke his heart by asking for a hamburger."

Lizzie had only once been to a restaurant with Michelin stars and, unfortunately, she didn't like the food then or now. "I don't see anything wrong with hamburgers," she said, giving up on the licorice sauce, let alone the peppercorns that weren't even ground up. "I'm a heathen."

Rohan took command of her plate. "You can't eat much if you want to be in movies," he told Etta, "but fish doesn't have any calories."

"I thought that was only women. You should see some of the women we get here, all skin and bones."

"I guess they don't ask for hamburger," Lizzie sighed.

"Don't tell your father about this heathen," Rohan said to Etta, forking up Lizzie's food. "He might not let us come back. Tell him every single plate is empty because we *adored* his food."

"I suppose that's a hint that you want me to go back and get you the next course." Instead Etta reached out and poured wine into Grey's unused water glass.

Lizzie eyed her.

"I'm Italian, remember? We drink wine from the moment we start teething. Is your yacht one of those huge ones?"

"We don't have a yacht."

"Bummer! Babbo still hasn't let me visit one of the really big ones, even when a kid my own age has invited me."

"Plenty of time for yachts when you're older," Lizzie said.

Etta plunked down her glass. "You agree with him!"

"I do. And I don't think he'd want you drinking a glass of wine," Lizzie said, moving it away.

"I am allowed to drink *acqua e vino*," Etta said, letting it go. "Kids in Italy drink watered wine from when they're two years old."

"Do you go to school on Elba?" Grey asked.

"No, of course not. I'm in middle school in New York, and I want to go to LaGuardia, but I'm not all that great at acting, so I might go to Beacon instead. For high school," she added, seeing that Grey had no idea what she was talking about. Rohan had turned away because the next table over were fans of *Diagnosis: Unknown.*

"So you and your mom and dad move to New York for the winter?" Grey asked.

Etta shot a look at Lizzie under her lashes. "My parents aren't together. My mom's in Milan."

Lizzie poured herself some more wine and took another piece of bread. Etta began a long story about how her mother was an international fashion consultant, which Lizzie highly doubted. She spent a lot of her childhood making up stories about her father, and she recognized the genre. Behind Etta's shoulder, Dante was moving around the kitchen with complete concentration, his hands flying.

It looked as if he was using a tweezer to place flower petals. Lizzie almost felt guilty, but licorice? With fish?

Grey was asking too many questions about Etta's mother, so Lizzie intervened. "You wanted to know what it's like to be famous," she said to Etta. "There it is." She nodded toward Rohan, who was genially signing napkins two tables away.

"My babbo got famous too, after *Hell's Kitchen*. He voted all wrong, though."

"Let me guess," Lizzie said wryly. "He awarded the best rating to a man, which led to another woman getting dispatched."

"He doesn't get it," Etta said. "I make him watch sometimes, just so he can see how fast the women's team gets knocked out, but it's not worth it. He gets too bent out of shape about the cooking."

Lizzie nodded. "Lately it's been better. The women's team wins. Does your dad ever make—"

"My babbo," Etta interrupted.

"Your babbo ever make beef Wellington, like Gordon Ramsay does? I'm curious how that tastes."

"No," Etta said, and then brightened. "He makes scallops all the time, though."

Rohan sat down again. "Your father's scallops are fantastic."

"If you told me some gossip, I could sell it to a website and make five hundred dollars," Etta suggested.

"I don't know any," Rohan said.

"So you and Lizzie aren't together?" Etta's eyes were way too innocent.

"I am not with anyone, and I don't wish to be," Lizzie said firmly. "Rohan lives in L.A., and I live in New York. I'm in Elba because Rohan will be directing a new film version of *Romeo and Juliet,* and I'm a Shakespeare professor."

"We had to write a paper on that last year," Etta said, wrinkling her nose. "I argued that Romeo's bloodline ended due to pure idiocy, and I got a B. Could you get me tickets to *Hamilton?*" she asked Rohan. "I entered the lottery four times, but I never won. I'm, like, the only person in the world who hasn't seen it."

"Nope."

A shout from the kitchen had them all turning around. Dante was staring out the window, hands on his hips. "Etta!"

"Gotta go." She jumped up and flashed them a smile.

"Do you think if I promised her tickets to *Hamilton,* we could eat here every night?" Rohan asked, once she was gone.

"No," Lizzie said.

Etta didn't bring back their *primi piatti*. The waiter did, giving Lizzie a baleful eye as he set plates in front of each of them. "There can be no changes to the menu, Signora."

"Yum!" Rohan said happily, picking up his fork and knife.

Lizzie looked down at her plate, and an entire octopus looked back at her. No, it was an octopus minus its head. In the panic of seeing all those legs, she hadn't realized. It sprawled across the white plate, suckers and all.

It was horrible.

"Do you want me to cut yours into small pieces?" Grey asked. "The way a mom might cut up a peanut butter and jelly sandwich?"

"I can do it," Lizzie said with dignity. When she thought about

Italian food, she didn't imagine whole animals snatched from the sea and thrown on a plate.

"Cooked to perfection," Rohan moaned. "I've never had *polpo* that melted like butter, not rubbery at all. No calories either. I wonder if he'd let me invest in this restaurant. He could fit twice the tables into the courtyard."

"He won't," Lizzie said, sure of that.

She sawed off one of the octopus's arms and contemplated cutting it into smaller sections. The suckers were a browner color than the arms.

With a flurry of squeaky barks, Lulu flung herself out the kitchen door, so Lizzie dropped her fork and knife to scoop her up.

"Hello, darling," she said, burying her face in her fur.

The extra chair scraped, and she looked up to find Dante sitting down beside them. Without a word, he took her plate and slid another in front of her. Then he pulled out a fork and knife and began to cut the octopus into precise slices.

Ridiculously, her heart sped up. He wasn't beautiful, like Grey and Rohan. Not at all. But she had never cared for perfection.

"I'm Dante. I met Lizzie on the beach." He looked at Rohan. "Good evening." Then he looked at Grey, eyebrow raised.

"I thought your name was Nicola," Rohan said, looking as delighted to be sitting with Dante as *People* readers were to see him wearing underwear or Captain Britain spandex.

"There was already a chef named Dante in New York, so my investors thought it was best if I took a pseudonym."

Grey put down his fork and knife. "It's a pleasure to meet you. I'm Grey Thuston."

Dante didn't blink, so he must not be a horror reader.

Lizzie dropped Lulu on the ground and looked at the plate he had slid in front of her. In the middle was a perfectly browned hamburger, with curly French fries extending around it like the rays of the sun.

"Thank you," she breathed. She picked up a salty fry and popped it in her mouth.

"I thought you never made substitutions," Grey said, in a reasonable imitation of the waiter's voice, albeit with a southern drawl.

"I do it for Etta all the time," Dante said. He was steadily making inroads on his octopus. Three legs down, fourth en route.

Lizzie didn't let herself smile.

Chapter Six

The next morning Lizzie found Rohan in the courtyard. "Time for *Romeo,*" she told him.

Rohan groaned, but put down the crossword and picked up his book. It was battered, which was a good sign. Either he'd been reading it, or he'd thrown it on the ground a few times.

"I got to the end. Romeo isn't all that interesting. Plus I realized that I'll probably get hit for encouraging kids to off themselves."

Before Lizzie could point out that practically everyone in the world knew how the play ended, the makeup artist Rohan had known as a kid came over and sat down.

"Hey!" she said.

"Ruby," Rohan said, putting down the book, "this is my friend Lizzie. Lizzie, Ruby—an old friend from when I grew up in England."

Ruby had a wide smile and a *Harry the Dirty Dog* T-shirt. "These days I'm going with Jamaican, because I'm not a Brexit fan. We moved to the UK when I was five. Hey, you snagged the mystery man. I was telling Roh that no one at home thinks he has a private life."

Lizzie blinked, wondering whether she could clarify the fact that she hadn't snagged Rohan, or whether she was supposed to act as a cover-up. It wasn't a cheerful thought.

"She's not mine," Rohan said, intervening. "Lizzie is a Shakespeare prof who's helping me out with *Romeo and Juliet*."

"Series or film?" Ruby asked.

"Film. But so far the play isn't as good as I remembered."

Ruby snorted. "Like all my exes."

"Because they sucked or because you have a bad memory?" Lizzie asked.

"Both. They sucked, and I can never seem to remember that in time to learn from it."

"Just before we moved to L.A., you had that guy with no chin," Rohan said. "Fuck, why can't I remember his name?"

"Shannon," Ruby said.

"No chin?" Lizzie asked, shaking her head.

"I know, right? Chinless, plus a limp dick. It was all laid out for me to see, but no, I had to decide he was sensitive. Like Taylor Swift with a beard and tats."

"I could make Romeo more manly by giving him sleeves or a tribal tat," Rohan said.

"God, no," Lizzie said.

"Leonardo DiCaprio would turn in his grave if you made his drugged-out sensitive soul into an ink warrior," Ruby said. She shrugged at Rohan's frown. "What? I had to watch that movie like ten times in Year Eleven. You were gone by then."

"Leo isn't dead," Rohan pointed out.

"He should be, just for being so dumb that he didn't crawl on that damn door and wait for rescue. Do you know how long it took to do that makeup?"

Lizzie laughed. "You are way too young to have worked on that movie!"

"Part of my exit exam from school was making a frozen aristocrat from the *Titanic*, so I have strong feelings about it."

"Do you prefer movies or real people?" Lizzie waved her hand toward a group of yachters on the other side of the terrace.

"I do movies or TV most of the time, but I like to escape, so my agency books me something like this."

"What is 'this'?" Lizzie asked curiously.

"Beauty makeup," Ruby said. "One of them got a Black girl-friend, so they booked me."

"The yacht people are already beautiful, by definition."

"Yeah, but they always want better."

"Better," Lizzie said. "What is that? Like, what would you do to me?"

"Are you telling me that you've never had your makeup done?" Ruby looked completely baffled. "How old are you?"

"Thirty-two," Lizzie said. "Shakespeare professors don't do that sort of thing. Unless maybe when getting married." She wrinkled her nose. "No, not even then."

Ruby leaned forward and peered at Lizzie's skin. "You know how fucking lucky you are, right?"

Rohan snorted, but Lizzie ignored him and just smiled. "Sure."

"The whole English rose thing going on with your skin, and that hair." She narrowed her eyes. "That's chemo hair."

Lizzie coughed in surprise.

"Still fighting it?" Ruby's eyes didn't have an ounce of pity in them. Not even sympathy.

"Yup, more or less."

"We're all there, right? More or less."

"You?"

"I'm a liquid chemical swamp," Ruby said with a distinct tinge of pride. "Thanks to breast cancer. Have you figured out the good news about this?"

"What?"

"We can eat all the Twinkies we want. You see my skin?" She tapped her cheekbones. "Not a spot—not ashy or blotchy. None of that. Not since the chemical overload." Sure enough, her skin was flawless, the sleek color of the bronze Etruscan statues in the hotel.

Rohan put down his paper. "You should both do yoga with me."

"Oh, hell no," Ruby said.

Lizzie grinned. "I like you."

"It's good for you, the best antioxidant ever," Rohan argued. "This morning didn't work out because fans were waiting on the beach, but the hotel people say there's a place on the roof that nobody knows about."

"Yeah . . . *no*," Lizzie said.

"Maybe at twilight?"

Ruby got to her feet and said to Lizzie, "You ever noticed how men just don't get broken into accepting 'no' the way women do?"

"Hashtag MeToo," Lizzie said.

"I'm not even talking about that. Just about your ordinary no-drama day that somehow turns into a sausage fest. Even the gay ones."

"Jesus," Rohan said. "I get it. No sun salutations."

"Ladies," Ruby said, and sauntered off.

"She just figured out you're gay," Lizzie said. "Is that a problem?"

"She's good people: Her mom and mine hang out together. Also, I don't want to keep that secret anymore."

"Grey said that you want to marry him."

Rohan nodded. "I just have to talk him into it. OK, I've been thinking. What if I use sword fighting to turn Romeo more manly? Maybe with a lot of choreography."

Lizzie thought that sounded boring, but she kept her mouth shut.

He squinted at her and then said, "Or not." He shook himself like a dog coming out of the water. "I have to talk to my agent at ten."

"Let me know when you want to have another discussion of

Romeo's testosterone," Lizzie said, standing up and then pausing to drop a kiss on his cheek. As powerful men went, he wasn't bad.

He whipped out the *Times,* folded to the crossword puzzle.

"You know, there's an app where you can get a load of those at once," she said, watching him.

"It's not the same."

"Why not?"

"This is the real thing." He looked up. "Did Grey ever tell you where I grew up?"

She raised one shoulder. "Maybe."

"I feel like I'm in a fucking threesome without the sex," he muttered.

"You're getting sex, and I'm not," she said, grinning.

He leaned forward and fixed her with the direct stare that made him famous. "I do believe you could be having some, Ms. Delford. If you wanted. Probably followed by better morning-after pancakes than I've ever tasted."

"What about your childhood?" she said hastily. "Your mother plugged the gaps between boards in the wall with newspaper to keep out the freezing cold, and you taught yourself to read from the crossword?"

He laughed. "Sometimes I wonder about you and Grey, and then I get it."

"Well?"

"Vocabulary. My parents speak Hindi at home, and if I wanted to make it in TV, I had to use English words, big ones, so I got into doing the crossword every day."

"Makes sense. OK, I'm going down to the beach."

"If you see a certain chef, will you tell him that I was in fucking ecstasy last night?"

"I probably won't see him."

"You could add that you need a good boning."

Lizzie whacked him with her hat. After Dante ate the octopus last night, he went back inside, and every time she had looked through the window, he was working. She had waved when they left and he had nodded to her, but that was all.

"I'll think about beefing up the testosterone in this damned play, and you tell yourself he's not coming to find you," Rohan said, chortling under his breath.

Lizzie marched away, down to the beach. Maybe she should catch a bus to somewhere else on the island. She'd heard about a beach with black sand. She didn't have to stay with all this insipid white sand and homicidal children.

But she didn't.

She sat down and read *Romeo and Juliet* all the way to the end. Rohan was going to need help with that last bananas speech of Romeo's. Though there was one lovely line, "My love, my wife."

Lulu hopped up on Lizzie's sunbed as if she had the absolute right to be there. After Lizzie said no to a man selling coconut slices, another selling watermelon, and a woman selling flowery shifts, they curled up together and went to sleep.

She woke up thinking that maybe Dante would be there, but he wasn't. Etta showed up a half hour later, wearing only a red bikini bottom.

"I forgot a towel," Etta said by way of greeting. She dragged a bed from under the next umbrella.

"That's rented to someone else. You could use my chair."

"They aren't here and the beds are better for tanning." She lay down, arms behind her head. "In case you're wondering, Italian women don't have to wear swimsuit tops. Not that I have anything to cover up, anyway."

"You aren't tanned."

"Russian women don't tan," Etta said airily. "My mother is a model from Moscow, and she will kill me if I don't put on sunblock every day." She turned her head. "You're tanning."

"Yup," Lizzie said.

"Are your breasts real?"

"Yup."

"Bras are breast prisons," Etta offered.

"Not if you have breasts like mine. If I hadn't started wearing bras early on, my breasts would be hanging around my waist."

"You said last night that you live in New York."

Lizzie glanced at her. "I teach at a university there."

"Columbia?"

"Fordham."

"I don't know that one. I'm not very academically minded."

"It's early days to decide that," Lizzie said, thinking of herself at twelve. Shoplifter extraordinaire was hardly a life plan.

"I'm not going to be a chef, but I might become a famous writer, like V. C. Andrews."

"You've read *Flowers in the Attic*?" Lizzie asked incredulously. "At twelve years old?"

"Five times," Etta said smugly. "I'm really thirteen. Like, almost there. Most of the kids in my class are thirteen and a half."

Interesting.

Lizzie had tried to get attention by shoplifting, perhaps because her mother passed away in prison, while doing time for grand theft auto. And drugs. Etta was getting attention with books. That suggested her father was a reader.

"Good for you," she said, and meant it.

"I'm thinking of reading *Lolita* next."

Lizzie was not going there. When she pictured parenting, she imagined an adorable baby, not a kid demanding to read about pedophiles.

Good thing she wasn't a mother. She would definitely mess this up. "Ask your babbo about that," she said.

"My babbo *likes* you," Etta said.

Lizzie turned her head and pulled down her sunglasses just enough so that she could give Etta a look. "Don't get cute with me. This is not *The Parent Trap*."

"That's an old movie, but I've seen it. If this was *The Parent Trap*, I'd have a twin sister," Etta said. "Are you looking forward to dinner tomorrow? Babbo says you're coming again."

"Sure." It wasn't true. No question, she was in the grip of that heady interest that comes with a crush. But did she want another octopus? No. The fish stew that followed was fine, but she didn't like to pick shells out of her food. It was messy, and Augusto hadn't offered them the lemon-scented washcloths they had on airplanes.

Well, the kind she got when traveling with Rohan, which translated to first class.

"You are *not* excited for dinner!" It was the kind of squeal kids make when they see their Christmas stockings.

"I have no palate," Lizzie confessed.

Etta giggled to herself, until she decided to change the subject. "Babbo says you're staying at the Bonaparte. Why aren't you at their private beach?"

Lizzie shrugged. "I found my way here instead."

"It's down that way. All those pink umbrellas with fringes."

There was a rosy haze off in the distance, like the Emerald City of pink. "This is better, because Rohan is there."

"You don't like him?"

"Of course I like him. But fans are on him like fleas on a dog."

"I didn't think you were with him," Etta said smugly. "I looked online last night, and I saw lots of photos of him with women, but none of them were you. Are you with that other guy?"

"No."

"Not even low-key?"

"No," Lizzie said.

Etta now had gossip that she could sell to a website—Rohan's sexuality being an ill-kept secret—but she didn't seem to realize it.

"My mother used to like his hospital show a lot. She watched it all the time."

"My mother died of cancer," Lizzie said flatly.

Silence. "Babbo told you about my mom, didn't he?"

"He said that he was raising you."

Lizzie was starting to feel nauseated, so she began mentally browsing over the vast collection of meds she'd left in the hotel room. "I'm going back to my room," she said, sitting up. "You can lie on my sunbed if you want."

Etta jumped to her feet. "Did I make you mad?"

There was anxiety but not fear in her voice. Good Dad award.

"Nope," Lizzie said. "I probably drank too much wine last night."

"That's not true," Etta said. "There's a tally right inside the kitchen door. Table Four had seven pitchers, but your table only drank one. I checked because the last thing Babbo needs is another alcoholic."

Lizzie had the feeling that *that* bit of information about Etta's mother was probably true.

"Too much sun," Etta said briskly. "I'll walk you back. Come on, Lulu!" She snapped her fingers.

"You can't walk back to the hotel without a top," Lizzie said, uneasily aware that she was nose-diving into motherhood. Or at least, sounding like it.

Then, at Etta's eye roll, she added, "The hotel is full of men. You're planning to read *Lolita*. Think about it."

"I'll wear your towel," Etta decided. She wound it around under her armpits. "I look fat in this."

Lizzie spared a moment to say thanks to the world that she hadn't given birth to a daughter. "You don't look fat. And if you did, who cares?"

"Someday I'm going to sail away with one of those rich boys," Etta told her. "I need to stay thin because my nose is too big."

"No, it isn't." Lizzie looked her over, slowly. "Your feet are too large."

"They are?"

"Everything else is great. Any time you decide you're fat or start peering at your nose, check out how big your feet are and complain about that instead."

"That's weird."

"Women seem to have to hate some part of themselves," Lizzie said, toeing on her flip-flops. "The key is to focus on something you can't change with dieting or plastic surgery."

Etta caught up with her. "What did you pick?"

"My knees."

She darted ahead and stared at Lizzie's knees. "What's wrong with them?"

"They aren't bony. I have plump, wrinkly knees, and they've been like that my whole life, no matter what I weigh."

At the worst of chemo, they were just as chubby. Very annoying.

"Whenever I feel negative, I focus on my knees and let the rest of it go. It'll help you avoid an eating disorder."

"I couldn't get one of those," Etta said. "Babbo would kill me. I think he loathes lollipop girls even more than Americans who want hamburgers. Not you, though."

They walked the rest of the way to the hotel in silence. Rohan was sitting under the trees, holding court with a flock of beautiful women.

"That's why I knew he wasn't with you," Etta said. "He could have anyone. Babbo could too," she added defensively.

"I'm sure that's true," Lizzie said, feeling completely flattened.

"You won't not come tomorrow, will you? You don't feel that sick?"

She did, but she'd get over it. "I'll be there."

"Babbo's never done this before."

Lizzie was about to go to her room, but she stopped, surprised. "Done what?"

"I can't tell. I promised."

"Served hamburger to the whole restaurant?"

"Nope." Etta gave her a lopsided grin. "Just come, OK?"

She ran away, taking Lizzie's towel with her.

Lulu stayed behind, following at Lizzie's heels as she went into the shaded hotel. When they walked into her air-conditioned room, the bed made up and new flowers on the bureau, she could have sworn that Lulu sighed with pleasure too.

Lizzie flopped onto the bed. Lulu tried twice to jump onto it, but she kept falling back. Just when Lizzie was going to force her limbs to move so she could pick her up, Lulu made it onto the bed and barked once in triumph.

Then they both went to sleep.

Chapter Seven

Lizzie slept until dinnertime and still felt so rocky that Grey brought her a plate of pasta and sparkling water. After sending Lulu home, she fell asleep again and woke early in the morning, her energy mysteriously restored.

Or not mysteriously. She'd never slept much before she got cancer. Now she could nap in the morning, and the afternoon, and easily fall asleep at night.

She pulled back her linen curtains and pushed open the heavy wooden shutters. The sea looked dark green near the shore and yellow on the horizon, where the sun was just coming up. Fringed pink umbrellas fluttered down to the right, where the sand had been raked into wavy lines like a Japanese prayer garden.

Down to the left was the public beach. The umbrellas were still tied down, the beds closed. A line of grey-green seaweed had come ashore and been left there by the tide. Last night the air had been heady with flowers, but now it was fresh and clean, with a delicate tinge of the sea.

Elba was seductive early in the morning. The water looked like lace, frothing when it met the sand, and if she held her breath, she could just hear it tumble onto the shore.

Lizzie stretched and then pulled off her Cure T-shirt and threw it on the bed. There she was, naked to the waist, though no one would see her unless she went out on the balcony. That was a step too far, though she found she was grinning like a fool. The sun on her breasts felt like a lover's first touch, hesitant and light, but all the more delicious for being new.

Grey would be writing; he rose at four to write, no matter where he was. Rohan probably wouldn't want to work on the script after yoga. She could leave and go to a market or a museum. But even in five minutes, the light had turned from pale gold to a deeper hue.

With sudden decision, she put on an old blue swimsuit, pulled a skimpy sundress over it, grabbed her book, and headed down to the beach. On the way she bought a *bombolone:* a puffy, still-warm donut that left her fingers dusted with sugar.

Down at the beach, she put the *bombolone* on the small round table attached to the umbrella pole and wrestled with her wooden sunbed until it gracelessly unfolded. Then she sat down, legs crossed, and watched as the sky turned pink and the sun came up like a lush orange.

The *bombolone* was stuffed with cream and had to be eaten with gluttonous speed or the filling would make a mess. Lizzie licked her fingers—more gluttony—and watched as seagulls streaked over the water and splashed down, squelching through the last inches of water before they stood still, their watery reflections looking all white bosom and no legs.

The beach wasn't quiet even at this hour: Seagulls kept her company and Italians began shouting at each other on the street that ran behind her. A guy raked up all the seaweed and then came, clucking, and opened up her umbrella. The smell of dark Italian coffee drifted her way with the sea breeze.

Contentment was a familiar feeling; she was a reasonably optimistic person, when she wasn't in the throes of chemo or grading stacks of *Hamlet* papers.

This was happiness, another emotion altogether.

She sat very still, letting it fill her up.

She spent the next hour there, reading about courtesans and eating whatever people offered to sell her: coconut pieces, watermelon slices, a small cup of coffee that made her heart pound.

"What are you doing?" Dante asked, coming up from behind her rather than along the beach, the way he had the other days.

"Congratulating my heart for speeding along the raceway," Lizzie said. She smiled at him, cautious, but knowing inside that she had been waiting for him. "No Lulu?"

"She's a late riser." He dropped his towel. "I'm going for a swim. Want to come?"

She shook her head.

He eyed her, still sleepy. "I didn't think I'd see you here until afternoon."

"Yeah, I don't really do mornings."

"All evidence to the contrary," he said, obviously amused. Then he walked into the ocean, pulling goggles over his eyes. She watched as he strode forward through the delicate green part then straight into the darker green. It looked like a forest, except he was swallowed up from the bottom, rather than stepping through dark firs and disappearing.

She turned back to her book, trying to care about sex workers who lived hundreds of years ago. Instead she thought about the way Dante looked at her. She remembered that male gaze from before cancer.

By the time he came back, more umbrellas were unfurled, and children were shrieking and running up and down the sand. He loomed over her, put his hands on the back of her chair, and shook his head like a big dog.

"Bastard," she said, wiping drops of salty water from her cheeks.

He squatted down before her chair. "Etta says that you're not with Rohan or Grey."

"No."

Was this the moment to announce that there were other impediments, as it were? His smile spoke of pure, brazen desire. It made all her senses come to life, as if the seagulls weren't screaming and the beach hadn't smelled like coconut sunblock before he walked from the sea.

"You may have noticed that my daughter has a flair for the dramatic," he said.

She nodded, eyeing broad shoulders glistening with seawater. Right at the moment she couldn't remember why she gave up sex.

"Etta's mother was Russian; she wasn't a model or a flight attendant or whatever else my daughter told you."

"Was?" Lizzie repeated, coming alert.

"She stayed around a week after giving birth before she took off. I wanted to marry her, but she wasn't interested, and she never came back for a visit. Her family sent me a letter a few years ago and said she'd died of liver failure." His tone was pained but accepting.

Lizzie thought about responses. "I know the feeling" seemed jocose.

He stood up. "I just wanted you to know, because Etta is excited about tonight."

"I see," she said cautiously.

"She's smitten with you, but I didn't want you to feel uncomfortable."

"I won't," Lizzie said, wondering what he meant.

"You'll see." His wry smile made her heart skip. "See you tonight."

Lizzie stared after him, enjoying the way his bathing suit clung to the curve of his ass as he strode away. Lust sizzled in the pit of her stomach. Nothing like this was supposed to happen. It wasn't part of her plan.

She could leave. She could run, which was the way she handled most emotional things; or at least, that's what Grey always told her. She could run away, back to New York, maybe even agree to discuss that new operation her oncologist, Dr. Weir, wanted her to try.

Or she could stay.

Chapter Eight

Etta Moretti's bedroom door,
from *The Perks of Being a Wallflower:*

Things change and
Friends leave and
Life doesn't stop
For anybody

"You have to trim your beard."

"I did it last week."

"You have to trim it again," Etta insisted. "Babbo! This is important."

"Lizzie either likes me the way I look, or she doesn't. She's traveling with a movie star, Etta. I can't compete with that."

"They aren't together. I told you; she's not with the other guy either. What'cha making?"

"Fiori di sambuco fritti." He was sorting elderflowers, clipping off stems so that the flowers could be dipped in batter before being fried.

"Not as bad as licorice and fish," she said. "What else are you cooking? Oh, I know what you should make her!"

He didn't look up. "What?"

"Gordon Ramsay's beef Wellington! She said she's never had it."

"Absolutely not."

"You said that you'd never serve hamburger, and you did the other night."

"Beef Wellington is foolproof. A good hamburger is not easy."

"She ate it all," Etta said. "So, your beard?"

Babbo rolled his eyes.

"Did you tell Ricardo that he has to be head chef tonight?"

"This whole thing is ridiculous, and it will serve you right if she turns around and walks off. She might even be married, Etta. I didn't ask."

"She would have told me. We talked about all kinds of things on the beach, the way women do."

His hands slowed down. "I went there in the afternoon, but she was gone."

"Too much sun. She promised to come tonight, though. I made you a playlist, light on Grateful Dead and Bob Dylan, because not everybody is crazy."

"I don't know if this is a good idea."

"I don't see why not. You haven't had a girlfriend since Rebecca, two years ago. Remember her?"

"Of course I remember her. Don't say anything rude, because Rebecca is a nice woman."

"Boring," Etta pointed out. "Dinner used to be so boring. She was always sighing over your food. Lizzie doesn't even like it!"

"No need to look so delighted. My food pays for your cornflakes."

"Adulation isn't good for you. I'm sure my mother wasn't like that."

"No, she wasn't," he said.

"You don't remember, do you?"

"Of course I remember. Your mother loathed fancy food."

Etta figured she'd made her point, so she jumped off the counter. "I'm getting your table ready."

Babbo groaned.

"In *The Parent Trap*—a movie that Lizzie *adores,* by the way— the twins use a checked tablecloth because it reminds their parents of their honeymoon in Italy. We don't have anything checked, but some candles are left from that wedding last month."

"The gold ones?"

"Tacky but fun," Etta shouted, running out the back door of the kitchen and through the storage room to the garden where the herbs grew. Augusto had kept his promise and put a small table and two chairs right in the middle of the tile sunburst.

This had to be just right, because Lizzie wasn't a sentimental person. You could see it. But she would think tacky was fun. Luckily, Babbo was always being asked to do weddings for famous people hiding from paparazzi, so the storage room had loads of tablecloths and decorative crap.

When she had the table set with a pink cloth, pink plates, and the gold heart-shaped candles, it wasn't quite right. Not funny enough.

She had to go and get Augusto to help. Between them they hauled out a huge wedding arch and stuck it right over the table.

"*Non gli piacerà,*" Augusto observed.

It wasn't important whether Babbo liked it; this was about Lizzie. Etta didn't do nearly as good a job weaving flowers into the arch as the wedding planner had, but that chick had four or five people to help, and Augusto went back into the kitchen to chop anchovies.

Still, it didn't look bad. She found some hanging candleholders, and stuck them in the arch as well.

Eat your heart out, *Parent Trap*!

This was cooler.

When she backed up and looked at it, she had a sickening feeling that it was all stupid. They were grown-ups, after all.

She was about to start tearing out the flowers when Babbo appeared from the back of the kitchen and started bellowing with laughter.

"I hardly know the woman," he pointed out, after he stopped guffawing.

"I lost my head," Etta said, rubbing her cheek against his shoulder. She wound her arms around his chest and thought violent thoughts about what she'd do if Lizzie hurt his feelings. He wasn't the most handsome man in the world, but he was the best.

Lizzie would be lucky to have him.

"Is it all right? You don't think it's lame?"

"It's sweet as you are," he said. "But, Etta, my love, you do know that Lizzie will come and go, the way summer people always do?"

"She lives in New York."

Etta actually felt him absorb that.

"She teaches at a university. Fordham, not Columbia. I might go there."

Babbo hugged her. "Sweetheart."

"I know, I know," she said, her voice muffled by his shoulder. "I can't go looking for a mother in every ditch. It's not mature."

"I get it," he said, rocking her a little bit. "I'm sure Lizzie does too."

"It's not a big deal," Etta said, pulling away and shrugging. "She likes the movie and she'll think the arch is funny. It would have been even better if you'd made beef Wellington."

His jaw firmed.

"OK, she'll settle for freaking fried flowers."

"The world must have given you to me to keep my ego in check."

Etta decided to ignore that. "I'm going to the movies with Lucia tonight. Her mom is taking us to Portoferraio. I'll sleep over."

Babbo groaned.

Etta grinned at him. "I put the speaker on the windowsill over there. The playlist is on your cell, named 'Lizzie.' Don't forget to turn it on."

She managed to avoid his swat and ran away laughing.

Chapter Nine

That evening, after a long nap, Lizzie felt better than she had in ages, so she put on a white lacy dress that showed off her tan. They had gathered Ruby into their group, so they all sauntered down the street toward the Principe Blu, bickering because Ruby hated yoga.

"It's dangerous to seek personal fulfillment by standing on one leg," she said. "Hey, did you recognize that line?"

"No," Rohan said.

"If he got fulfillment from balancing on one leg, he wouldn't be always trying to get us to do it with him," Lizzie pointed out.

"*The Incredible Jessica James,*" Ruby said. "I've memorized the opening because she's my hero. *I think it's really dangerous to seek personal fulfillment through romantic relationships.* That works just as well for yoga. Dangerous, dude. Dangerous."

"Yoga is all about personal fulfillment," Rohan said, with the patience of someone explaining the Bible to infidels. "Relationships are about sex. And love."

"It's not personal if you require an audience," Lizzie said, which wasn't entirely nice. But really? He was always nagging them to join him.

"It's not about having an audience," Rohan said. "It's about sharing. I tried my daily practice alone, but I realized that I like to teach. I can't teach on the beach with everyone watching."

"You're too famous," Ruby said. "I bet you get mobbed in Sainsbury's."

"Talk to the hotel. They'll hold off the crowd," Grey said. "They promised."

Lizzie fell back and trailed after them, trying to get the flutters in her stomach under control.

Two years ago, she would have hopped into bed with Dante. But now? She had scars, for one thing. Lots of them. And sometimes her meds made her fart.

She was supposed to be done with this.

After breaking up with Grey, she'd had dates and a few hookups, and even a relationship long enough that she started referring to Ben as her partner, until it began feeling too serious and she ran away, according to Grey. In reality, Ben moved to North Carolina. It wasn't like she could give up a tenure-track job for a man.

Six months ago, on New Year's Eve, she'd decided that she was done trying to find a mate, or even a one-night stand. She and her friend Hannah had swigged champagne to celebrate being done with men. She could still hear Hannah's voice in her ear. "Reason to Celebrate, Number One: You will never again hear a man telling you how much his ex liked giving head."

They had drunk to never worrying about what a man thought of her belly, or the way her breasts slid into her armpits if she lay the wrong way, or whether she tasted good, top or bottom.

Even the hangover had had a congratulatory feel.

Plus, there was Etta to think about: Etta who was obviously shopping for a mother to replace a dead Russian woman.

Lizzie put that thought to the side, together with her longing for the adorable baby she might have been mothering, if the world had been different.

No wonder the mayor wanted to renovate Dante's building; it

looked as wrecked as exploded firecrackers on July 5th. As worn out as an Airstream trailer belonging to hippies. As . . .

She didn't get to the third metaphor, because the lady guarding the entrance to Principe Blu said, "You're on time."

"We didn't know where we were eating the other night," Rohan said. He tipped forward as if he was about to kiss her hand, but then thought better of it.

"You three come with me," the signora said. "You, you, and you." She stabbed her finger at Rohan, Ruby, and Grey.

Lizzie stood at the entrance by herself, feeling irritated. Presumably this was what Etta had been talking about. She was going to eat alone with Dante, which made her feel as if he had assumed that she would sleep with him.

I don't fuck for supper, she told herself. And almost laughed, because if she *did,* it wouldn't be for an octopus.

But maybe for a man with eyes the color of seawater. Chilly seawater, where it goes dark green near the rocks.

The lady came back before Lizzie could make an idiot of herself coming up with two more similes about Dante's eyes.

"You're in the back," she said ungraciously. "You can go through the kitchen, or you can walk around the building."

Lizzie opened her mouth, and caught the woman's smug, beady eyes. She was waiting for Lizzie to be rude. She *wanted* her to be rude.

"How kind of you, Signora," Lizzie said, beaming. Then she headed around the building because there was no way she was going to walk through the kitchen. Talk about a walk of shame. Maybe Dante picked up Americans on the beach every week and paraded them past his staff.

Not fair. He wouldn't.

Arriving from the side of the building meant that she had a preview of one of the most absurd, and absurdly romantic, scenes she'd ever seen.

Etta's work, obviously.

The wedding arch had pink and white flowers sticking out in every direction. The tablecloth and everything else seemed to be pink. Except for Dante, who was sitting under the arch reading a book by the light coming from a window into the kitchen. He didn't have on his chef's coat; instead he wore an old grey T-shirt.

He had shaved his beard even shorter.

The only deal breaker, Lizzie realized in a rush, would be if he was reading Shakespeare.

She walked toward him as quietly as she could. When she could almost see his book—after being momentarily distracted by the tackiest heart candles she'd ever seen—he looked up and said, "Have you read this one?"

He was holding up *Mort,* one of her favorite Pratchetts. She grinned. "I love *Mort.* After the police, that's my favorite series."

"I started *Unseen Academicals,* but I went back to *Mort* instead."

"Yeah. I should like that one because it's all about university life, but it was boring. I don't think I finished it, even though I bought it in hardcover."

Lizzie came to a halt in front of the arbor, looking up and around, and back at him, eyebrow raised.

"She's twelve," Dante said. He said it in just the right way: not apologetically, with a hint of pride. "I try not to deflate her when it comes to small stuff." He nodded at the other chair. "Won't you join me? Although, if you'd rather eat in front, we can join your friends. Etta will never know because she's taken herself out for the night."

Lizzie burst into laughter and dropped into the chair. "Clearing the decks for her ancient father to have a reckless night of sexual excess?"

"She made me a playlist, which we would have called a 'fuck tape,' back when cassettes were a thing."

"Better put it on," Lizzie said, chortling. "I can't wait to see what a twelve-year-old thinks we should be listening to."

"Hopefully she pandered to me," he said, pulling out his phone. "There should be some Grateful Dead."

"Leonard Cohen?" Lizzie asked hopefully.

He shook his head. "Unlikely. The theme song to *Beauty and the Beast,* though? Almost certainly, given her sense of humor."

A speaker on the window looking into a storage room behind them burst into "The Look of Love."

"Dusty Springfield!" Lizzie said. "A little obvious, but hey, showing great musical range. You've done a good job raising her."

He was the sort of man who looked effortlessly confident, so it was odd to see a flash of uncertainty in his eyes. "We're coming up on the worst time, though. She's going to hate me because she doesn't have a mother."

"No, she'll find lots of other reasons to hate you," Lizzie said. "Somewhere deep inside she knows that she is lucky/unlucky."

He poured wine. "Our meal is here, by the way." He nodded to a big cooler. "We can start whenever you're hungry. I refused to make beef Wellington."

"It hadn't occurred to me," Lizzie said, taking a sip of wine. Elba wine was more addictive every time she tasted it. At this rate, she'd start to hate champagne for being aggressively bubbly and bitter.

"What'd you mean by lucky/unlucky?"

Lizzie was trying to figure out if she had ever, in the whole of her life, had a more romantic evening than this. The answer was no. Not even when Jake talked her into losing her virginity after he won State in football. He'd done his best, throwing wilting rose petals on the bed and putting Beyoncé's "Crazy in Love" on repeat.

But this was ridiculous. Bananas.

"Some people are unlucky," she explained. "Everything goes

wrong. A lot of others are lucky and live pretty decent lives. But then there's the hemophiliac princes, who are lucky/unlucky."

"What?"

"You know, those Romanovs with hemophilia, doomed to die before they hit twenty. Rich and titled, but short-lived. Lucky/unlucky."

"My daughter is not doomed." Dante growled that.

"Of course she's not!" Lizzie said quickly. "What I meant is that she's unlucky in not having a mother, and lucky in having you as a dad, and she knows it. Making up stories about her mother isn't a bad sign. I did that about my dad."

"So your mother was a single parent?"

Lizzie shrugged. "Something like that."

He bent down to the cooler. Soft grey cotton clung to his muscled back, and desire wrapped around her like a favorite blanket she'd forgotten about. He straightened with a plate covered in tinfoil and put it between them. She had to swallow, because it turned out that green eyes made desire turn to pure lust.

She'd be damned if an erotic undertow was going to push her into activities that she'd celebrated giving up. For good reason.

"Are you planning to expand my palate?" she asked. "I just want to brace myself."

"Of course."

"I didn't mean— I used to try everything."

He started untucking the tinfoil, moving precisely around the plate. "What happened?"

"Life," she said flatly. "I love this song!" She wasn't lying either.

One side of his mouth crooked up. "'Po' Boy' is one of my favorites. Since I think of Bob Dylan as the Second Coming, that's saying a lot."

"Mumford & Sons doesn't do it for you? You know, maybe I should play 'Po' Boy' for my Shakespeare students," she realized, cocking her head and listening to the words.

He pulled off the tinfoil and revealed not a plate but a wooden board, covered with grilled vegetables, fanned slices of cheese, olives, and curls of prosciutto. In her hands, it would have been a chaotic, incoherent heap of food.

In his, beautiful, deep rich colors harmonized into one of those Renaissance still lifes. "That's prosciutto," Dante said, pointing. A darker red, spare-looking meat was *bresaola*. Little glistening cheeses were *mozzarella di bufala*.

"I didn't know that they had buffalo over here," Lizzie said. "What's this one?" It was a paler meat, embedded with slices of green, like pastel emeralds.

"Mortadella," Dante said, pulling off a piece and giving it to her. "Poor people eat it instead of prosciutto. It's studded with pistachio."

Lizzie followed the fatty, delicious mortadella with a mozzarella ball that had a creamy center. She let out an involuntary moan and then felt herself turning pink.

Dante's eyes were happy. "Perfect with salty meat," he said, taking up a curl of prosciutto and holding it to her lips. She smiled at him because they both knew exactly how the evening was going to go.

Screw all those decisions she made in the life before she met Dante.

She was going to eat every delicious thing he had prepared, and then they were going to go to bed in his house—because she didn't want him to see all the medicines she'd scattered around her room.

He kept pulling miraculous things from his cooler. Chilled pea soup, the color of early spring, served in old jam jars so it wouldn't spill. Two more jars were unscrewed to reveal an icy drink made from basil and mint, with lemon and crushed ice. "I can add vodka or tequila," he said, holding up little bottles.

Lizzie shook her head. She hadn't had sex with another person in a couple of years, and she wanted to remember every moment.

They listened to "Po' Boy" a few more times, parsing the line about time and love.

"I feel 'branded with its claws,'" Dante said.

"Time or love?"

"Love. Etta was an accident, and I was dreading her birth. Then I picked her up. She had her eyes closed, but she peed on me, and her eyes flew open as if she'd surprised herself."

Lizzie was struck by such a bolt of desire for a baby, for that moment, that she actually felt dizzy.

"I thought there was a good chance that her mother would want to take her back to Russia. I decided right there that I wanted every minute with Etta, even if I had to move to Moscow." He gave her a wry smile. "Etta wouldn't like to be thought of as branding me with her claws. 'Love' sounds better."

"I have the feeling that you might invite me to your house . . . unless you sleep in that storage room?"

His smile was slow and warmed every inch of her. "I live down the road."

"If you're branded by love, I'm branded by time," Lizzie told him. "You might notice later that I've had an operation or two."

He spread out his hands and told her where each of his scars came from. He'd cooked all over Europe, and had the burns and cuts to prove it.

They drank sweet, dark Vin Santo for dessert, with hard cookies that tasted of anise. He had made them from the same licorice herb that he'd used for the fish sauce.

"Much better," Lizzie told him, waving her third cookie. "This is almost as good as red licorice, the kind that comes in long strands."

He snorted, shaking his head but giving her delighted eyes.

"Mrs. Bedrosian, one of my foster moms, used to drop us off at the swimming pool in the morning with lunch and money for candy," Lizzie said, before she thought better of it. "I always got red licorice, and Grey got candy necklaces."

Dante didn't show any visible reaction to the whole foster care thing. "How old were you then?"

"Thirteen. Grey and I had been placed together the year before."

"He seems like a decent guy."

"He's the best. We had swimming lessons from a chemistry teacher, who ended up tutoring us in the afternoons. We both decided we would be teachers, so we could have the summers off."

"Grey is a professor as well?"

"No, he's an author, so he gets the winter *and* summer off. He writes horror novels."

Dante raised an eyebrow. "Published?"

She nodded happily, taking another cookie. "Four bestsellers. He's *New York Times* gold. His readers love him."

"Does he live in New York too?"

She shook her head. "He and Rohan live in L.A."

It wasn't her imagination: His shoulder relaxed a fraction of an inch. Mr. Dante Moretti was surprisingly hard to read.

But when she spilled Vin Santo, he took her hand and licked golden wine from the tips of her fingers. Their eyes met, and she knew that his heart was beating as crazily as hers, both of them waiting for words to turn to kisses, for clothed to turn to naked.

The whole meal was a seduction. The candles burned low, turned to puddles of garish gold wax, and still they talked, Dante's Italian accent making her restless for their first kiss and scared of it at the same time.

"This can't be anything," she made herself say, over a final glass of Vin Santo. "You know that, right? You have Etta."

He was silent. Then, "You live in New York."

She couldn't do it, she really couldn't bear to tell him. No pity. She was as honest as she could bear. "I don't want a relationship. I can't be a mother to Etta. I—can't."

"I see."

Lizzie was world-class at shrugging off uncomfortable thoughts. He looked at her, heavy-lidded and Italian. She polished off her glass and then smiled at him. "Play that song one more time?"

She hummed along this time, going high when Dylan growled "Po' boy." Yes, it was the right song for the night, with the growling blues sound of it.

"I don't get the *Othello* reference," Dante said. "In the song, Desdemona poisoned Othello, but didn't he suffocate her and stab himself?"

"It's about love. The whole song is about love that poisons and drives you mad. Desdemona was mad with love for Othello and gave him *that* poisoned wine: love. She basically proposed marriage, you know. He went mad for love."

"That's dark, even for Dylan." Dante got up and her heart stuttered. He bent his head, avoiding the arch, and held out a hand.

"If you ask me to dance, I might die of sweetness overload," she warned, coming to her feet.

"I hadn't thought of it. I'm rubbish at dancing." But he grinned at her and tapped his cell once again.

They swayed back and forth in the moonlight to "Po' Boy."

Between one verse and the next, he kissed her for the first time.

"I'm thrilled by your kiss," he whispered sometime later, voice rough, quoting the song's quiet promise. *"I don't know any more than this."*

The song changed, and Jo Stafford sang "You Belong to Me," but Bob Dylan's words filled Lizzie's heart and spilled through her body.

Dante brushed her curls back from her forehead and kissed her again. She tightened her arms around him. "I think you know more than this."

"Maybe."

They walked around the kitchen. Rohan, Ruby, and Grey were gone, but the tables were full.

Dante ignored everyone who called his name. He held her hand and pulled her through the courtyard as if they were kids escaping school.

Chapter Ten

A big quiet house, white linen sheets, open windows.

Sex—or making love?—making love was never uncomplicated. Lizzie kept freezing, unsexy thoughts crowding in, but Dante had no restraint and in no time she was naked, all her secret scars silvered by moonlight.

Dante may have been hard to read on the beach or at the dinner table, but in bed, he was pure abandoned desire: touching, kissing, licking everything, everywhere, shivering, panting, laughing.

No longer laughing.

Muttering hoarse words in Italian, his forehead against hers, her fingers sliding over damp skin.

Lizzie clung to words she couldn't understand and let herself forget the body that had betrayed her. She let desire fill her like an empty cup.

No more awkwardness, just joyful craving.

"Did you know that moonlight has no color?" she asked much later, turning her head to look at Dante's face. The light was strong enough to see that he was still winded, staring up at the ceiling with a crooked grin. Looking satisfied. Proud of himself, even.

Which he should have been because, honestly? Getting her to come was no easy feat at the best of times.

He'd done it.

She couldn't quite get her mind around that, kept circling the memory of pleasure as if it might disappear and the backs of her knees wouldn't be sweaty.

He raised his hands and scrubbed his face. "Moonlight . . . Isn't moonlight blue? Bluish?"

Dante's bedroom was square with big windows that splashed moonbeams around the room.

Lizzie held up her arm and it glowed. "I could be the Silver Surfer," she suggested.

"Is that one of those guys with a YouTube channel?"

"No, he's a superhero from the sixties. All silver."

He rolled to his side, propped up his head, and his grin got bigger.

"All right," she said, poking him. "*You* get to be Silver Surfer for the night. That was pretty fucking . . . amazing. Not usual for me."

"*Tesorino, mi terrorizzi.*" He said it matter-of-factly, maybe thinking she couldn't understand.

"*I* terrify you?" Lizzie made sure the sheet was tucked right under her armpit. Maybe he'd seen everything, all those scars, but maybe he'd missed a few. There was no way she was turning on her side and letting her belly relax without a sheet.

Once everything was in order, she turned onto her side and gave him a casual smile, as if she did this sort of thing all the time.

"Yeah, you do," Dante said. He seemed fine leaving it there, because then he said, "It's not that moonlight has no color. It just doesn't cast enough light for our eyes to pick up the whole spectrum. Right now, your hair is standing out all over your head, silver as your skin." He eased closer, grinning.

The problem with looking silver all over was that a small part of

Lizzie's mind translated it to looking dead, but she pushed it away. "Did they have comics in Italy when you were growing up? Not the Silver Surfer, obviously."

"Yes." He wound his fingers into her curls.

"Rohan just signed up to do another Avengers movie, but he's thinking maybe they'll let him direct a superhero series on TV after."

"Netflix?"

"No, streaming Disney, because he works with Marvel."

"Etta finds it irritating that I am uninterested in the fancy Hollywood actor," he stated. "I am no Shakespeare professor, but I think his production of *Romeo and Juliet* sounds abysmal."

"Cruel," Lizzie said, giggling, "given that Rohan is so interested in you."

He shrugged. "Most interesting subject: you. What are you like?"

Lizzie raised an eyebrow, aiming at urban sophisticate. "I'm sick of artisanal cocktails, I like hot dogs from a cart. I like teaching freshmen, and I don't like to quarrel."

"Why not?"

"Life is too short," she said, hunching her shoulder. "Do you like to quarrel?"

He looked faintly astonished. "I'm Italian. A good fight clears the air. What do you read besides Pratchett?"

"Poems by musicians," she said promptly, grateful to get away from a conversation that sounded too much like a future. As if he was imagining the two of them quarreling and making up. She could hardly tell him that her New Year's resolution had been to be done with sex—and anger.

And she was, mostly. Her therapist kept pointing out that dying is enraging. They never talked much about her mother, but Lizzie nurtured a little anger there too, because it would be idiotic not to. Like being dead already.

Mothers were supposed to stay around. The whole cancer narrative describing a person's last months involved adoring parents, like the ones in that John Green novel, who had money and more. Who cared.

Perhaps if her mother hadn't died of cancer, she would have been at Lizzie's side during chemo. She didn't have enough memories to know. All she remembered was that her mother went to prison, supposedly for five years, but she never came back.

Dante was looking at her hopefully, saying something important to him. "Do you read Dylan? He's a poet."

His favorite poet, obviously.

"I haven't really listened to him in years," she confessed. "The year after Grey and I graduated from college, we listened to a lot of Dylan. We didn't bathe as much as I would have liked, which fit the ethos."

"Dylan probably smoked too much pot to bathe often."

"We were of the same mind," Lizzie said wryly. Really, it was a wonder she hadn't gotten lung cancer. She didn't have to ask to know that Dante Moretti hadn't smoked much pot, if any. He was a man who wanted to be in the moment.

"If not Dylan, which poet songwriters?"

"Leonard Cohen. Mirabai. Mark Knopfler."

"I went to a Leonard Cohen concert once, but I don't know who Knopfler is." His brows had drawn together, and Lizzie reached out to touch the furrow.

"Knopfler wrote for Dire Straits," she said, leaning forward and brushing his lips.

"You could be the moon, you know, not the Silver Surfer. I can feel your undertow."

He leaned in for a kiss, and Lizzie let that happen but kept her mouth closed.

"I can't do it again," she whispered. He was on top of the sheet.

So she could see golden Italian skin and an erection bobbing next to his thigh.

"We don't have to."

"That was the first orgasm I've had with another person in two years," she blurted out. "I kind of lost my head, but normally, I can't do that, and I don't want to . . . to let you think it happens every time."

Silence. His eyelashes were too long for a man. "Can we try again at some point?" he asked, with a very satisfying hunger in his eyes.

Lizzie couldn't help it and beamed at him. "Even though I'm lots of work?"

He ran a finger down her nose. "God damn, Lizzie, has no one ever told you that it's the best work in the world? Better than cooking, even. Even trying to be sensible, I'd say that fucking you was the best experience I've had in years."

Lizzie cleared her throat because what was she supposed to say to that? *My best, ever?* Embarrassing, but she ended up saying it anyway. Then she didn't let the sentence end, because he might think he had to say something else. "I almost married a gay man, so what do I know?"

He blinked, eyelashes flickering in the moonlight. "Huh."

"Yeah."

He touched the edge of a scar left by a PICC line. "You weren't joking about those operations."

She shook her head, her throat tightening with silent pleas that he not ask anything more.

He leaned closer and brushed his lips over hers. "You know Leonard's 'A Thousand Kisses Deep'?"

"That's a poem as well as a song," Lizzie said, feeling happiness fill her like a boat with water. A sinking boat, with all this emotion.

"Will you consent to be wrecked, a thousand kisses deep?" His voice was husky, and his Italian accent curled around the edges of each word. Lizzie had the unnerving feeling she was living a movie.

Or, even better, one of Leonard's songs.

"Only kisses," he added, because she must have taken too long to think.

She rolled on her back and gave him her version of his crooked smile, his invitation.

Chapter Eleven

Etta Moretti's bedroom door,
by Eleanor Roosevelt:

Do what you feel in your heart to be right—
For you'll be criticized anyway.

Etta tiptoed into her house the next morning, thinking that maybe Lizzie would be there, drinking a cup of coffee, the way they did on *Friends*. Etta planned to be incredibly cool about it.

She'd say "Ciao," and then tell Lizzie and Babbo about the movie, as if that sort of thing happened every day. She didn't want to scare Lizzie. There was something wary about her. The opposite of Lulu, basically.

But no one answered when she called "Ciao!" The house was silent and cool, as if Babbo had run the air conditioner all night. That was a sign, right? He would never run it for himself.

After a while she realized that of course he'd gone to the market. Even after a date for the first time in years—at least, as far as she knew—he wouldn't sit around in the kitchen in the morning.

She tiptoed over to his bedroom and peeked in the door, to see if there was a sign that he'd entertained a visitor, but she was kind of glad there wasn't. If she'd seen a condom or something, she might have barfed.

It looked as if nothing had happened, which was freaking annoying.

"All right," she said aloud. "I'll go to the beach."

Her babbo never told her to take a shower because that was something mothers did, which meant she often didn't take one, just to show the world. But now she took one, because she didn't mind grossing out Babbo, but not Lizzie. And then she put on her red bikini, with the top as well, because Lizzie was probably right about old men.

Lizzie wasn't at the beach, which made Etta remember that Lulu hadn't been in the house.

She went up the boardwalk and along to the restaurant. No Lulu. When she walked over to the kitchen window and peered in, her babbo was making tricolor pasta, which always put him in a bad mood. He was a perfectionist and wanted every single ravioli to have the same size stripes.

Her heart bounced.

Babbo was feeding great ribbons of red, green, and white pasta into the roller, and he was smiling. *Smiling.*

Smiling to himself.

Listening to Dusty Springfield, who was Etta's favorite singer, not his.

Back on the street, she decided that a great detective wouldn't give up. She headed for the Bonaparte, walking into the courtyard as if she belonged there.

A hotel man—one of those guys sent out from Rome for summer—moved toward her, but he backed away instantly when someone shouted, "We're over here!"

She smiled at the attendant with just the sort of lofty disinterest that she'd seen on the faces of yacht kids. Then she waltzed over to Rohan and the other guy whose name she couldn't remember, as if she always hung out with Hollywood people.

"Hey, kid," Rohan said. He was doing a crossword.

"Nettie, right?" The other man had a lovely southern accent. He was almost as beautiful as Rohan, in a more relaxed way.

"Etta," she corrected him. "I'm sorry, I don't remember your name."

"Grey. Have you had breakfast?"

She didn't actually eat breakfast in the summer, because her babbo always left for the market by five in the morning. He thought she ate, but she didn't. She wasn't fat, but she had no intention of getting fat either. She shook her head.

"Hungry?"

"Sort of," she said cautiously.

Rohan raised a hand, and a moment later Gabriella, who sometimes babysat her, showed up and gave her a confused look. "Breakfast," Rohan said, in the same deep voice he had on TV. "For Nettie."

"Etta," she said. *Pane e marmellata di mirtilli, per favore, e un tè caldo.*"

"What is your father cooking tonight?" Rohan asked, the moment Gabriella was gone.

"Tricolor ravioli," she said. "I smelled duck confit too."

"What do you think he'll put in the ravioli?"

"Maybe lamb tongue. I know that sounds gross, and it *is* gross, but it tastes great. Today is Tuesday, which means that my friend Lucia's dad will have been at the market. He raises lambs. It's late in the season, but he keeps all the tongues for Babbo because no one else is crazy enough to eat them."

Grey cleared his throat. "So, Etta, have you seen Lizzie recently, by any chance?"

"No!" Etta said, bouncing in her chair. "I went out to the movies and stayed over with my friend. There's no one home now."

"We haven't seen her," Grey said.

"Are you her brother?" Etta asked. He had an adorable worry wrinkle in his forehead.

Rohan snorted, and Grey shook his head.

"My dog, Lulu, is missing too."

"Is that new?" Grey asked. "I found Lulu on the beach a couple of days ago, and the third person I asked said that your dog ran free all the time, and I should let her go. So I did."

"I could check Lizzie's room," Etta said. "Just to see if Lulu happened to be there. I'm getting concerned."

She thought about putting on a worried expression, but Rohan was an actor so she probably couldn't pass muster. Last winter, Miss Hallburton said her audition for Anne Frank was the worst she'd seen in years. Not nice but perhaps accurate.

"Sixteen, on the second floor," Grey said promptly.

"Didn't she tell us never to bother her in her bedroom?" Rohan murmured, writing a word into his puzzle.

"*We* aren't bothering her. *Etta* is," Grey pointed out.

"That's right!" Etta leaped to her feet. "I'll be back for my *pane,* so don't let Gabriella take it away."

She'd never actually been inside the Bonaparte. Gabriella was lucky to have a job, because they staffed the whole place from Rome. They even shipped in their own tomatoes until the mayor threatened to raise the hotel tax by four thousand percent.

No one noticed her, so she ghosted over to the elevator like Harriet the Spy. On the second floor, she knocked on Room 16, her shoulders twinging from trying to look as if she were one of those super upright girls who spent their summers on yachts.

"Yes," Lizzie said from inside, her voice thinner than it had been on the beach.

"It's me, Etta."

"I'm not feeling terribly well, Etta. I'm sorry."

"I might get caught at any moment," Etta said. "I'm not supposed to be in this hotel. Nobody from town is supposed to darken its door. They'd probably think I am—"

The door opened.

Etta dropped the rest of the sentence. Lizzie turned right around, went back to the bed, and lay down on her stomach. She was wearing a T-shirt and white shorts. Lulu sat up on her haunches and gave a bark.

"Too much Elba wine?" Etta closed the door behind her, then climbed onto the other side of the bed and propped herself against the headboard. "Too much fish? Too much of my babbo? 'Cause some days I can only take him in small doses myself."

"I'll feel better by afternoon," Lizzie said.

She was turned in the other direction, so Etta peered over. Lizzie's face was kind of pale under her tan.

Lulu climbed onto Etta's lap and demanded attention, so Etta pulled her ears a few times. Then Lulu trotted around Lizzie's feet and curled up against her stomach.

Etta was trying to figure out how to bring up the subject of last night's dinner, but before she figured out what to say, she realized that Lizzie had wrapped an arm around Lulu's stomach and closed her eyes. Asleep.

Etta stretched out her toes and examined her pedicure. She had to stop getting blue on the edges of her toes. Then she looked around the room. Maybe every room in the Bonaparte looked as if it belonged on *The Crown*.

The curtains went all the way to the floor, with a border of little bumblebees, because of Napoleon. She knew that because every year when her babbo's sister came to stay, she always insisted on going through Napoleon's villa.

Maybe she could talk Babbo into taking Lizzie to Napoleon's house. She was a little afraid that he would go back into the kitchen and pretend nothing had happened. Especially because it seemed as if he'd poisoned Lizzie the night before.

There was a heap of sea glass on the windowsill; Lizzie must have been picking it up on the beach. Their beach was rotten for that. If she really wanted sea glass, like enough to fill up a bowl, she had to go to the black beach.

The room was quiet with nothing to hear but Lulu's snorty breath. Etta slowly, slowly pushed herself down on her back. She wasn't really pretending, but this was the way that a mom would take a nap with her daughter.

The daughter would have lots of important questions about periods and stuff, but she would know there was time to ask them later.

The ceiling had a design of bumblebees too, which put it over the top, in Etta's opinion. When Lizzie woke up, she would ask her whether it wasn't kind of ridiculous to be so bolshie about bumblebees. Maybe she'd even use that word: "bolshie." She'd learned it from one of her babbo's old songs and she wasn't quite sure what it meant yet.

She felt like it all the time though.

Chapter Twelve

Lizzie woke up right on the edge of panic. She was about to feel . . . She sucked in a breath. She didn't. Her bones had that empty, hollow feeling that followed a bout of pain. She could just imagine what Dr. Weir would say about the last twelve hours.

Had great sex.

Had the best sex of her entire life.

Let an Italian man with green eyes talk her into sleeping in his bed for just an hour or two, and she *did* sleep, the way she hadn't in ages. So deeply that when she woke up she was already two hours late. She'd let the pain get ahead of her, which every cancer patient knows is the worst thing you can do.

She'd kissed sleeping Dante, and left a heart drawn in sugar on the table because she couldn't find a pen or paper. A small Elba village is chilly and dark as pitch at four A.M. Her iPhone flashlight had bounced and jittered all over the street, but it was only two blocks before she was nodding to the night attendant of the Bonaparte.

She got upstairs knowing she was in for it, and even so she couldn't stop grinning at herself in the mirror. Six miserable hours later . . .

She stretched, rolled on her back—froze.

She wasn't alone.

Second time in two days that she'd managed to fall sleep with someone else in her bed, if she didn't count Lulu.

Etta was sleeping on her back, her arms at her sides. Lizzie marveled at that. Etta didn't have a mom, but it didn't matter. She was so safe, so secure in her place in the world and the people who loved her that she slept without defenses. She was wearing a pair of jean shorts and a red top that was meant to be pulled down the shoulders. Too old for her.

Not that it was any of Lizzie's business.

"What are you thinking?" Etta asked, without opening her eyes.

Lizzie startled. "You're awake?"

"Now I am. Have you ever read *Harriet the Spy*?"

"Of course."

"Well, Harriet wouldn't sleep with someone staring right at her, would she?"

"All I remember about Harriet is that she was a frightful sneak and deserved it when everyone found out and hated her."

"She didn't think she was being mean. She didn't know. She didn't have a mother to tell her not to."

"I didn't have a mother for most of my life, and neither do you, and we aren't running around creeping in people's windows and writing things down in a book." Etta opened one eye so Lizzie gave her a direct look. "Unless you are."

"I'm not. Most people are boring. Books are better."

"What's your favorite book, other than *Flowers in the Attic*?"

"Harry Potter, of course."

"Hermione?"

"Yes. She's very bolshie."

Lizzie tried to remember what "bolshie" meant. Maybe its meaning had changed.

"Tough," Etta elaborated. "Her teeth were too big, but she

zapped them to a perfect size. So how was dinner with Babbo last night?"

Oh God.

What was she supposed to say? She should have asked Dante. She'd never been interrogated about a one-night stand by a kid before. Hell, she'd never slept with anyone who *had* a kid before.

"I loved the flower arch!" she cried, suddenly remembering.

Etta's face turned endearingly pink. "I was worried you might think it was stupid."

"It was perfect. And the playlist was great too. I'd forgotten how much I love Dusty Springfield. Do you want some breakfast, by the way? I think I'll order some toast."

"Yes!" Etta said. "Here, let me. My breakfast is downstairs and they can just bring it up. Unless you want to join Grey and Rohan."

"No," Lizzie said, meaning it. Grey would take one look at her and know that she'd gotten off schedule. He'd stayed with her for two months during the worst of the first round of chemo, cracking jokes as he handed over a trash can so she could vomit. Shaving her hair. All that stuff that lasts five minutes in movies and truly sucks in real life.

Etta grabbed the phone and started talking in Italian so quickly that Lizzie couldn't parse the words. "Just toast?" Etta asked, twisting about.

"And tea."

More Italian, but Lizzie caught *tè caldo*.

"Can they make the tea from spring water, please?" she asked hastily.

Etta rolled her eyes but said some more, before she laughed and hung up.

"Are they horrified by my fussiness?" Lizzie asked.

"Nope," Etta said. "They always use spring water because Brits complain about the taste of Elba water in their tea."

"It changes it."

"Are all those medicines yours?" Etta was frowning at the bureau.

Lizzie twitched. She would go over and push them into her traveling bag but . . . too late. "Who else's could they be?" she asked, countering a question with a question.

"I guess no one's. You aren't a drug addict, are you?"

"No." Etta had her father's eyes, but green-blue, like the Adriatic on a cloudy day. "What do you want to do when you grow up?" Lizzie asked.

"I might go on *Project Runway*. I inherited Babbo's creativity, but not when it comes to food. I have a lot of passion from my mom. What did you get from your parents?"

"I might have inherited my mother's ability to steal cars," Lizzie said. She folded her hands over her stomach and then glanced over at Etta. "I haven't tested it out. I don't think she was all that good at it. Unfortunately she got ill and died in prison, so she didn't teach me."

Etta's eyes rounded. "You're the daughter of a con!"

"You sound like a movie from the eighties," Lizzie observed, smiling because Etta's tone was just right.

"She didn't teach you anything? Not even how to hot-wire a car?"

"I don't think it's possible to hot-wire cars these days. They all run by computer."

Etta rolled her eyes at that, and Lizzie figured out that twelve-year-old girls aren't impressed by being put off with facts.

"I grew up mostly in foster homes, so I didn't know my mother very well. She died a long time ago now."

"That sucks," Etta said.

Lizzie rolled onto her side. "Not really. How could I have become a professor if my mother had taught me how to steal cars? I was lucky and ended up with a foster mother who really cared about homework."

"Yeah, but everyone knows that the foster system is broken because they're all predators and—and the rest of it."

Lizzie shook her head. "That didn't happen to me. Grey was placed with me, and after that it was great."

Etta narrowed her eyes. "Nothing bad, like *Lolita* kind of bad?"

"Luckily, no."

"Foster homes, jailed mom, *and* you're sick and have to take meds? That's not fair!"

There was something so appalled about her tone—appalled but not particularly sympathetic—that Lizzie burst into laughter. "Fairness has its place but not in the big things."

"Everything big should be fair," Etta said, her mouth set in a stubborn line. Lizzie could imagine her at two years old, learning that the world didn't always agree with her.

"Yeah. And no. If life was always fair, there'd be no winning, and it's fun to win."

"What did you win?"

"I'm not in prison. I do something I love. Right now I'm on an island, staying at a fifteen-star hotel. I'm in love with Elba."

Etta thought that over, her brow furrowing the way her father's did, except her skin smoothed out like lake water after a stone skips. "I'm not going to be an alcoholic. Or have a baby and leave it behind."

There was a brisk knock at the door, and Etta lunged from the bed, trotted across the room, and opened it. There was a tray with domed covers, but they weren't stainless steel. In fact, Lizzie suspected they were made of silver.

"Wow," Etta said a minute later, peeking under a cover. "I feel like Napoleon. You know he used to live on Elba, right?"

Lizzie nodded and didn't get up because lack of pain doesn't mean energy. Right at the moment she didn't have any.

"Could we eat in bed?" Etta looked hopeful.

"Do you generally eat at the table?"

"Yes. Italians like to eat and eat. I grew up having dinner at four, right after I came home from school, so that Babbo could go back to the restaurant. My friends get to have dinner watching *The Office* or *Friends,* but we always sit down and have two courses, sometimes three."

"You do a tragic look very well," Lizzie observed. "Come on, bring over the toast, then, and let's eat in bed."

"It's more than toast," Etta said. "You look as if you need something more nourishing, so I ordered lots of food, the good stuff in case you don't like eating lambs' tongues tonight."

Lizzie prided herself on not throwing up in most circumstances. But . . . "You're kidding, right?" Her voice sounded high and squeaky.

"Is it a deal breaker, and you won't go out with Babbo again? Because he was happy this morning. He must have liked the date, even though I think the arch embarrassed him."

"Lambs' tongues might be a deal breaker," Lizzie said, meaning it.

"You could tell him you've gone vegetarian."

"Yeah."

"But then, no more hamburgers." Etta handed her a thick slice of bread slathered in butter and honey. She was a caregiver, this twelve-year-old. She was making sure that Lizzie ate, because she loved her babbo.

In short, Etta was matchmaking, for herself and her father.

"True," Lizzie managed. She should kick Etta out of her room right now. She should insist on flying to Paris. Or just go home because let's face it, Rohan's *Romeo* was a car wreck.

"If you were vegetarian," Etta went on, "you couldn't have lamb patties either. But if you *did* have a lamb patty—because, be real, they are the absolute best—they have to come from a baby sheep. And there are all these parts left over."

Lizzie groaned. "I'd rather not think about it."

"It's not nice," Etta said, grinning. Her lips were shining with youth and butter. "Little lamb ears are left, and tiny curly tails, and funky eyes, and soft baby noses."

"Oh, for God's sake," Lizzie said. "Baby noses? Really?"

"Probably somewhere in the world they're eating those noses," Etta said. " 'Cause of not wasting food. And you'd better hope that my babbo never thinks about it, because he'll get the recipe. He can't stand wasting food."

"Still. *Lambs' tongues?* That's everything I hate about Michelin star restaurants in two words."

"He puts them in ravioli and they're pretty wicked. Ha! I saw that look. You're not going to even try his ravioli, are you?"

"Nope," Lizzie said. She was rather surprised to see that she'd finished the toast. She felt a lot better.

"You'll have to feed them to Lulu under the table, then. He's really proud of the way he does them in three colors and it might make him sad—"

"Shut up, Etta."

Etta grinned, unrepentant. "Lulu loves lambs' tongues." She put down her empty plate and weighed the silver dome in her hand. "Do you think I could get five hundred dollars if I melted this down?"

"No. Why are you so fixated on five hundred dollars?"

"*Hamilton,*" Etta said. "That's how much it costs. A girl in my class told me." She swung her legs off the bed. "I'd better get going. I have to chop vegetables for an hour every day. It'd be child labor in the States, especially because Babbo doesn't give me an allowance."

Lizzie said it without thinking, the words coming from some place deep inside her that she didn't know existed any longer. A part of her that believed in Hogwarts and spells that could zap big teeth to just the right size. "Want some help chopping?"

"Babbo always needs help."

Lizzie had to give it to her: Etta did a good job of keeping her grin to a manageable size.

"So you want to go to LaGuardia High School?" Lizzie asked, once she'd had a shower, and they were heading out the door, Lulu following.

"I used to, but I'm *done* with acting. Done."

They found Rohan on the way through the courtyard. He leaped up and said he wanted to chop as well. Obviously, he really wanted to get Dante to let him turn the restaurant into a moneymaker, which would never happen, in Lizzie's opinion.

More people would mean more demands for French fries from infidels who didn't think that licorice paired with fish, or that eating lambs' tongues should be legal.

The restaurant looked even more dilapidated in the light of day, without twinkling lights and the general air of excitement that came from the yachters arriving for a meal they'd reserved months before.

Maybe Rohan thought that befriending Etta would get him more reservations. Just now she was telling him about a failed audition for *Anne Frank* and one of the most famous actors in the U.S.—soon to be a famous director—was nodding his head sympathetically. "You have to pick your roles," he said as they walked through the restaurant's courtyard. "Anne just wasn't right for you."

"Yeah," Etta said. "Or I suck as an actor!" She didn't sound too bothered about it. She pushed open the door into the kitchen. "Hey, Babbo, look! I brought along a couple of prep cooks, and we don't even have to pay them."

Lizzie felt desperately uncertain. They hadn't talked. Maybe Dante wanted to pretend last night didn't happen. After all, she had said that they couldn't have a relationship.

But his head jerked up and there was no mistaking the look in his eyes.

"Damn, girl," Rohan whispered in her ear. "You must be good in the sack."

She swatted him. "Shut up." She walked over to Dante, trying to look casual because there were three other people in the kitchen, one of them the tattooed waiter, who was giving her that beady look again. "Seriously, can we help?"

"Do you have any knife skills?" He was flat out grinning at her.

"Sure!" She could cut bread.

"No, you don't. Rohan, how about you?"

"None."

"I'll show Rohan how to cut up celery," Etta said. "He's giving me valuable insight into my future life as an actor. You teach Lizzie something, Babbo."

"Yeah, Babbo, teach me something," Lizzie murmured, looking up at Dante.

He cleared his throat. "Have you ever filleted fish?"

Lizzie shook her head. His hand had casually landed on her hip and she felt a delirious zing right up her spine. His sea-green eyes had a ring of black around them.

"I do it in the backyard because it's a messy business."

"Ah."

"Let's go."

The minute the door swung shut behind them, they came together in a wordless, eager rush and kissed until she started giggling from pure joy. He pulled away, then pushed curls behind her ear and glanced behind him at the closed door.

"She's curious," Lizzie said, nodding.

Curious or not, Etta didn't appear, and they kissed between every fish. Dante's knife was so fast that shining scales flipped in the air, turning over, catching sunlight. "I will always think of you when I smell raw fish," he said an hour later.

Lizzie felt a drop of cold run down her spine. She was going to have to tell him.

Instead she snuggled closer and put her cheek against his chest. He smelled like sweat and sushi.

Rohan poked his head out the back. "I've chopped enough celery for an army so I'm going back to the hotel."

"Thanks," Dante said.

"Will that celery earn a reservation tonight?" Rohan's smile glinted, just as it had from a hundred billboards.

"Rohan adores your food," Lizzie told Dante. "He bought an apartment in Chelsea because it's near your restaurant."

"Christ."

"I'll take that as a yes," Rohan said. "Good work, Lizzie. I can see you're learning a lot about fish." He disappeared.

"Tell me you're joking."

"Nope. Rohan can't eat much because of having to look good, so he makes it count. He hasn't had a McDonald's French fry in years."

"And you *have*?"

"You needn't sound so horrified."

Where there used to be a tub of glistening fish with iridescent scales, now there was a platter of fillets, all exactly the same size. "I *am* horrified," Dante said, turning his head and kissing her forehead.

"I'd better follow Rohan," Lizzie said. "Maybe I can talk him into discussing the play. I feel guilty because he's made no progress."

"I want to put you on that table and show you that last night was no accident."

His voice was a sexy growl, but she laughed at the very idea that she, who could scarcely relax in the dark, would ever be ravished in daylight. And then she gasped because he pulled her tightly against him and desire flamed in her belly.

"How much longer do you have on Elba?"

The question hung in the air, meaning all sorts of things that had nothing to do with time. Lizzie let the truth of it melt into her bones. This was no one-night stand. She wasn't going to run away. "A long time. Five more weeks."

Dante nodded, stepping away. He nudged the last fillet into precise alignment with the one beneath. A thick curl of hair had fallen over his forehead. His face had blunt angles and a solid jaw. His nose was too big.

"What's your last name?"

"Delford."

The gap between Dante's eyebrows narrowed to a centimeter. Or an inch. "Grey is the guy you almost married, right?"

"Think *Romeo and Juliet:* young and doomed," she said, shrugging. She raised a hand to shade her eyes, wishing she had worn her sun hat. "We stayed together until we weren't in love any longer."

"Then you broke up?" His voice growled.

"In 2015," she said. "It took us a while to settle back into being best friends, but we are."

"You broke up because he's gay."

"Yup."

"Lizzie Delford, I'd like to fuck you every single one of the nights you have on this island."

He'd chosen that word deliberately so that she couldn't bleat about not wanting a relationship. She knew that, and still the word thumped onto the ground between them. He took a step closer, eyes wary. A glistening scale clung to the side of his cheek. It looked like a version of those black patches that Marie Antoinette put on her cheeks.

A beauty mark.

She had the unnerving feeling that the two of them were turning from single notes to a chord of music.

Look what it did for Juliet when Romeo died. Not that she and Dante were thirteen-year-olds.

"Fucking is OK," she said lamely. "Maybe some chopping."

Dante didn't say anything to that, just looked at her.

He was going to move into her story and change things more than he already had. But that was the point, right? Romeo fell in love with Juliet because she was so beautiful, but the story changed after she proposed marriage.

A shared sonnet at a ball wasn't dangerous. A few weeks of sex wasn't dangerous.

"OK," she said, gulping air. Words hovered in her head. *I get sick sometimes. I am sick. I am . . .*

In the last six months, she had begun to feel like a blown dandelion, floating along, shedding things and people. Giving away her books. When the end came, she'd have nothing to say except "I love you" to Grey.

The danger of weighing down a dandelion is obvious.

Dante slid his hands up her arms.

It was all very well for Bob Dylan to reduce everything he knew to a simple thing, a kiss. Dante started kissing her again, so she let that thought go, because something was welling up in the middle of that kiss, and maybe there was knowledge there.

All I know is this.

Chapter Thirteen

"I can leave the rest of the prep to Augusto," Dante said over his shoulder as he washed his hands one afternoon, two weeks after that first night. "I want to take you somewhere because Etta is not coming back until supper."

Lizzie couldn't stop smiling, a fizzy smile that made her feel as if she were in middle school again. At first, Dante stuck to a strict routine in the kitchen. But these days he was leaving the stove, spending hours at the beach with her, even returning from the market in time to have breakfast at the hotel with all of them, Etta too.

Day by day, they were coming together, not just Lizzie and Dante, but Rohan, Grey, Ruby, and Etta. Eating and squabbling and sunbathing. Ruby was teaching Etta how to knit, and Rohan was teaching Dante how the *Times* crossword worked, and Dante . . .

Dante was teaching Lizzie that if she waited for pleasure, it would come. Every time.

"Are we going to a new beach?" she asked.

"Nope."

It had to be going on four in the afternoon, but Lizzie didn't have her phone, so she didn't know. She *never* forgot her phone. It had a special app on it that reminded her of her meds. It also had an app that messaged directly to her doctor, and three apps that reminded her to breathe and stay in the moment.

The irony was obvious. She was having no problem staying in this moment.

Dante had a battered little white car, a Fiat 600, he said. She got in and rolled down the window because it didn't have air-conditioning.

"It's old," he added, unnecessarily.

They headed out on the road that led alongside the sea, which was on Lizzie's side. As they climbed higher, the sea turned from a clear blue to a darker, moodier shade with more green in it. "Do you like Disney movies?" she asked.

No hesitation: "Absolutely not." Dante glanced at her. "Too silly to waste time with."

"I love Ariel." She sang the bit about the sea.

"Great voice," Dante said.

Lizzie blinked, because she never sang without thinking about it first. In fact, she rarely sang at all. The most she did was hum. "Thanks."

They turned away from the sea and began climbing up into the mountains. The air changed almost immediately, and a smell of pine forest blew through the car. There wasn't a railing on her side, just a steep fall into a deep forest that went down and down to the little ribbon of road they'd already climbed, and from there an even steeper fall to the sea.

Dante took his right hand off the wheel and reached toward her, but Lizzie squeaked and pushed it back toward the wheel. "Are you kidding? This road reminds me of an entrance to the subway: too narrow and steep for all the traffic."

He laughed and put both his hands on the wheel. "It's really quite safe. See that mirror?" They went around another curve.

It would be rude to clutch the side of the car, wouldn't it? Cars that don't have air-conditioning definitely don't have airbags.

"Yes," she said, not managing to sound anything other than scared.

"The mirror lets me know if something large is coming along, like a bus."

"A bus!" Lizzie peered out her side again. "There's no room for a bus." Trees hugged the curve of the mountain far below her. It was like looking from a helicopter—not that she'd ever been in one—swooping over a sea of green, from pale jade to avocado and glassy emerald.

"We would pull over," Dante said, nodding toward the other side of the road. "There isn't much traffic during the afternoon. It's different when people are coming home from work."

"There is rush hour traffic on *this* road? I'm guessing your car doesn't have airbags."

It was irritating how much she loved his laugh. Loved? *Enjoyed.* She enjoyed his laughter. Who wouldn't? It was deep and joyful. Like a child's—except, had she ever laughed like that?

Maybe not.

They were almost at the top of the mountain.

"We're here," Dante said, turning onto a dirt road.

"Thank God, without meeting a bus," Lizzie breathed. "Where's here?"

"One of my favorite places, an abbey from the 1300s."

Lizzie got out slowly. The abbey had fallen down hundreds of years ago. Trees had grown around it, and in it. Vines had turned heaps of stone into blurry green creatures, like the elephants and giraffes carefully shaped by British gardeners.

These would be whales or sleeping dinosaurs.

The forest towered on all sides, the air so cool and pine-scented that it was hard to imagine that they had recently left behind the sweaty, sandy shore.

Dante was striding around the side of the abbey, heading toward the back. Lizzie stayed where she was, knee-high in grass and weedy, white flowers—Queen Anne's lace, she thought.

When he disappeared, she stood there alone, in a silence broken only by birdsong. The abbey almost seemed to breathe, slumbering under the trees. If she was ever to find herself believing in God, this might be the place. She held her breath, but no quiet voice offered wisdom, or prophecy.

Still . . . there was a feeling. Perhaps because of the monks who had lived here, praying, offering blessings, singing.

Following Dante around to the back, Lizzie felt as if she could almost hear the echo of the Tallis Canon, though perhaps that wasn't old enough to have been sung by these monks. She rounded the remains of buttresses to find Dante sitting with his back to a great tree, eating a plum.

"This must have been the courtyard," she said, squatting down and clearing away fallen plums to make herself a seat.

"As a boy, I read a great deal of science fiction," Dante said, tossing away the pit. "I used to bike up here and read, pretending that I could walk through time and find myself in the 1300s or the 1400s."

"You *biked* up that road?" Lizzie said, hearing the squeak in her own voice.

He lifted the back of her hand to his lips, eyes smiling. "There was less traffic back then. If a car came, I had more than enough time to pull over."

"What else did you dream about?" She began to gather plums from around them, throwing away the ones that had been sampled by birds and making a pile of dusky purple fruit.

"Screwing," Dante said simply. "Some days that was all I could think about, so it was a damn good thing that I didn't walk through time and shock the monks."

"Are you saying that you used to *masturbate* back here?" Lizzie started giggling. "I was thinking that it felt like a blessed place."

"Could you think of my spare DNA as offerings?"

"No!" Lizzie leaned against his shoulder. "I'm trying to imagine you as a boy. What were you like?"

"Solitary," Dante said, picking a plum from her pile and eyeing it critically before he bit in. "Masturbatory, obviously. Fascinated by food, but secretive about it."

"Secretive? Why? Don't Italians think about food all the time?"

"Sure we do, but my parents have other people prepare the food."

"Oh." Lizzie absorbed that. "You're rich, then? Your house is big, but I thought that was because of the restaurant."

"Not rich like yachters," Dante said, licking his fingers. "The house belonged to my grandmother. My babbo is a professor, and my mother is a judge."

"Wow!"

He shrugged. "I used to hang around my grandmother, learning how to cook *polpette,* which took two days, *tricolore* pasta, the difficult stuff. I was an only child, so she always said that she was teaching me in case my wife turned out to be as disappointing as her daughter. The judge," he added.

"That's harsh."

"That's how she saw things. Italian families function because there is a revolving door of women to care for the house."

"Yeah, a lot of households around the world are set up that way," Lizzie said, keeping an edge out of her voice.

"My parents thought I would be a judge or perhaps a senator. Not a professor, as the academic system in Italy is highly corrupt . . . but a judge. A good one, like my mother. The only problem being that I was entirely uninterested." He shifted, pulling Lizzie over his leg so that she was sitting with her back to his chest. He wrapped his arms around her, tucking his chin into her neck.

"Did you bring me up here to fulfill some sort of adolescent fantasy?" she asked, tipping her head back to peer up at him with a mock frown. "Because I am a respectable thirty-two-year-old woman, and I do not screw in sacred spaces. Nor on the ground either."

"Nope," he said amiably, kissing her forehead. "I just thought you'd like it."

Lizzie snuggled back against his chest, wrapping her arms around his.

"What about your parents?" Dante said a while later, when Lizzie had been almost lured into sleep by the hum of bees.

That woke her up.

"They were *not* judges or professors."

His chin descended on her head. "I forgot you told me that you used to make up stories about your father, the way Etta does. What about your mother? What does she do?"

Lizzie opened her mouth—but theft, drugs, and dead to boot? Something like that should be kept from casual lovers. Still, she had told Etta. "My mother passed away a long time ago," she said finally.

"Did your mother know your father? In more than the biblical sense," he added.

"That seems to have been the extent of her knowledge," Lizzie said. This peaceful air was like a drug, a sweetness drug that made painful facts seem unimportant. "You were up here masturbating about movie stars," she said, "and I was busy pretending that my father would appear and whisk me away. I would have specified a yacht, except I don't think I knew they existed."

"Lizzie," he said, and his arms tightened.

"Grey and I were together in foster care for years," she said, pitching her voice to just the right level of cheer. Dante's silence was warm and interested, so she said, "Our foster mother's name was Mrs. Bedrosian, and she was very devout. This place would horrify her, though."

His chin lifted from her head. "Why?"

"It's a church, but no one cares for it," Lizzie said. "We don't have many old things in America, and she loved old things. She's the reason I'm a Shakespearean; she used to have movie night with popcorn whenever one of his plays showed on PBS. If it was up to Mrs. Bedrosian, this would be fenced off, and there would be docents wandering around telling you where the medieval toilets used to be located, and where the modern ones are now. It would cost at least twelve dollars to enter."

"Lucky us," Dante said. He shifted again, moving her so that she was lying in the circle of his right arm, her legs draped over his. Then he kissed her nose.

"How does extraordinary devotion translate in foster care?" he asked.

"There was a lot of praying, but basically, God had told her to save our souls, which meant we were clean and fed and she tried hard to make sure we were happy. She cared if one of us was sick, and she made everyone do their homework."

"How many of you were there?"

"Children came and went all the time. The most was fourteen, after a crisis with an abusive foster parent."

A shiver went right through him. "I hate it that that happens."

"Yes," Lizzie said. Then she tilted her head and kissed the scratchy underside of his chin. "But not to me, thankfully, nor Grey."

"So . . . devotion," Dante said, his voice deeper, perhaps from relief.

"A great deal of singing," Lizzie said. "Sunday school, of course, and hymns all Sunday afternoon, and at least two before supper every night. In parts."

"That sounds rigorous."

"It was. I think that may be why Grey and I . . . well, why we turned out the way we did. With college degrees. Singing, real singing, requires discipline, and we both had good voices, so she made us work harder and harder at it."

"It's important to learn to work," Dante said, nodding.

"*She* worked all the time, taking care of her foster kids. And praying. Praying was work for her, a life's work. Plus singing. Those three things sound separate but they weren't. Any girl who landed with Mrs. Bedrosian was identified first, before her name, by whether she was a soprano or an alto. Unless she was too small, of course."

"What are you?" He sounded amused.

A pulse of relief went through Lizzie. He wasn't sorry for her. Over the years, she'd developed a Disney version of foster care with Mrs. Bedrosian, though the reality wasn't terribly far off.

After all, she and Grey did go to college. She *was* a professor and Grey *was* a novelist. Thanks to Mrs. Bedrosian.

"I'm a contra-tenor," she said, drawing her tongue along the prickly line of his jaw.

"Huh. I don't know what that is. Or what I am, for that matter."

"Do you know any hymns?"

He shook his head. "I'm baptized but not confirmed, much to my grandmother's disapproval. I think she found that harder to forgive than my mother's career. The ghosts of monks—who are surely wandering around here, and likely remember all the sperm I spilled in their courtyard—would love it if you sang a hymn, Lizzie. And so would I."

"I don't sing very much these days," Lizzie said. An understatement. She kept her voice to herself and had for years.

"Got it." He bent his head, caught her mouth with his own.

Dante had an instinctual sense when a person wanted to change the subject, Lizzie thought dimly. It was a sign of deep kindness.

But the thought slipped away, because kissing Dante was not a thinking pursuit, unlike everything else in her life.

Except perhaps singing.

He enveloped her, and after a while, with a great deal of laughter, a younger, eager Dante shone in his eyes. And he managed to talk Lizzie into allowing herself to be adored in a grassy bed, perhaps observed by ghostly monks.

"They would be very happy for me," he said later, lying on his back, chest heaving.

Lizzie stared far up into the trees, letting happiness fill her the way pleasure just had. Letting it take over her body as if the other things that had taken over her body didn't exist.

"I could sing something for them," she said. "I never feel like singing anymore, but here . . ."

"I wish I could sing with you, but I can only do the Grateful Dead and the Beatles," Dante said, putting an arm behind his head in a way that showed off his rather marvelous arm muscles.

"It's all right," Lizzie said. "I have sung a lot of solos." She got herself to her feet, because the monks wouldn't sing lying down, their robes pushed up to their waists. She shook out her sundress. Then she looked down at Dante. "I thought of the Tallis Canon when we first arrived."

"No idea what that is," Dante said, "but I'd love to hear it."

She took a deep breath through her nose and let it go through her mouth. *Warm the air*, Mrs. Bedrosian said in her head. "Shall I sing all four verses, or just my favorite?"

Dante looked up at her, the unmistakable heavy-lidded look of a man who'd just had an orgasm and was already thinking of the next one. "All of them."

"All praise to you, my God, this night," she began softly. *"For all the blessings of the light."* She looked at the abbey dreaming in the late sunshine, but she saw from the corner of her eye when Dante sat up. Her voice tended to do that to people.

"Keep me, O keep me, King of kings, beneath the shelter of Your wings." Her voice was perfect for an abbey open to the rain and sunshine. Usually she hated the way it disrupted the world. But here?

It seemed one with the quiet, not too loud, not too flashy.

The second verse done, she wrinkled her nose at Dante and said, "I'm skipping the third verse, because I hate that one," and took another deep breath with a sudden piercing wish that Grey was there. It was his favorite song. She had avoided singing with him for years, which seemed selfish now.

"Praise God from whom all blessings flow," she sang, dropping to a deep, quiet plea. *"Praise him all creatures here below."*

Dante was standing now, hands on his head, with that trans-fixed look some people got when she sang. She let it all go for the last two lines, waking the old silence, and the sleeping monks, and the drowsy birds. *"Praise above, ye heav'nly host; Praise Father, Son, and Holy Ghost."* Her voice was too big for her body, but just right for an entire abbey.

When the last note died, Dante said, "Jesus Christ" with such stupefaction that Lizzie burst into laughter.

He came over and wrapped his hands around her upper arms and didn't say all the things that people usually say once they heard her, like, "Why are you a teacher? You could be a millionaire! Susan Boyle has nothing on you!"

"Thank you," he said instead, kissing her. "Thank you from the monks, from the memory of a randy boy, from the adult that I am now. That was the most beautiful song that I have ever heard."

A funny squeaky giggle burst from her mouth. "You went to a Leonard Cohen concert!"

"You're better," he said, pulling her into his arms.

He didn't ask her to sing again or tell her that he couldn't wait for his friends to hear her. None of that. None of the things that would have made her stiffen.

Instead, he kissed her again and said, "Time to go home and cook, my Lizzie."

All the way down the mountain, there was song in her heart, but it had nothing to do with hymns and everything to do with those words.

"My Lizzie."

Chapter Fourteen

Lizzie spent the next morning at the beach with Lulu and walked back to the hotel with silent laughter bubbling up inside her. Was it normal to find oneself flung into an affair so intense that it felt as if one's blood was running faster?

Sure, in high school.

But now? A thirty-two-year-old woman on the verge of something momentous—i.e., death—who should be preparing herself for that big leap? Visiting Peru, learning how to meditate so she could breathe in synchrony with the universe, finishing a great work of art?

Or even just learning how to knit?

As she walked into the courtyard, Grey stood up and strode toward her. "Where have you been?"

Lizzie stopped in front of him and looked up. Grey was scowling down at her. He wasn't a scowly man, by nature. He tended toward easy good humor, served up with a lashing of southern charm.

Grey *was* charming. But Lizzie hadn't decided yet just how much Rohan saw of the real Grey, the man who took his fears—of which there were many—and shaped them into terrifying books.

"Lazing down by the beach," she said, putting her hands on his chest. "Mmm, nice shirt. Is it Rohan's?"

His frown deepened. "Do you think a gay relationship is an extension of a dorm room where we rifle through each other's clothing?"

Lizzie sighed and let her hands drop. "Let's go sit down, and you can tell me what's the matter."

"Nothing's the matter. I just wanted to know where you were. I went to the hotel's beach, and you were nowhere. I've been under that tree, trying to figure out how to start a new chapter, for two hours."

"What happened to Rohan?"

Grey looked around as if Rohan would appear and she could blame him too. "I don't know. It's fine."

Obviously, it wasn't fine. Lizzie tucked her hand into Grey's arm. "Shall we find Rohan and have lunch somewhere?"

Grey snorted. "No. God, no. This is— *No* to Roh. He's probably inside, talking on the cell to his agent."

"All right, let's go," Lizzie said, tugging on him. "You and me. I found a great restaurant the first day here. Well, actually Dante told me—"

"No Rohan," Grey said, his accent thicker and more southern by the moment, "and no Dante either."

The good thing about having the same best friend for years was that Lizzie could tell when he was wound as tight as a wire vibrating in a tall wind. The bad thing was that she could have no idea why, because Grey rarely got angry.

"Come on, then," Lizzie said. Two minutes later they were seated in the corner of Fabrizio's.

"Bolognese sauce," Grey said, pointing to the paper menu that doubled as a placemat.

Lizzie took longer and ordered twice as much. She didn't have a bucket list, but somehow, improbably, greed hadn't deserted her.

"We're going to have dessert too," she told Grey. "Now what's the matter?"

He grabbed his wine. "I like this bubbly stuff. I could drink it for breakfast. Better than toothpaste. Definitely better than champagne."

"*Grey.* What's the matter?"

"I've been thinking about when we were placed with Mrs. Bedrosian."

"You, dead beautiful. Me with braces, kinky hair, and a temper."

"I was so lucky to find you."

Lizzie reached about and grabbed Grey's hand because when men's voices fall to that gravelly texture, they need a hug. "I was mostly worried about my braces. They shouldn't put braces on kids in foster care. The orthodontist tells you that you must come back for checkups and then you get a new placement, and who knows if you'll ever go to an orthodontist again, and meanwhile your teeth are fenced in by a metal jungle."

Grey turned her hand over and examined her palm. Back then he had looked around at all the kids, then sidled over to Lizzie—who he had entirely ignored in the minivan on the way over—and hissed, "You're my girlfriend."

His southern accent had been so strong in those days that she hadn't understood what he said and just stared at him.

"One of the favorite moments of my life," Lizzie said. "A gorgeous boy comes over and wraps his arm around me and suddenly I feel like Anne of Green Gables, noticed by Gilbert."

"I remind you of someone called *Gilbert?*"

"Anne was an orphan," Lizzie explained. "She went to a new school, and everyone was mean to her except for Gilbert, the cutest boy in the whole school. You climbed into the minivan, looking like a—a rock star or something, and then when we were in Mrs. Bedrosian's house, you came over to me."

"Survival instinct. I knew that you would become the most important person in the world to me."

"No, you didn't," Lizzie said, putting her elbows on the table. "I was the only possible female, given that Jinx was nine. Were you . . . ?" She hesitated. Of course he didn't know he was gay back then. He would have told her years earlier than he did.

"They put me in a group home for a couple of weeks while they tried to figure out if my dad had any relatives. An older boy had told me that I should find a girlfriend the moment I got a placement, to stay safe."

"Thank goodness, then. What's that ancient history got to do with your bad mood?"

"I haven't hardly seen you in the last three days," he said, his voice growling even lower. "You're—" He stopped.

"You've been writing," Lizzie said. But that wasn't really what he was saying. The thing about cancer, dying of it, is that you spent a lot of time dealing with everyone else's discomfort. Her colleagues at Fordham were freaked out. When the first chemo failed, her therapist had cried harder than she had. Grey . . .

Grey never cried, and she should have remembered that. "I'm sorry. I know this sucks."

Plates went down in front of each of them. Lizzie stared down at her *primo piatto,* a bowl of golden chicken broth with pasta rice floating at the top. Simple, perfect food.

Grey had a manly jaw, the kind that came along with the Ken DNA that turned him into what he was. Or what he looked like, anyway. Right now that manly jaw was clenched.

"There's that operation we've talked about a few times, the new one that they do with heat."

"Yeah." She poked at her food.

"You're with Dante now, so no more giving up and not doing it, right?"

His eyes looked so hopeful. "Not giving up," she objected. "Just perhaps not— There's no cure, Grey."

"There isn't if you think that way," he snapped.

There wasn't another way to think, but she kept that to herself.

"You're supposed to get better," he said, voice raw.

"But—"

"I know what they said. But when I was there, in the round of chemo last fall, they said that it didn't matter what the PET scan showed because of the stuff you're on now, and the new operation might work."

"Dr. Weir," Lizzie offered. "His optimism in the face of terminal cancer is either idiotic or awe-inspiring."

"I considered him factual," Grey said flatly. "The doctors haven't given up, have they?" He paused. "You have."

Lizzie looked away. The water below the window of the restaurant wasn't the gorgeous turquoise green that it appeared to be from far away, from the window of an airplane, for example. It was a bit mucky, with seaweed and globs of Styrofoam bobbing on top.

Avoidance, or so her therapist said, was Lizzie's defining trait. The wish to run away. It was no excuse that she had so many reasons for it, going back to a parent with no particular interest in mothering. Before she came to Elba, she had gone back and forth with Dr. Weir, talking about this operation. He didn't know if the operation would work. He couldn't promise her anything.

"You turned it down," Grey persisted, revealing the drawback of being friends with someone who knew her too well.

"You are trying to make me feel guilty," Lizzie said, looking from the water to the paper placemat. "I haven't turned it down. They wouldn't schedule it until after this round of pills is finished. But . . . I'm thinking about it."

She hadn't said that aloud to anyone but her therapist, and then she felt guilty because her therapist started sobbing, using the Kleenex that was scattered around her office for patients.

"I feel like a coward," she said. "But I am a coward who is making a decision that no one else can make for her." She finally looked at him, eyes hot.

One of the reasons she and Grey were so well matched was that *his* defining trait—in her opinion—was that he couldn't stand conflict. Conflict avoidant. Willing to walk away rather than raise his voice.

Who were these perfect people anyway, the ones who weren't cowards, and weren't conflict avoidant, and weren't . . .

"You're breaking my fucking heart," Grey said, his voice flattening even more. "You don't get that, do you?"

Lizzie swallowed hard. What could she say? *It's my fucking life? I can't do it any longer? I'm sick of it? I hate the smell of sheets washed in hospital bleach? I hate pain? I hate fear?*

"If I begged." He stopped and cleared his throat. "If I begged, would it make any difference?"

"I love you, but you don't get it."

He didn't say anything, just reached for her hand.

Lizzie was so angry that she curled her hand into a fist and only let him enclose it, as if her hand were a closed clamshell. "You don't think that I'd rather stay here with you? I would. I *would*."

But then the words dried up and she couldn't speak, so she stared fixedly at the placemat. One corner curled up. Probably they had been stored in a damp place for a long period of time.

All winter, in some back room.

"You're so good at stepping gracefully away." Grey stopped.

"It's a useful quality," she said.

"Do you remember the end of our relationship?"

She snorted. "Did you really just ask me that?"

"Yes."

"We were going to move to London for my dissertation year," she said obediently. "You had an advance for a book—"

"*Untimely Frost.*"

"Weird, 'untimely frost' is from *Romeo and Juliet*," Lizzie said. "You gave me the title."

She nodded and tugged her hand free.

"My point is that I told you this thing," Grey said, "that I may be—that men were— And you acted as if I'd said that I couldn't go to dinner next Tuesday. We had one conversation, and then you left for London without me, and that was *it*."

Lizzie glared at him. "Are you telling me that you wished I'd signed you up for a weekend in conversion therapy? What was I supposed to do?"

"Cry," Grey said. "I thought you'd cry. Or maybe try to talk to me about it."

"I know that you are selfish," Lizzie said, willing her voice not to shake. "But are you really angry at me for not crying in front of the man I thought was about to propose, who told me he was gay instead? Do you realize how totally fucked up that is?"

"Is it?" Grey leaned forward, and Lizzie saw with a shock that he was absolutely livid. His face was white, and his eyes were ferocious. "I didn't want you to cry because of some weird self-gratification, Lizzie. I wanted to know that I *mattered* to you. That you cared how I felt and who I was."

"Fuck you," Lizzie whispered, her throat closing. "You are—you're—" She pushed back her chair.

"You can't leave," Grey ordered. His voice caught and a weird strangled noise came out of his throat. "Don't. Don't."

Lizzie swallowed hard and edged her chair back to the table.

"You're already leaving me, and you just told me that you're fucking *choosing* to leave me, so you don't get to walk away now," Grey said. His voice was raw, and tears made his eyes bluer.

Fury was making Lizzie's spine stiff—because really? Was this all about him? Men, testosterone, privilege, it all tumbled about her brain as she watched Grey sob without making a sound.

That was a foster care trick everyone learned on their first placement.

"I haven't made up my mind about the operation," she said again. But that wasn't really it.

She'd be *damned* if she'd apologize for dying. Women apologized for too much. Always apologizing for someone else getting sick, for example. The nurses, touching her gently on the arm, whispering, "I'm sorry."

"I just— You matter so much to me," Grey said, gulping back tears, voice hoarse now. "You're everything to me, Lizzie. If you'd asked me to, I would have stayed with you and gone to London; if you'd needed me, I would—"

"Grey, don't be ridiculous," Lizzie said, interrupting. "You can't stay with a girlfriend if you're *gay*."

"That's sex," Grey said. "Just sex. I hadn't had sex with anyone but you. I wouldn't have either. You saw it so black-and-white. I didn't. I wanted to tell you that I was surprised that men suddenly seemed desirable. Not anything else."

"What about biological imperatives, et cetera?" She let a burst of fury straighten her spine. "You seem to be overlooking the fact that I would have liked to have sex."

"We *did* have sex!"

A quick image of Dante flashed through Lizzie's mind. Sex . . . and sex. Like a firefly to lightning.

A beat of silence, and Grey's mouth quirked into a near smile. "I gather Dante is as great in bed as he is in the kitchen."

"Grey, stop. It's not a competition. My point is that you're making this all about you," Lizzie said. "Why in God's name would you blame me for breaking up with a man who told me he was attracted to men?"

"Because it wasn't just any man who said that. It was *me*," Grey said. "I wouldn't have left you if the opposite was true,

Lizzie. At the very least I would have asked you what you wanted to do."

"*What?*"

"I told you this thing, and you ripped our life in two without asking me for my opinion. Without . . ."

"You're bananas."

Grey pulled out a handkerchief. They sat there silently for a while. "I guess."

"Why didn't you say all this years ago, say, five minutes before I started packing my bags?"

"Because you didn't want me," Grey said.

Lizzie shook her head. "Me? Give me a break. I wasn't the one whose lover just told her that he wanted something she couldn't give him. I'm not a man."

"Oh for fuck's sake," Grey said, "sex doesn't matter."

"Love does."

"Yes, and I loved you then and I still do. I love you more than I will probably ever love Roh, and I suspect he's my future husband. It's not about *that*."

Lizzie fiddled with her spoon. A horrid, weary exhaustion descended on them, between the plates of exquisite Italian food, between the squawks of seagulls patrolling the shore, between the muted cacophony of a German family at the next table.

"I'm so sorry that I failed you," she said finally. And then looked up. "And I'm so fucking angry that I'm apologizing for dying."

"Lizzie, our breakup happened well before you got cancer."

Lizzie sat with that for a moment. She tended to forget there was a time before cancer. The cancerous Lizzie, the Stage Three Lizzie, was the only one available to look back, after all.

"My point is that it's happening all over again. Of course you have the best of all reasons to leave me, and you're doing it so politely that I should be grateful."

Lizzie waited, reminding herself that she didn't yell at people.

"You want to go quietly into that good night, or however that poem goes. You're the one with cancer. You're the one who was vomiting and in pain and all that stuff. I should be grateful to have spent any time with you. I suppose that's what I'm supposed to say at your memorial service, that I loved the time I had with you, no matter how short."

"I generally shy away from envisioning my memorial," Lizzie said. She turned around and waved at the waitress. "We need more wine." Neither of them had eaten a spoonful, but the squat little pitcher of sparkling wine was empty.

"I'm supposed to be lavishly grateful for those minutes, and yet I'm so furious I could reach across the table and strangle you myself. You're abandoning me—again. Leaving me before you have to leave."

The waitress turned up and looked at the bowls. *"Peccato!"* She reached out to take them.

Lizzie grabbed her bowl and pulled it closer. "More wine. *Vino, per favore.*"

"You can take mine," Grey said, nodding at his soup.

"No!" Lizzie pointed. "Eat it. All of it."

The waitress muttered something about Americans under her breath, grabbed the pitcher, and walked away.

"I'm not allowed to waste away from grief like a Victorian heroine?" Grey's eyes crinkled at the corners.

"No," Lizzie said, willing away tears. She watched Grey eat his soup and then took a deep breath. "I'm sorry I broke up with you like that, without talking about it."

His eyes softened, meeting hers. "Just don't—don't do it again, OK?"

"At the risk of saying the obvious—"

"Don't walk away as if I don't matter. As if we don't fit together like puzzle pieces. As if you didn't save my life back in foster care. I never would have gone to college except that you liked studying and you wanted me to go with you. You're acting as if you aren't everything to me. You know you are." He paused. "You act as if you don't matter to me."

Lizzie's mouth was trembling, so she spooned up some rice from the bottom of her bowl and put it in her mouth. For a moment, she thought it would come back out, spat inelegantly into her napkin. But then her taste buds recognized chicken broth that had no relation to the sandy cubes she used at home.

She put down her soup spoon, because when you're at a climax, an emotional climax, you aren't supposed to just want to drink soup and pretend you were in another room listening to a version of it on *This American Life*.

Synonyms for avoidance, her greatest skill: evading, dodging, shirking.

"It never occurred to me that you wanted to stay with me."

"I figured that out very quickly." His voice was wry.

"Is there another woman you think would have responded differently?"

"The Lizzie of my heart?"

Lizzie felt her stomach clench. "That's mean." She cleared her throat. "That's a cruel thing to say. I'm sorry not to be the person you thought I was . . . a woman who would stay."

He put his head in his hands. "I don't want you to be that woman. I'm not making any sense. It felt as if you were rejecting me for being gay. I told you a secret, my deepest secret, and you left me."

"I didn't leave you because you were gay! I mean I did, but because you were literally telling me that I wasn't the right . . ." Her voice trailed off. "Listen, are you going to tell me that making love to me was anything like making love to Rohan?"

Grey flinched.

"It wasn't," Lizzie said for him. "You're making me feel like I was homophobic, but I wasn't. I avoided. I ran away. I know that. I didn't see any point in couples therapy or talking it out. Plus I suck at confrontation."

Lizzie poured another glass of wine because the pitcher had reappeared when she wasn't looking. Then she poured some more for Grey as well.

They sat there and drank bubbling wine, listening to seagulls scream at each other.

"I love you," Lizzie offered, after a while. "More than anyone else. As much as my inadequate heart is able to. And I'm sorry that I didn't realize what was at stake when you told me."

"Now it sounds like a test," Grey said, giving her a crooked smile. "I'm such a wanker, as Roh would say."

Lizzie reached over and wound the fingers of her right hand through the fingers of his left. "We are matching puzzle pieces, Grey. You're right. And if it makes you feel any better . . . I left the apartment that night, remember?"

He nodded. "You wouldn't answer my texts."

"I went to a hotel, and I cried all night. And most of the next day too. I called down to ask for late checkout but I started sobbing and they just said, 'Yes, yes,' and hung up on me. The fact that I never cried in front of you . . . It wasn't a measure of my grief."

His fingers tightened. "How can you love me when I'm such an idiot?"

"You're *my* idiot. And I'm yours. I didn't know . . . I didn't want to drag down your joy."

"Joy?" He said it incredulously. "*Joy* when it meant—when it meant you left?"

Lizzie felt the Germans next door pause to look. Didn't all of Germany learn English in the cradle?

"If you didn't feel it then, you do now, right?" she said. "The whole time you were telling me, I was divided between wanting to kill myself for being such a fucking cliché—the happy woman who missed the obvious—and wanting you to be happy."

"I was happy."

"Happier."

"You're saying happiness is measured by who we sleep with. That's bollocks."

"Do you realize how much English slang you've picked up from Rohan?"

"There's some good words over there. I was gutted by not being happy enough with you."

At that, Lizzie actually started laughing, just a little. "OK, then, I can be British too: I was gobsmacked by your announcement. The only way I could keep breathing was to stay calm. Detach." She wrinkled her nose. "Dr. Weir told me that I won the Calmest Patient award when he told me about being Stage Three. I felt as if I heard it from another room, spoken about another person."

Grey's mouth wobbled again, and this time the sob burst from him, so Lizzie pushed back and went over and sat on his lap. He smelled so familiar, like blackberries and fresh clothing.

He was silent crying again, so she fished out a wad of Kleenex, clean ones, and pressed them into his hand. Then she closed her eyes, leaned against his chest, and pretended they weren't surrounded by curious tourists. Or curious Italians.

When his arms tightened and she heard him say in a very thick way to the waitress that they didn't want anything else, she popped her eyes open and said, "Au contraire, darling." The waitress was looking confused anyway, because when Grey was upset he sounded like deepest Georgia, and most Americans couldn't make their way through that accent, let alone an Italian trying to understand a foreign language.

"We would like dessert," she said. "All of them, one of each."

The waitress was less curious than exasperated, which was strangely reassuring.

"No one orders all of them, Signora."

"How many are there?"

"Eight." She started to list them, "Tiramisu . . ."

"All of them," Lizzie said, staring defiantly, with tearless eyes. The waitress probably wasn't being judgy, but Lizzie felt as if she was not living up to her part in the dramatic scene by staying calm while Grey sobbed. People probably thought she was a bitch.

"I reckon I'm about cried out," Grey said, his accent thicker than pond mud.

She didn't move until eight plates landed in front of them. "We have to eat the tiramisu first," she said, standing up and going back around the table, careful not to look at anyone around them.

"Why?"

"Do you know what the word means? *Tira* is a verb, like pull or pick, and then *mi* is me, and *su* is up. So it's a pick-me-up." She took a bite and let her mouth be incredibly happy about the combination of coffee and cream and cookie with just the right amount of sogginess.

"Are you more interested in food now that you're doing a chef? Even though you hate his food?"

"You're no good at being a BFF," Lizzie said, talking through a second bite because it was too good to wait. "Shouldn't you be emotionally supportive or, at the very least, polite about the guy I'm *doing*?"

Grey ate two bites so fast that Lizzie had to pull the plate closer to her side.

"I suck at being gay," he said. "I want to be with you and I want to love Roh, both at once. I don't want to talk about feelings, and I definitely don't want to make an ass of myself crying in public."

"That wouldn't have worked for me," Lizzie said. "I'm not a sharer."

"I didn't mean it that way."

"You should marry him." She finished the last bite of tiramisu. "You love me but you're in love with Rohan."

"Are you giving me permission?" Grey said wryly.

She looked up and met his eyes because this was important. "No. We don't have the right of refusal. You don't get to say whether I take chemo or not. I don't get to say that you should let your lover come out and be himself and marry you. I mean, I do get to *say* it, but it's not up to me, and you get to be in the closet if that's what you want."

Grey scowled at his plate.

"Next, *panna cotta,*" Lizzie said. The plate held a creamy mound that was flat on top, like a snow-covered volcano that exploded a million years ago.

"It looks like a boob." He took a bite. "Custard with a hint of orange. Mmm."

"You can have that one if I can have the zabaglione. Look at these strawberries." They were small, like dollhouse strawberries peeking out of frothy deliciousness.

"I don't like strawberries." He pointed his spoon. "How could you calmly turn your back on a giant boob? Or any of this? *Elba?* How can you give up?"

The vomiting nights, the loneliness of a nurse's visit at three A.M., the smell of those damn sheets, the freaking pain—it all went through her head, but she held her tongue.

Silence said it for her, because he scowled and said, "Zabaglione looks like semen."

Lizzie broke into choked laughter. "Foam?"

"Yeah, Jove's love butter." He stole a bite of hers. "Better than 'panna' whatever."

"Jove's *love butter*?"

"Oyster stew? White honey? French dressing?"

"Men are always trying to get someone to dress up that pig," Lizzie said, grinning.

Grey laughed and sang in a low voice, *"You see, we believe, well, let me put it like this."*

Lizzie squeaked. "Monty Python!"

"*Every sperm is sacred,*" he caroled low and sweet, smiling at her with the innocence of a choirboy. He had a honey-deep alto.

Lizzie took up the soprano without a second thought, their voices twining effortlessly after five years of Mrs. Bedrosian, singing a hymn in the morning, lessons after school, a hymn before dinner, a hymn before bed. "*Every sperm is great. If a sperm is wasted, God gets* quite *irate.*"

"Everyone is watching us," Grey sang, almost under his breath, "Shall we keep going?"

Lizzie grinned, happy that her back was to the room. "*Let the heathen spill theirs on the dusty ground . . .*"

Grey joined in, "*God shall make them pay for each sperm that can't be found!*"

"If this was a movie, the room would have joined in," Lizzie said. She didn't dare look around.

"You mean if life was a version of *Mamma Mia*? They enjoyed it," Grey said. He waved at someone behind her, and his eyes shifted down. "Especially this little fellow."

Lizzie turned and found a child standing at her knee. Curls fell over his forehead.

"*Ancora.*"

"I think he wants more."

An Italian woman approached. "If you will excuse," she said, "Alessandro loved your singing. One more song?"

The father of the German family at the next table flashed a white smile and said, in perfect English, "We love Monty Python! We will listen to anything you sing, Signore."

The endless afternoons singing shoulder to shoulder with a skinnier, younger version of Grey went through Lizzie's head like a slideshow on fast-forward. A side effect of cancer—at least in her brain—seemed to be an annoying habit of turning one's own life into a PowerPoint presentation.

Grey met her eyes. He was used to her refusing to sing with him, even in private. But she nodded and watched his eyes lighten.

"Of course we will," he said to the room at large, with his lovely smile. Then he stood up and brought Lizzie to her feet. "'O God, Our Help,'" he said in her ear. "Verse one, then four to the end."

"I haven't sung it in years," Lizzie said, looking around. The restaurant had maybe ten tables, and every single person was looking at them.

He shrugged. "Falling off a tree."

"A log, you idiot. All right."

From the moment she hit puberty, she realized her voice was embarrassingly gaudy. It surprised people. It drew attention. But Grey knew how to tame that big sound and wind around it, subduing the way her voice vibrated. It only took the first verse, about the stormy blast and endless years, to adjust their voices back together.

In her mind, she could hear Mrs. Bedrosian shouting, *Sing it with meaning, kids! Mean it! Mean it!*

"Now verse four," Grey said. He pulled her close to his body, smiling at their audience. It *was* an audience now. The diners at individual tables had magically aligned themselves, their faces open, not blinking.

"A thousand ages in Thy sight are like an evening gone; Short as the watch that ends the night, before the rising sun." They had it now: Their voices blazed with joy. Lizzie leaned her head against Grey's shoulder as no professional singer would do. But her voice was more than enough for this small room.

She could hear Mrs. Bedrosian in her head. *Go quiet on this one,* she would say, *rein in your voice, then bring out the trumpets at the end.*

"Time, like an ever-rolling stream, bears all its sons away." She sang soft and high, so that Grey could carry the sound from be-

neath, trying not to listen to the words, hearing them anyway. *"They fly forgotten, as a dream dies at the opening day."*

She didn't want to sing the last verse. She wanted to fly like birds do, in the stream of time, without acknowledging the eternal home she didn't believe in. Grey shifted so he stood behind her, wrapping both arms around her body, as if he could be her home.

She dropped from a soprano to an alto, playing the part of God's trumpet, and Grey effortlessly followed her. *"O God, our help in ages past, our hope for years to come."* His voice roughened, and she could hear tears in it. *"Be Thou our guard while troubles last, and our eternal home."*

In the second of silence that followed, powerful hands clapped together. Lizzie's eyes flew to the door where Dante was standing, his eyes fixed on her.

The silence broken, the German man rose to his feet, clapping. The two-year-old climbed on a chair, hooting happily. The Italian woman was wiping away tears. Chairs scraped as the other diners rose and clapped.

Dante threaded his way among the tables.

"Thank you," Grey called to their audience. "Thank you."

They sat back down. Dante had been caught by a table of bright-eyed Italians.

Lizzie picked up her fork and turned it over, looking at the desserts they had left. Around her, everyone was talking. The table behind them had decided, with polished British restraint, that she would do well on *The Voice*.

"Simon Cowell," someone said, and then, "Beautiful too. Hair . . ."

She looked up at Grey. "If someone pesters me on the beach tomorrow, I'm blaming you."

Grey's eyes were shining; he had loved Sunday performances as much as she had hated them. To this day, she lip-synced "Happy

Birthday," embarrassed by the way her voice boomed out and shocked people into saying absurd things.

The day she gave herself permission to stop singing—the day after breaking up with Grey—was . . .

Now, from the vantage point of Stage Three, it felt as if she might have overreacted.

"Thank you for singing with me," Grey said.

"You remembered that hymn was my favorite," Lizzie said, allowing one side of her mouth to curl up a bit.

"I remember everything about you," Grey said, just as Dante sat down.

"One of those Italians is connected to the TV channel Rai Due, and he'd like to talk to you," Dante said.

Lizzie pressed her lips together, but he kept talking. "I said no, you were a terrible diva and they shouldn't have anything to do with you, because you were an example of Americans at their worst."

"Thank you!" Lizzie said, a grin bursting out on her face.

"Damn, you're good," Grey said appreciatively.

"And straight," Dante said, the faintest edge to his voice.

"Yeah," Grey said. "If I was, you wouldn't get within ten feet of her."

"What a testosterone-y moment," Lizzie observed.

Dante shrugged. "Angelica's *torta della nonna* is famous all over the island. She's Fabrizio's wife, by the way." He picked up a fork and took a huge bite of cake.

"I'm full," Lizzie confessed.

Dante pushed the plate toward Grey. "Try it. It's good."

"Just look at that," Lizzie said, giggling. "Détente by means of sugar."

Grey flicked a look at her under his lashes. "I think I'll go find Rohan."

"He's in the hotel courtyard, digesting the fact that I don't need a restaurant partner, nor do I want to cook for more people." The edge in Dante's voice sharpened. "He appears to think I might change my mind if I were offered enough money."

"Right," Grey said. "I'll try to explain to him."

Dante glanced at him. "Tell him it's like being gay."

Grey scowled. "I see no similarity."

Masculinity was practically poisoning the air, but Lizzie couldn't think of anything to lighten the moment.

"Owning my restaurant is at the core of me," Dante said, his voice hard. "Everyone in this room realizes what you sacrificed due to an equally incontrovertible fact."

Grey leaned across the table. "You listened closely to the hymn?"

"Grey!" Lizzie said sharply.

He didn't look at her, so angry that he'd gone pale under his tan. "Then you should know that time and that ever-rolling fucking stream is the *only* thing that will take Lizzie from me."

"That's enough," Lizzie said, standing up. "You're both acting like idiots. I'm no restaurant," she said to Dante. "I'm not your possession either," she told Grey. "Idiots, both of you."

She walked out and people clapped for her as she went among the tables, and she thought with a lurch of her stomach that perhaps she couldn't come to Fabrizio's again.

But the waitress didn't bother with a smile. Maybe she understood enough English to be insulted by singing about sacred sperm. "Are you paying, or shall I give the bill to him?" She nodded behind Lizzie, presumably at Grey.

"Him," Lizzie said. "See you tomorrow, Signora."

Chapter Fifteen

Etta Moretti's bedroom door,
from Mark Drought, op-ed columnist:

We humans have an exaggerated view of our
place in the cosmos. We inhabit a small planet,
circling an ordinary star on the periphery of an
unremarkable galaxy—one of 200 billion stars
in the Milky Way, which is itself just one of 200
billion galaxies. Nonetheless, we consider our-
selves the "crown of creation," as if the goal of
the universe's 14 billion years of evolution has
been the ascent of mankind.

Teenagers are always in bad moods. It's practically a requirement
of turning thirteen that you start pouting and farting around in
your room looking sullen and maybe even suicidal. Staring at zits
in the mirror. Whatever.

Yay for not being there yet.

The truth is that grown-ups are just as prone to pissiness. It isn't as if an extra thirty years make that thirteen-year-old complainer disappear.

Witness whereof: Babbo was in the kitchen, glowering instead of glowing. Lizzie answered the door in her room, but shook her head and closed the door before Etta could say a word. Grey was reading under a tree in the courtyard. He looked up, and Etta almost tripped over herself.

He looked sick. Like, really sick. He probably drank too much the night before, the way adults do when they're on vacation.

"Do you want some gelato?" she asked cautiously.

Grey shook his head. "Lizzie insisted on trying all the desserts at lunch." He looked back at his book.

No one needed her or wanted her, which made her feel unexceptional. And unnecessary, which she also was, except to Babbo.

Grey probably thought she was spoiled, but he was wrong.

For one thing, Etta had to cut vegetables when other girls her age were going to camp. In Italy, camps for kids happened in four-star hotels, or at worst, three-star hotels. Everyone got to keep their cell, and no one had to weave baskets or learn to swim. They ate ice cream and sat around under the pine trees, because the camps were in the mountains where the air was better for children.

But Babbo had said no to camp again this year. It wasn't money, because he had plenty of that. "I want you around, Noodle," he had said back in June, and it had seemed so sweet that Etta didn't push. If he got together with Lizzie, like really got together, next summer she could go to camp, because he wouldn't be alone.

She sat down on the opposite side of the courtyard from Grey and watched him through her sunglasses. They were very cool sunglasses: big orange frames from the 1960s. Firenze had fantastic vintage stores, better than anything in New York. Someday people would notice how cool she was, and what great stuff she had. Meanwhile she was just practicing her look.

The glasses turned the world a watery green. Maybe that's why Grey looked sick. Maybe everybody in the sixties walked around with frizzy hair, peering through green lenses.

"May I bring you something to drink, Signorina?" It was one of the waiters from Rome who didn't know she didn't belong in the hotel. He couldn't be more than seventeen, though, of course, that was fantastically old compared to her.

Before Etta could decide how to reply, Grey barked, "Room sixty-three" from the other side of the courtyard.

The waiter smiled. "An ice cream?"

He thought she was American because Grey was. Well, she *was* American.

"Yup," she said, in a very New York way. "Chocolate, vanilla, and . . ." Heck, what was *stracciatella* in English? Not chocolate chip. "*Stracciatella.*"

His eyes narrowed a little because she slurred her C's like a Florentine, but she just looked at him, calm, like one of those sleek girls who spent all their time in hotels like this one. "Room sixty-three," she added pointedly.

Then he bowed, and said, "*Un minuto.*" That was some Roman accent he had. It went with his hawkish nose.

Ruby walked out of the hotel just as the gelato arrived. It came in a pink glass, like a fat wineglass, with three wafer cookies stuck into the gelato and fanned out like a peacock's tail. Plus *fragole di bosco,* wild strawberries.

"Hey, that's a gorgeous pudding—what we Brits call dessert," Ruby said, coming over. "I love that T-shirt too. Hermione rules."

Etta grinned at her. Her shirt read *I may be frumpy but I'm super-smart.*

"Another gelato," Grey called, nodding toward Ruby.

"Room sixty-three," the waiter replied, scurrying away.

Ruby sat down, shoved her sunglasses on top of her head, and looked over at Grey. "Looks like he's throwing a wobbly," she said to Etta.

Etta was eating all the strawberries first. "What's that?"

"Pissed off, visibly. Let's take our ice cream down to the beach and find Rohan."

The afternoon had made Etta achy because no one wanted to be with her, but now she had Ruby and fancy gelato, so she couldn't stop smiling. Once another glass of gelato arrived, they headed toward the arch that led to the path that went down the side of the hill to the private beach.

Etta had seen the hotel's beach before. No one could stop Italians from walking up and down the whole seaside, including the part that belonged to the Bonaparte.

At the private beach, the umbrellas weren't made of straw, but some sort of plastic with pink fringes that blew in the wind. Pretty. Not environmentally sound, but really pretty. Every beach bed had a pink table, and all the beautiful people were out here, being beautiful and poking at their phones.

As they reached the bottom of the stairs, a man bowed and said, *"Buona sera, Signore."*

"Buona sera," Etta said. "Have you seen Mr. Das?"

"I'm in his party," Ruby put in.

He squinted at Ruby and jerked his head. *"È di là dal paravento."*

Sure enough, Rohan was behind a privacy screen they'd set up on the beach. He had five women in front of him. The hotel had a man standing by to shoo away anybody trying to get around the screen and take photos.

They walked over and watched as the women stuck the bottoms of their bare right feet against their left thighs.

"Look up to the sky," Rohan said, his voice very deep and calm. "You might stay in prayer pose, or you could lift your arms to the sky and be a tree. You might raise your eyes to the heavens, or even close them."

At Etta's shoulder, Ruby whispered something under her breath that definitely wasn't a compliment.

They all waved their arms around, while Etta spooned the last of her gelato into her mouth. Rohan looked like a great stork on one leg.

"Feel the sand," Rohan said, so Etta toed off one flip-flop and curled her toes into the sand. "I say to you something that my teacher says to me every day: 'If one's mind has peace, the whole world will appear peaceful.'"

He brought his hands into a prayer position and bowed his head. "Namaste."

The women all chirped "Namaste" and clustered around him, chattering, until he said something that made them all turn around and stare, so Etta raised one hand and waved, feeling very good about her orange glasses, and less good about her faded T-shirt.

None of the women seemed ready to shout out "Hermione!" the way Ruby had.

One of the women, the one with her hand curled around Rohan's arm, was wearing an amazing one-piece swimsuit that had V's going down the front, with the sharp point right at her coochie. Sunflower earrings, lots of chunky bracelets, and an orange gauzy thing that billowed behind her. And a big scarf wrapped around her head like a turban.

She was gorgeous and expensive. She didn't even look stupid. She was too expensive to be stupid. All the same, she couldn't be more than eighteen. Maybe seventeen.

Etta put down her gelato glass on one of the pink tables and reminded herself that she was only twelve. She could find the boy equivalent of that girl and transform herself, using his money, unless her babbo finally started giving her an allowance.

But somehow she couldn't imagine that she would ever be able to wear a tall turban without looking silly.

"Let's go," Rohan said, striding past them, his shoes in one hand.

"Not yet," Ruby said, snickering. "I'm busy growing roots."

Etta ran to catch up. He was heading up the stairs to the Bonaparte superfast. "Wait up!" she called. "Ruby's still eating her gelato."

He didn't stop until he was halfway up. Then he looked over his shoulder, so Etta did too. Ruby was just starting to climb the stairs, and the women were standing together, looking up at them.

"Are you kidding me?" Etta demanded. "You think they're going to chase you up the stairs so they can namaste you a few more times?" She clung to the railing. "Ugh, I'm out of breath, and if I sick up my gelato, it's your fault."

"You should do yoga with me," Rohan said. Of course, he wasn't out of breath at all. He held his sunglasses up as he stared at the beach. He had the kind of face that was hard to read, but the corners of his mouth were tight, like pinch pleats on fancy curtains.

"Why do you teach yoga if you don't like them?" Etta asked.

Ruby had caught up, so Rohan snapped his glasses back down and started climbing again. "I like teaching. And, of course I like them."

"Even that one with the turban?" Etta asked.

"The one who's hiding another life-form on top of her head?" Ruby added.

"Yeah, maybe she is," Etta said, grinning. "She's an alien and she's covering up the bulbous part of her head where her ESP is stored. Or she's got another person in there, like Voldemort. Maybe the captain of her spaceship or something. He's a different species and—"

Rohan stopped again. "Jesus, kid."

"Yeah, OK," Etta said. "You're not going for the Voldemort scenario. Have you even read Harry Potter?"

"I saw the first movie."

They were moving again, and Etta could see the arch leading into the *albergo*. "That's lame," she said, trying not to sound gaspy.

They walked through the arch and found the courtyard still empty except for Grey. It had big trees all the way around that made it shady but noisy, because the cicadas sang loudest after lunch. The singing and the heat gave it that sort of dreamy-afternoon-ness that never seemed to happen in New York. In Italy, afternoons puddled like tide pools left behind in a rocky seashore.

"I'm thinking about a nap," Rohan told Grey.

Grey stood up. "I'm not sleepy. What are you doing?" he asked Etta and Ruby. He had his hands stuck in his pockets.

Etta barely stopped her mouth from falling open because, really? He wanted to do something with her? Well, her and Ruby?

His shoes were soft and worn, but they were dark red and probably cost a ton. He was wearing baggy white pants that managed to look cool, and a Captain Britain T-shirt. He looked super Gucci and not like someone who would want to hang out with her.

"We could go to the black beach," Etta said, making it up as she went. "Lizzie is collecting sea glass, and we could get her some."

"What's a black beach?" Rohan asked.

"The sand is black. There aren't any umbrellas there. No tourists either."

"A secret beach," Ruby said. "I like it."

"Where is it?" Grey asked.

"We catch the bus, or maybe Mario can drive us," Etta said. "He's got a job for the summer, driving hotel guests to and from the ferry."

Rohan went into the hotel to find Mario.

"Text your father," Grey said.

"My *babbo*, not my father. He can't drive us. He's cooking."

"No, to make sure it's OK."

"I can go anywhere, within reason, as long as I'm home by six." She was proud of that, because last year she couldn't take the bus alone.

"You have to ask your dad. Babbo. Whatever."

"Why?"

"Oh for God's sake. Because you're a kid and I'm not—we're not. You're a little girl and I can't believe I'm even thinking about going to a beach. I hate beaches."

"Too late, you already said you'd go, and Ruby is going, Rohan too."

"I'm thirty-three and way too old to be jaunting around in company with a—what are you? Ten?"

"*Ten?* You think a ten-year-old has the freedom to get on a bus and go around Elba?"

"Seventeen-year-olds aren't allowed to go around L.A., so cut me some slack."

"I'm almost thirteen." She stuck out her phone so he could read it. "Babbo says sure."

He peered at it. "Does he know that Lizzie isn't here?"

"I said, 'with Gray and Ruby.'"

"That's not how I spell my name."

"Phonetic spelling," Etta said. "My generation is all over that. No more grammar. No more spelling. Anyway, Babbo knows it's you guys."

She tagged along as the hotel people fell about getting Rohan a car and driver, who turned out not to be Mario, but a guy in a Mercedes.

"*La spiaggia nera,*" Etta told him. "*Vicino a Porto Azzurro.*"

"I'll get you as close as I can," he said.

His voice was thick Roman. Babbo would hate him on sight, or rather, on sound. That's the way it was for Florentines and Romans. Also Florentines and Milanese.

The Roman drove them partway around the island.

"You guys should leave your phones," Etta told the others, putting hers on the seat. "We have to climb, and you'll break the screen if it falls."

"Climb?" Rohan asked.

"Over there." She waved her hand. From here, the black rocks looked soft and round, like black pillows.

Grey and Ruby left their phones, but Rohan kept his.

"You need both hands to climb," Etta told him.

"I don't go anywhere without it," he said, shoving it so deep into his pocket that he almost pulled down his own pants.

"Your funeral," Etta said. "Come on."

To get to the black beach you had to climb over a hill made up of volcanic rocks, smooth and rounded by the wind. Rohan took a call, leaning against the car, so she and Ruby and Grey set off without him.

Ruby climbed fast, arms swinging, while Grey trailed behind. Etta could hear him muttering to himself as they picked their way across the rocks, skipping tiny rivers that filled up when the tide came in, or if there was a storm.

She called him over when she found a tide pool with anemone. "See that red one?" It was hanging out, all its tentacles just drifting around. She poked at it with a rock and it shut up tight.

Grey squatted down.

"Wait a minute," Etta said. Sure enough, it didn't have enough brains to stay closed for long and it turned itself inside out, gleaming red through the water. "There are yellow ones in the ocean. Like daisies, but sea daisies."

"I could use those in a book," Grey said, almost to himself.

"You mean like in a horror novel?"

"Maybe." Grey got up. "That secret beach is coming up in the next day or so, isn't it?"

"We'll see it soon." They followed Ruby, clambering down the rocks and then along a narrow path. The air started to smell good, like her babbo's kitchen, because of wild fennel and rosemary. Then they scrambled over some big chunky pieces, and there it was. "Black, see?"

Grey nodded. "Looks like murder on the feet."

"That part, inshore, is rough, but at the shore it's regular sand, but black. The sea glass is near the water anyway." The beach was completely empty, with just one yacht anchored a ways out. It wasn't one of the floating apartment buildings, just a regular boat.

"At least it's quiet," Grey said, as he came down to the flat part. Ruby was already at the shore, crouched down and scooping up black sand.

"No cicadas," Etta pointed out. Herby bushes led down the mountain to the beach, but no trees for the cicadas to hide in. "Did you know what you hear is the male cicadas singing together, trying to get females to come over?"

He didn't answer, but she kept telling him anyway. "Every type of cicada has its own song. They just discovered a new Italian cicada when they realized it had a different song that hadn't been heard before. Well, not a new one, because it's millions of years old, but new to us. To scientists."

They got to the shore and Grey walked past Ruby, right into the water, his red shoes looking like blurry anemone.

"See how your shoes look like anemones?" Etta asked. "That's what I think, anyway. How would you describe them?"

He shrugged.

"You're a writer," Etta pointed out. "Doesn't it come easy to you? What color would you call the water here? Not blue, something better."

Grey looked out at the cove.

"Blue," he said.

"Turquoise," Ruby said over her shoulder. She was walking along where foamy water hit the shore.

"Indigo," Etta suggested.

"Maybe you'll be a novelist. You talk a lot," Grey said.

Not very nice. Etta narrowed her eyes at his back and then said, "Fine. Let's go find sea glass."

"Not me." He turned again to look out at the ocean, shading his eyes.

"That's what we came here for! To find a present for Lizzie!"

"*You* came here for that."

Etta put her hands on her hips, and straight-out glared at him. "What's the matter with you and Lizzie? I thought you were friends, like, best friends."

He twitched like he was about to say one thing, but changed his mind and said something else. "Do you hear that? I think I can hear a cicada or two." He cocked his head.

"I don't hear anything but you being weird."

He scowled at her. "I'm an adult. Shouldn't you be more polite?"

"Why are you being so weird about Lizzie?"

"You don't see what's happening?"

"What do you mean?" Etta said, exasperated.

"She's falling for your dad."

Happiness can come with a thump, as if an adult pounded you on the back in order to celebrate but overshot the mark. It can shake up your inner organs.

"Yeah," Etta managed. She kept a smile off her face, just barely. "I know that. So?"

Grey pushed his glasses up on the top of his head. "This is absurd."

"I don't get it. You should be happy for—for Lizzie. *I'm* happy for Babbo."

"I'm happy," Grey said, his mouth thin. "I'm not having this conversation with you. I'll find some damn sea glass, OK?"

He had that look her babbo got sometimes, as if he was about to storm out of the room.

"Good!" Etta said, going over to where the black sand met the water. The sea was clear, indigo blue, and there was a little wavy line of foam going down the beach, like a lace ruffle.

Ruby was farther inland, down on her knees.

Etta went over to her. "The best sea glass is right at the edge."

"Look at this sand," Ruby said, picking up a handful and letting it stream out of her hand.

"Lizzie likes glass, not sand."

"It's pearlescent," Ruby said, sounding kind of awed.

Etta squatted down. "It is shiny."

"I could do something with this," Ruby said, letting another handful stream back to the beach. "I think it's pumice but I've never seen anything like it."

"What could you do? Put it in a bowl?"

"Make a skin rub," Ruby said. "Or maybe a hair mask. A shimmering black sand mask."

"I'm going to find some sea glass." Etta went back to the water's edge. It didn't take too long to walk the whole beach. A while later, she came back with a heavy pile of sea glass in the rolled-up bottom of her T-shirt.

She waved at Ruby, who had dug a bunch of holes in the sand, and kept going.

Rohan was sitting with Grey right on the edge of the sea, where the sand turned to rocks.

"Did you find any?" she asked Grey.

"Yeah." He patted the ground next to him, and sure enough he had a few.

Etta plopped down and started sorting. She didn't want to give

Lizzie bad ones, with sharp edges or the wrong color. The best sea glass was hazy, like the deepest green sea, frosted over.

"I'm not jealous of your babbo," Grey said abruptly. "I love Lizzie. We grew up together."

Rohan muttered something in another language.

Etta kept sorting glass, tossing bad ones as if she were barely listening. As if the conversation weren't important. "I don't have a brother, but if I did, he wouldn't mind if I fell in love."

"It's more complicated than that, kid."

"I don't see why. You're gay. Lizzie's not a guy."

"Yeah," Rohan said. "You're gay, and Lizzie's not a guy."

"Why are you throwing so many pieces away?" Grey asked Etta, ignoring Rohan.

"They're not perfect." And, at his raised eyebrow: "What? I want her to love every one of them."

"You're both saying 'gay' as if it meant something," Grey said, looking back out to sea.

"It does mean something. It means who you want to have sex with. Unless you're pansexual, which means you're not limited in sexual choice. *What?*" Etta said again when they both turned their heads and looked at her. "I had health class just like everyone else. And you needn't look so condescending. I know all about being bi."

"You do?" Grey asked.

Etta pointed at him. "Don't you dare smirk at me."

"I'm not!"

He was, but she let it go.

"My cousin is queer, and she says that straight people aren't allowed to say anything about it, because we'll always get it wrong."

Grey reached toward her pile of perfect sea glass and let them fall through his fingers. "Love is more complicated than who you sleep with."

She pounced on a piece of sea glass that glinted, showing a shining green edge, and threw it toward the ocean so it could be tumbled in the sand. "We talked about that in English class. Romeo is in love with Juliet, but he loves Mercutio too, maybe even more."

Grey muttered something that sounded like "Fucking Romeo."

"Romeo loved Mercutio more than Juliet," Rohan said, kinda slow. He was sitting with his hands dangling over his knees and his sunglasses pushed back on his head. From where she was sitting, he didn't look like a movie star: His nose was too big.

"I love you, damn it," Grey said to him.

The tension was pretty thick so Etta started talking just to say something. "You could get married in my babbo's restaurant. Famous people do that because there aren't any paparazzi and no cameras, even for weddings. It's a rule."

"Can't do that, kiddo. Italy doesn't allow gays to marry," Grey said.

"Not that you would," Rohan said.

"Maybe I would."

They looked at each other, and Etta was definitely feeling like she wished she was somewhere else. She started scooping all the sea glass into her T-shirt again. "I'll go see what Ruby is doing."

"You can't climb over the rocks like that." Grey got up too. He took a handful of her glass and poured it into his pants pocket. They bagged down, making Etta giggle.

"You look like a teenager trying to shoplift candy bars," she told him.

Rohan was still staring out to sea.

Grey rolled his eyes. "I would have shoplifted cigarettes, if anything." He reached out a hand, and Rohan took it and got up.

Ruby came back, her pockets bulging too, and told Grey and Rohan about the sand, the pearly black sand.

They went back faster than they came.

It was always like that.

Chapter Sixteen

Lizzie had walked back from Fabrizio's in a fog. Grey was furious at her. *Furious.* How could she not have known it?

But what the hell?

He was angry at *her* because she broke up with him? Isn't that what every woman in the world would have done? The problem was that Grey was so endlessly genial. He oozed southern charm, even when he was angry. His version of a tongue lashing would be a compliment from a New York cabbie.

She sat on her bed feeling sick to her stomach. Her best friend in the world had been . . . whatever he was, and she hadn't known. Of course, at the time she'd been busy trying to crawl out of a pit of grief and shame.

New Year's Eve, and they'd gone out to dinner, which was a big deal because he was only writing his first book, and she'd been a grad student. No money.

She had been certain, dead certain, that he was going to ask her to marry him.

It was a logical step. All her girlfriends thought so. They'd been together, really together, for years. Perfect time to pull out a ring.

But instead . . . She'd never forget the way her heart beat quickly all the way through the meal, waiting for the moment—he wouldn't do a ring in champagne, that was too trite. Over dessert? *In* the dessert?

Instead, he put down his fork and told her that he was attracted to men.

And now he was blaming her for their breakup? *He* was the one who had made love to her so sweetly, for years. She started grinding her teeth, thinking of it. Making love to Grey was nothing like making love to Dante. That was a fact.

Still, it hadn't been bad. It had been *good*.

Images beat their way through her mind: Grey smiling at her, loving her. Grey being tender and sweet and making her feel beloved and lovely, even her knees.

Then, after he said that at dinner, the way she felt shamed and ugly, even though she knew he loved her.

But Dante? Having sex with Dante was all body. It was sweaty and gasping and *base*.

It was fucking.

She sank her head into her hands. Her whole body had jolted when she saw rage in Grey's eyes. He was her other half, her protector. During chemo, he had mopped her head and coaxed her to drink broth and watched endless Bollywood movies with her. Movies that weren't even in English and didn't have subtitles. They made up stories about what was going on.

He had left Rohan in L.A., where God knows what could have happened to the sexiest man alive, surrounded by predatory beautiful people. Obviously nothing did, because here they were, still together.

But all the same, something could have. She could have broken his heart, and then broken his relationship too.

It was all just so—so fucking awful.

Out of her control.

There was nothing she hated more than being out of control. It went back to her mother, she knew that. Years of therapy told her that. Four foster homes, with the thirty-day notice always hanging over her head.

Stuff happened. She had been in her first foster home for two years before Mariana got pregnant, then started throwing up all the time and couldn't handle being a foster mom anymore. Lizzie had been just eight when she moved in, but by ten she had fooled herself into feeling safe.

She'd actually tried begging, promising to help.

Stupid.

Mariana cried so hard that she got sick and then her husband was angry, and the social worker took Lizzie and the two other kids away the next day. Not even waiting thirty days. Later, Mariana wanted her back, the social worker said. She felt guilty. She had stopped throwing up.

Lizzie said she would run away if they put her back in that house, and they believed her. She couldn't control much but to go back to Mariana? No. Lizzie was the one to reject her that time.

After that, Lizzie did exactly what needed to be done in order to make the next foster mom happy, no more, no less. After two placements, she ended up with Mrs. Bedrosian, which meant she had to learn how to sing.

The only hard part was when Mrs. Bedrosian wanted her to sing at church. Or, God forbid, do a solo.

Cost of doing business, Grey would tell her. *Cost of doing business, Lizzie-Liz.* Mrs. Bedrosian had been his first and last foster home. They'd been together there until they graduated from high school.

A sob was pressing on the back of her throat, which was fucking annoying, so she rolled onto her back and stared at the ceiling.

What was she crying for? Little Lizzie, safe and warm, if not loved? Not-so-little Grey, less loved, except by her—and she had apparently dumped him, because she thought *he* was dumping *her*?

He was gay.

How could he possibly think they wouldn't break up?

But he had. He had. This afternoon she'd seen in his eyes that he had believed their relationship would survive his announcement. Her heart thudded slowly in her chest and she could taste surprise and regret in her mouth.

No, not regret.

She refused to regret what was obvious common sense.

Grey looked at Rohan the way Dante looked at food. Dante was so passionate about the way it smelled and tasted and looked that it made her hungry, not for his food, but for his broad shoulders, for the smell of him, for the thrust of him, for the startling, lucid way that lust and erotic energy grounded her in her body, for those orgasms he gave her.

Dante orgasms, she should call them. The ones he coaxed and commanded her into. The ones that were vulgar and took so long. Leonard Cohen would say that generations of butterflies died waiting for her, waiting for that final rush of feeling, the curled toes, the bolt of joy.

Were they worth breaking Grey's heart?

Not a fair question, because Grey had broken *her* heart.

She had cried for a year, in cafés, in grocery stores, once, horrifyingly, in class while teaching *The Winter's Tale*, because Hermione's little boy dies. She had cried in front of a room of students, because she wouldn't have a baby with Grey.

She hadn't imagined then what lay ahead.

No babies at all. Not so many more years either.

That thought was familiar, a grating horribleness that she'd come to terms with, more or less. She pushed it away and opened

her courtesan book only to close it. Finally, she resorted to counting Napoleonic bees on the ceiling until the grief and anger slipped
away enough so that she could sleep.

But she woke hours later, in the early evening, still thinking
about Grey.

He was objectively beautiful. When he was singing about sacred
sperm and laughing, his face was too pretty to be real. His mouth
was perfect, with a deep lower lip and a pout on the top, like a girl
from the 1920s who had just discovered lip color.

But when he growled at her in the restaurant, his eyes went
squinty and hard, and she could see lines around his eyes and in his
forehead. Then he wasn't beautiful anymore, but a man whose girlfriend and best friend had broken his heart (albeit for the right
reasons). Lots of people weren't married as long as they'd been
together.

The thing was that they had become each other's family. Foster
care was full of unmoored children, and the two of them formed a
unit. So there had been so much at stake when he told her the truth.

It wasn't her fault that he was gay. And it wasn't her fault that
she was dying. It wasn't her fault that Grey already looked like a
survivor, and he already had survivor's guilt, and probably depression to go along with it.

The hard thought that showed up next?

It *would* be her fault if Dante got that look, that survivor look.
If Etta's bright, curious eyes turned into survivor eyes. She'd seen a
lot of those eyes. People with those eyes walked the hallways in
hospitals. The worst was on the peds floor.

Right. No survivor eyes for Dante, and certainly none for Etta,
which meant she had to go. Go. Leave Elba.

She curled up at that thought, pressing her stomach against her
knees. It wasn't fair. That wasn't fair. All of this shit wasn't fair,
but Elba . . . she was in love with Elba.

Maybe with Dante too.

She wanted to keep going to the beach, and sleeping with Lulu, and eating *bombolone* for breakfast, and having dinner at the Principe Blu, followed by sex with Dante.

Last night he had traced her scars with one finger, so she really had to tell him soon. But meanwhile, she had just been gobbling the days, all the hours she was awake.

Still, she didn't want Etta to change, like a robin whose bright red breast faded.

Maybe she was making too much of her influence on Etta, but she didn't think so. She remembered what it was to look for a mother to replace the one who wasn't there.

She had made that mistake with Mariana, let herself think that she was loved because she had cereal every morning, and because Mariana sang her funny songs and read her stories. It turned out that Mariana had just been practicing.

Practicing being a mother.

Practicing loving.

If she was Etta's mother, it would be a temporary thing. Practice for nothing. Even when the social worker closed the door of the car to drive Lizzie away from Mariana, she hadn't really believed it.

She could still remember the way her fingers looked pressed against the glass.

Mariana hadn't come out and said it was a mistake.

There was no going back from being Stage Three either.

Chapter Seventeen

Etta Moretti's bedroom door,
by Dr. Seuss:

Today you are you! That is truer than true!
There is no one alive who is you-er than you!
Shout loud, "I am lucky to be what I am!
Thank goodness I'm not a clam or a ham
Or a dusty old jar of sour gooseberry jam!
I am what I am! That's a great thing to be!"

The morning after the black beach Etta went to the hotel first thing. Babbo was at the market, so she put on a sundress and walked through the archway and sat down under a tree as if she belonged there. When a Roman waiter showed up, she took that as a sign and ordered breakfast. "Room sixty-three," she told him.

"*Sì, Signora,*" he said, and bowed a little. *Signora!* That's what it was like to have money. You could be twelve years old, and people thought you were grown up. Or pretended you were, because you had money.

"Hey, there." Ruby sat down across from her.

"Would you like breakfast?" Etta asked. "I can call him back."

"I didn't know you were staying here."

"I'm not. This breakfast is Grey's present."

Ruby had a way of making one eyebrow go up by itself that Etta meant to copy. "Does he know? No, don't answer that." She turned around and looked for the waiter.

He came outside, but he didn't notice that Ruby had her hand up and went back in the door. Etta stuck her forefingers in her mouth and whistled. The sound bounced around the stone walls and sure enough, the waiter jerked his head out the door and headed toward them.

"*Non sai chi è?*" she hissed at him.

He gave her a squinty Roman look.

"*È una famosa attrice in America. Può farti licenziare in cinque secondi!*" He looked pretty startled, so Etta added, for good measure, "*Lei possiede il più grande yacht. E tu l'hai ignorata.*"

After that he gave Ruby a deep bow and said "Signora" a bunch of times.

"What did you say to him?" Ruby asked after the Roman had gone.

"I told him you were a famous actress with the biggest yacht out there," Etta said.

The waiter showed up with a big tray of pastries. Ruby winked at her and played up being a famous person until Etta started giggling.

He finally left and Ruby took a bite of a brioche and moaned. "I think this is one of the best pastries I've ever eaten."

"Does it have red filling?" Etta peered over. "They're pretty good. Signora Antonella makes them from the sour cherries in her garden. Babbo thinks she uses too much sugar, but he's wrong."

Ruby took the last bite and then licked her fingers. "Your babbo is nuts. This stuff is addictive."

"If you like the smell, she makes other stuff too. Candles and stuff like that."

"I love the smell," Ruby said. "Does Antonella have a store?"

"No, but you know those little shops on the way to the beach, the public beach? They all sell her essential oils. Elba oils."

"I need some Elba oil," Ruby said, finishing her brioche. "And sour cherry perfume."

Rohan walked out of the dark hotel and ambled over to them. He was wearing a pale yellow linen suit with a vest. It would have looked ridiculous on almost anyone, but he looked great.

"Hey, girls," he said, sitting down.

"You have to eat one of these," Ruby said, pushing the last brioche toward him. "Some lady makes them out of the cherry trees in her backyard."

"Huh." He ate a bite and then finished the whole thing in two more bites.

They ordered more brioche and tea.

"I have to leave today," Ruby said, wrinkling her nose. "I came to say goodbye."

"Why? Job to do?" Rohan asked.

"The French girl I was doing makeup for hopped yachts yesterday and left with a Swiss guy sometime after lunch."

"Hell," Rohan said, pouring tea. "Are you OK to get home?"

"Sure, it's all set up in the agency agreement. My agent said I can work with Ava DuVernay, if I go back immediately."

"She did *A Wrinkle in Time*," Etta said, feeling her eyes widen. Rohan was one thing, but honestly, his stuff was too old for her. But Ava DuVernay? *Cool.*

"Did you like the movie?"

"It wasn't terrible," she said cautiously. "Except in places, if you had read the book. The makeup was great. Do you know how they got jewels to stick on Oprah's face?"

"Spirit gum," Ruby said. "You make dots first, to get the shape you want, and then glue the jewels on with spirit gum."

"Were you there?"

"Yup," Ruby said. "A friend of mine, Derrick, was in charge of Oprah's look, but I worked on the cast."

"So cool," Etta breathed.

"You don't look too excited," Rohan said.

Ruby shrugged. "I have to go in as an assistant rather than artist, because I'm last minute. Lots of arms and legs."

"You should be key, not assistant," Rohan said. "Key makeup artist," he told Etta. "They design makeup for a film."

Etta looked between them, thinking it sucked that she didn't have an old friend. Ruby and Rohan had been friends forever, and so had Lizzie and Grey. Maybe it wasn't too late.

"Maybe in a few years," Ruby said. "Anyway, I'm starting to think about creating some of my own products. I found this sand yesterday—pearly black sand—and I'd like to create a face wash or mud mask."

"Can't you just stay here and make face mud?" Etta asked, wishing she would.

"In a perfect world," Ruby replied.

"I'll hire you," Rohan said.

"What for?" she asked, frowning at him.

He put down his teacup. "Lizzie's makeup?"

Etta hooted. "Lizzie doesn't wear makeup!"

"She could," Rohan said. "Come on, Ruby, just tell your agency you're staying with me, and they'll bill my people."

"Lizzie is not someone who wants to put on makeup," Ruby said. "She doesn't need it either. And I don't take charity, even from old friends." She reached out and punched him on the shoulder. "Ass."

"Not charity. Listen, why don't you be key for *Romeo and Juliet*," Rohan said, eyes all lit up. "You can design the makeup."

"You don't even know my work," Ruby said, snorting.

"I know *you*," Rohan said.

"But we haven't seen each other in years."

"Doesn't matter. My first chance to direct . . ." Rohan said. "It's everything, Ruby. I need people who I can trust."

Ruby didn't look convinced. "I could bollocks up the whole thing."

"You won't. Unless you want to go back to L.A. and slosh base onto legs and arms."

Ruby narrowed her eyes, so Etta decided to help. "Juliet would love to have jewels stuck on her face. Sparkles!"

"It's not a sci-fi," Rohan pointed out.

"Yeah, but she's thirteen years old, right? Why not? On Instagram, girls glue jewels and glitter all over their faces. You can practice on me!" Etta turned to Ruby. "Oh, please, please design Juliet's makeup and use me. Please!"

"I'm happy to bling you up, Etta, but makeup is *serious*. It can make or break a production. It has to grow from the idea, from the heart of the script as the director sees it."

Sometimes Etta had to remind herself that she wasn't a teenager yet, and this was one of those times. She couldn't flounce out of the room—or the terrace—without seeming like a baby.

But really? That was crap.

"Got it," she said. "Well, I'd better go cut some vegetables or something. Babbo is likely back from the market by now. Have you guys seen Lizzie this morning?"

She happened to know that Lizzie had not spent the night in her house last night, the first time in a couple of weeks. If you could count "spending the night" as tiptoeing into the house holding hands with Babbo and sneaking up to the third floor for a few hours before she went back to the hotel.

Not that Etta was playing Harriet the Spy or anything, because she wasn't. But the stairs creaked.

Last night, the stairs didn't creak under two people's feet, just one pair.

"I haven't seen her," Rohan said. "You might have something with a blinged-out Juliet. Romeo says she shines like a jewel at night."

"*Like a jewel in an Ethiop's ear,*" Ruby said. "I remember that due to being the only Ethiop in my Year Eleven class."

"Is that junior year?" Etta asked.

"In England," Ruby said, nodding. "Mind you, my mom came by way of the Caribbean, so I'm not really an Ethiop."

"I tried to get Babbo to send me to England for boarding school," Etta said, feeling a pang of longing at the thought. "You know, because of Harry Potter."

"I was in boarding school for a year," Rohan said. "They all called me sausage because I was plump. Boarding school is more *Lord of the Flies* than Harry Potter. I'm getting to an idea," he said, mostly to himself, as far as Etta could see. "Jewels, homo-eroticism, boys, bullying . . . dead boys."

Etta was trying to be cool about it, but she couldn't help being thrilled because she was sitting around, brainstorming with a famous actor about his film. No one in her class would believe her, even if she took a selfie.

"They're all lying around dead in the tomb at the end," Ruby said. "Actually, I can do some wicked dead makeup. It's a strength of mine."

"Beautiful when dead," Rohan said dreamily. "Perhaps bejeweled. For marriage and for death. That would be great, with the right lighting."

"Mercutio could rock some jewels," Ruby said.

Lizzie would say this idea was bananas. Etta was sure of it.

"I'd need incandescent light," Rohan said. "Maybe limelight."

"What's that?" Etta asked.

"The stage lighting used in music halls, basically torched quicklime. If Romeo enjoys bedecking himself in jewels, the whole fight makes more sense. I don't want the plot to come from their fathers' quarrel. I need something more vital. Something kids actually fight and die for."

Etta thought it sounded crazy. Romeo in jewelry?

"Kids die in their fathers' battles all around the world," Ruby said.

Etta kept trying to bite back a smile, because this was the most interesting conversation of her life. She looked around carefully, memorizing everything. If she ever became a novelist, she needed to remember the details.

The air was muggy and still under the trees. The Roman waiter finally showed up with more tea. She could still smell a buttery brioche smell even though they had all been eaten, and a brown tea smell, and the sunny coconut smell of sunblock from the table under a neighboring tree.

Cicadas were singing and she thought that maybe she should try to distinguish different songs. It would be cool to say years later that fourteen different kinds of cicadas serenaded them.

But it sounded like one big choir to her, all singing the same song.

Chapter Eighteen

After deciding to leave Elba, Lizzie hid in her room claiming a headache, nurturing a heartache. Then to make everything worse, she slept late and missed breakfast.

Still, ferries ran all day and she could eat something on the boat. She pulled out her suitcase and started putting everything she'd brought along inside, folding everything quickly, even inside out.

But it turned out that she couldn't just get on the ferry and cry all the way to the mainland, cry all the way to the U.S., and then take a lot of Xanax, enough to get over the whole vacation.

Because: Grey.

Survivor Grey blocked the door of her room and glared at her as if he'd never heard of the South, and didn't know that southern people were supposed to be syrupy sweet.

He looked like a burning bush, and she was about as likely to get past him as Moses was. Was Moses the one who was blindsided by a burning bush?

"Shut up," Grey said when she asked. Then he walked into the room, picked up her suitcase, and threw it across the room. It burst open and badly folded clothes went everywhere.

Lizzie backed up and sat on the bed. "I didn't mean to run away from *you*."

"More excuses?" Grey said.

He looked savage and ravaged. The two words were oddly similar. If she was a better linguist, she might even know whether they had the same etymology.

"It's not you," she said, discovering that the sob that had pressed her chest bone all night had dissolved into simple tears. One slid down her face. "It's Dante. Don't you see, Grey?"

"No."

But there was something in his voice. He got it. Maybe he didn't want to, but he got it. Lizzie sat and waited, brushing tears off her chin.

"I don't want him to hate me, the way you do."

He laughed at that.

"You love me too," Lizzie said wearily. "It's complicated, right? But I look at you, Grey, I looked at your eyes at lunch yesterday, and I knew. . . ." A big sob strangled her words for a minute, but he waited. "I know you will always love me even when you hate me. Or hated me. *Will* hate me, because I'm leaving you."

He stopped, took a breath before he sat down next to her. The bed tilted in his direction. "I hate the fact that you're thinking of not having that operation. I don't hate you."

"You don't get it."

"No." He turned, survivor eyes drilling into hers. "I never will, Lizzie, so what's the point of telling me? I would never do that to you." He got up again and went to the window.

She hunched her shoulders and cried silently.

"Never," he repeated after a while.

It's easy to be definite if you haven't faced a situation. Like when Lizzie was eager to marry Grey. The choice was clear, until it wasn't.

She would have said the same if Grey were ill, and meant it: *I will never leave you. I will hold this vomit-filled trash can forever. I will make you organic chicken soup. I will love you even when you can't talk, and you have no hair, and you smell terrible all over, even after a shower.*

She would say that now.

But he wasn't sick. She was. He wanted her to fight, but it just seemed so impossible. The doctor had told her the truth: There was no curing her cancer. She could hold it off, but at what cost?

"I haven't decided for sure. I'm afraid," she said, her voice grating out from somewhere in her gut.

"I am too." He didn't come back and put an arm around her, didn't pull her close, wouldn't give up his anger.

Silence.

"If you're afraid of death, is there any reason to run toward it?"

"Running toward is better than running away." She took a deep, shuddering breath. Then she saw his face again.

Five minutes later they were still sitting in silence, but she was next to him, his arms around her, his tears falling onto the back of her neck.

"It's Dante," she said, sniffling. "And Etta too. I don't want to hurt them."

"I like him," Grey said. "He's good people. Solid."

Lizzie sniffed again. "I know."

"Here." Grey reached over and grabbed a Kleenex from her bedside table. "Damn it, I feel like I've been run over by a tank."

"Me too. I hate crying."

"Don't go back to New York, Lizzie."

She sniffled but the decision was already made, between one tear and the next. "OK."

He rocked her back and forth, both of them out of words. After a while, he said, "I told Roh that we would go with him onto some yacht tonight, but we don't have to, if you want to stay in bed."

"Who's on the yacht?" Lizzie asked, blowing her nose. "I didn't think anything could lure Rohan away from Principe Blu."

"One of the finance guys, the type who back movies. I didn't listen very hard. Something to do with *Romeo and Juliet*. He wanted to bring Ruby to talk about jeweled makeup and you for Shakespeare. Dante too, if we can pry him away from the kitchen, and Etta, because she told him that she's never been on a yacht."

"Does Rohan always want people around him?"

"No. You're not *people*, Lizzie. Not to him."

Lizzie thought about contesting that, but what did she know? Maybe Rohan was fond of her, but it was hard to tell with all his charm.

"It isn't easy, being Indian in Hollywood," Grey added. "They make Roh a sex symbol in *People*, but he never gets that sort of leading role. Captain Britain never gets the girl. So he likes having friends around."

"OK," Lizzie said, throwing a Kleenex toward the trash can and missing. "I'll go on the yacht and pretend he has a coherent plan."

"He spent a few hours last night ripping through the play and scratching things out. Or adding words. But obviously if he has a tame Shakespearean under his wing, it makes him look more together. I'll send up some food, OK? Meet us downstairs later if you feel up for the yacht. If Dante doesn't lure you into his kitchen."

Late that afternoon, Lizzie woke to a loud knock. When she opened the door, it wasn't Etta, who she half expected, or Dante, who she secretly hoped for. Ruby smiled at her from the darkened corridor.

"Makeup express," she said cheerfully.

Lizzie's hands flew up to her hair, undoubtedly flattened by her nap. "I don't—"

"I know it. But you got me anyway. Rohan has booked me as key artist for *Romeo*, which is a major step up, in case you're wondering. I'm doing makeup for you out of guilt, because even a key doesn't get a fancy hotel room. I'll powder your nose or something."

"Powder?" Lizzie stared at her. "I don't wear powder! That sounds like something from the fifties."

But she stepped back because she got it. After all, she was supposedly brainstorming about Shakespeare but actually lying around in a fancy hotel room that Rohan was paying for.

Ruby walked past her into the room, carrying a square case, like an old-fashioned jewelry box. "Lipstick, if not powder."

Lizzie chewed on her lip, thinking unkind thoughts.

Ruby pivoted, the side of her mouth quirking up. "If I don't suggest liner?"

"Liner? Like a trash can liner or eyelash liner?"

"Lipstick liner. You don't know what that is?"

"I've been too sick to give a damn about makeup," Lizzie said flatly.

"Yeah, and I was never too sick for makeup. Everything is easier with a new lipstick. I practically mortgaged my soul to Topshop's BeautyMART during chemo."

"Don't—don't argue with me," Lizzie said, closing the door before she went over and sat on the bed. "Please. I've had my full share lately."

"You don't care about makeup because you've never had to," Ruby said. "You get in the shower, and I'll try out my first homemade product on you. Ruby's Glow. I made it this afternoon. Please?"

"You made it yourself?" Lizzie didn't like face masks at the best of times, but Ruby's eyes were shining. Her heart sank.

"From the black beach." Ruby said, nodding. "Excellent for chemo skin. I've tried it five times already. After that, I'll find you something to wear and put on a little lipstick without liner."

Lizzie sighed.

"I told Etta to come over because she wants jewels pasted on her face," Ruby said. She looked at Lizzie's bureau, which was covered with plastic bottles of pills. "Gotta get these out of sight." She pulled open the drawer and swept them on top of Lizzie's under-pants.

Lizzie found herself laughing. "Does anyone ever tell you no?"

"Not since I went through chemo," Ruby said. "There's a lesson there, by the way. I stopped hearing 'no.'"

"Huh." In the shower, Lizzie leaned against the wall and listened to Ruby singing unselfconsciously. Off tune.

Lizzie heard "no" a lot.

Ruby was singing about feeling good, lifting Nina Simone's dark voice into a different place: younger, shinier. *"Fish in the sea . . ."*

Did fish know how anyone felt? Did they care?

Lizzie thought about joining in, but then Ruby would hear her voice. She listened to another verse, thinking about saying no.

A foster kid can't ever say no. But an adult can, and it was probably time she understood that.

"Dragonfly out in the sun," she sang, coming in under Ruby, slurring the words the way Mrs. Bedrosian liked. Mrs. Bedrosian was an Episcopalian, but she loved a good gospel song. Lizzie leaned back against the white tile and let warm water hit all her scars, took a deep breath, and set her voice free.

Ruby went silent, shocked probably, so Lizzie sang the last verse alone. But Nina never stopped with just words, and Lizzie could hear her experienced, tired voice in her head. *"Mmma . . ."* she sang, dropping low, Nina's scat in her head, blowing it like a trumpet, ending with *"feeling goooooood."*

Which was when the curtain was ripped back. Lizzie squeaked and slapped her hands over her breasts. Ruby turned off the water.

"You!" she shouted. "You've got that? Hiding away?" She waved her hand. *"That?"*

Lizzie grabbed the shower curtain and pulled it across her body. "Yeah."

"I would kill to be able to sing like that."

Lizzie brushed past her and grabbed a towel. "It makes people look at you differently."

"I'm Black," Ruby said. "You can't tell me anything about being looked at differently. OK, come over here, lie down faceup."

She had covered the pillows with towels. Lizzie lay back, keeping her towel wrapped around her. Evening was drawing in. Out the open door leading to the balcony, the sky was a violet blue. Somewhere between periwinkle and lavender. A tender color.

Ruby came back with a bowl in her hand and nudged Lizzie to move over so she could sit on the edge of the bed. "See?"

Lizzie peered into the bowl. "Looks like mud."

"Pearlescent mud," Ruby said. "Shiny. I'm thinking that if I ever have my own makeup line, everything will be pearly, like this. I'm going to pull your hair back, OK?"

Lizzie closed her eyes, and Ruby ran her fingers down her left cheek and then, more quickly, over her forehead, down the bridge of her nose. Lizzie had always avoided facials due to the intimacy: a woman breathing in your face, peering at your skin. But Ruby's touch slipped like a caress over the other cheek, back to her forehead, rounding her chin.

"Did you ever play with mud as a kid?" Ruby asked. "It's one of those things we're supposed to do, like sitting on a strange man's lap because he put on a red velvet outfit and a fake beard. Sounds good, but bollocks in reality."

"No," Lizzie said. "I grew up in the city. Did you?"

"The mud is drying faster than I'd like. I'm going to add some more oil." Ruby reached for something. "There wasn't a lot of mud to play with in Brighton, at least not the part where Roh and I grew up. Think orderly flower gardens."

"Were you happy?" Lizzie asked.

"Definitely. I have a great mum. Although she didn't want me to become a makeup artist. Or move to America: That was the worst."

"What does she want you to do?"

"Run a newspaper, the way she does, would be good," Ruby said. "Lead a congregation in prayer. Be a VP of something. Something *big*. But I got cancer right after I finished my GCSEs, before I could dutifully go off to uni. So I went on a makeup course instead."

"She didn't like it?" Lizzie asked. She could feel herself sinking into the bed, boneless with pleasure. Ruby's fingers were stroking her neck now.

"Tragedy," Ruby said. "I'm the only kid, and she had big plans that didn't include 'shellacking the vain to make them more so.' That's a quote, by the way. I've always loved that makeup transforms a person. She doesn't get it."

"This mud feels so good," Lizzie said, realizing she sounded a little drunk. "Will you go back to the UK someday?"

"Maybe." Ruby's fingers slowed. "I get bored, you know? That's why I'm here. Originally, I was offered artist rather than assistant on the DuVernay movie, but it was filming on set in L.A., and I wanted to get away. My mom hates that I hop around. Always on a plane, she says."

"I get it," Lizzie offered. "Cancer is way more than the diagnosis."

Ruby's fingers came back, covered in more cool mud. "Yeah."

"Do you . . . I mean, I'm guessing you don't have a partner?"

"Nope. Not my style. I'd like a baby someday, so I might have to lower my standards. Though internet sperm would be OK too."

"You don't sound very certain."

"Cancer," Ruby said. "I only know what I don't want: to stay in one place, to have a big career, to be tied down by responsibilities. Babies are a huge responsibility."

"I used to think I'd have a baby," Lizzie said. "One of those babies in tire commercials that looks as if it laughs all day. I was going to be the best mother ever."

"I'm sorry," Ruby said. "You're not going to die, though. You know that, right?"

"No, I *am* going to die," Lizzie said. "Sooner rather than later." She almost added "sorry," and choked it back. No apologizing.

At this point, people got tearful or started telling her about a miracle drug they read about. There was a pause, and Ruby said, "I guess we all are, right? Pointing out the obvious here: You might not get a baby, but you seem to have a twelve-year-old girl."

"I'd have to have given birth to her at twenty," Lizzie said. "I could have handled a baby, but Etta will be a teenager next year. I don't think I can do it."

"I get it." Ruby's hands slowed again, making little swirling motions. "So have you always been able to sing like that?"

Lizzie nodded and mud cracked on her throat. "This feels great, but could I wash it off pretty soon?"

"Sure," Ruby said. The mattress jolted when she stood up. "Go check out your nonexistent pores."

"Thank you," Lizzie said. She opened her eyes, swung her legs off the bed, and waited a moment for her head to stop swimming.

Ruby came back out of the bathroom, drying her hands. "I need a drink," she muttered, pulling open Lizzie's minibar. "We're having some wine. I met a white version of freaking Ella Fitzgerald, and I need a drink."

Lizzie got up. She didn't think Ruby needed a drink because of her voice. It was the whole death thing. "I'd give you a thanks kiss, but I'm shedding like a lizard."

Face washed, she glanced in the mirror and then came back out. "I look miles better," she told Ruby. "Not a pore to be seen."

"I'm going to make a fortune on Ruby's Glow. Or Ruby's Grit and Glow if I make a scrub."

"I bet your mother would like CEO even better than VP," Lizzie said. She went out on the balcony in her towel and sat down, pulled up her legs, and wrapped her arms around them. The sun was almost gone for the day, and the surface of the sea glittered.

To the right, the town spilled down the hillside, yellow and orange buildings falling on top of each other as if they were sliding out into the sea.

Seagulls were swooping about, looking as if they were following the steps of a dizzy waltz. There was too much giddiness in the way they flew for mere fishing.

Ruby came out, holding two glasses of white wine, and sat down, handing one to Lizzie. "I left the door ajar for Etta."

The sun sat on the rim of the sea, marking a space between dark blue ocean and violet sky. And then, with no adieu because it happened every day, it was gone.

All that fire and beauty, finished. Or, to put it another way: the singing, teaching, loving, reading . . . gone.

Why in the hell did it feel so personal? Grey cried when Douglas Adams died, and then again for Terry Pratchett. Nina Simone was gone, Aretha too. John Lennon, Prince . . . For God's sake, Shakespeare wasn't still wandering the world as a zombie or otherwise.

People, regular people, died every hour, every minute. Mrs. Bedrosian, and Etta's mother, for example. Her own mother.

"It's not so bad, dying," Lizzie said, putting down her wine untouched. "Not that you're dying, because you beat back the cancer."

"You don't beat back the fear," Ruby said.

"You can look past it," Lizzie said. "Not that I'm an expert. I'm trying to focus on how scary it would be to mother a teenager instead."

"I was god-awful at fourteen," Ruby said. "You want water instead of that wine?"

Lizzie sighed. "That would be great."

"Do you need any of those meds before Etta shows up? I threw them in the drawer so I might as well fish them back out."

"Zofran," Lizzie said. "Thanks."

When Ruby came back, they sat watching as two hotel men lit a line of torches down the beach that glowed yellow in the twilight.

"Smell that?" Ruby asked.

"Perfume?"

"White orchids," Ruby said. "See those little boxes attached to the torches?"

Lizzie squinted.

"They fill them with white orchids every night, and the heat of the torches makes the hotel air smell like flowers all night."

"Squashed in the box?"

"No need to go dark with it," Ruby said. "Could be that they're nestled in wet paper."

"I like the ocean better." Lizzie took a loud sniff. "It's there too. Salty and real."

She and Ruby sat there for a while smelling the air and not talking.

Etta burst through the door without knocking. "You're not dressed! Get dressed!" she screeched, throwing something on the bed with a thump.

"She's a little Napoleon," Ruby said. "Littler Napoleon." She didn't turn her head, just sipped her wine and looked out at the dark sea.

Etta zipped onto the balcony, whirling and holding out her arms. "Do you see this?"

She was wearing a white T-shirt with a linen vest over it, leggings, and black combat boots. "Isn't that Rohan's vest?" Lizzie asked, recognizing the yellow suit.

Ruby raised an eyebrow. "You recognize the content of his closet? There's something weird about that."

"It *was* Rohan's," Etta said. "He took it off in the restaurant, and I found it."

"He'll probably recognize his own clothing. It's not mine and *I* recognized it," Lizzie pointed out.

"No, he won't," Etta said. "Rohan's yacht people, nicer than most, but still. They drop clothing all over the place and never know the difference. You can't just sit around and drink wine. We have places to go! Yachts to visit!"

Lizzie groaned but got herself out of the chair and went inside. She opened her wardrobe and peered inside, hoping something marvelous and yacht-worthy would appear. Nothing did. The one good thing was that the hotel staff spirited away her clothing every morning and returned them clean and ironed.

She pulled her white dress off a hanger and headed into the bathroom.

"Don't forget your underwear!" Ruby shouted after her.

"Yeah," Etta shrieked. "Put on a bra or your boobs will be at your knees by the time you get home!"

Lizzie closed the door and let her towel drop to the floor. After a lifetime of picking up her towels, she was turning into a heathen. Hands on her hips, stark naked, she looked into the mirror that covered the whole wall in front of her.

"Geez, kid," Ruby said on the other side of the bathroom door. "That's on the negative side. Lizzie's bosom is a thing of beauty, and she doesn't need it compared to a pair of knee socks, OK?"

" 'Bosom'?" Etta started giggling. "That's what grandmothers call boobs."

Lizzie's hair was drying in a curly mass. Her face looked great, thanks to Ruby's mud. Her scars looked like the shadows of tattoos, as if she'd had complicated polka dots and more arcane designs traced on her body before she lost her nerve and had them lasered off.

Just silver outlines left.

If she had the operation and the next treatment, if she didn't give up, then someday there'd be the operation that removed part of her colon, because from what she saw in support group, that's what happened. Then she'd have a bag of one type or another that turned into a secret belt you had to wear under your clothes.

The feeling that she would never, ever allow Dante to see her wearing that belt was so fierce that she felt as if her temperature rose at the thought.

Since she didn't bring a bra into the bathroom, she just pulled the white dress over her head. It fell with a whisper of soft folds. Sans bra, her breasts were soft and pillowy, very Italian.

They looked good.

Why the hell should she worry about having breasts at her knees? There wasn't time for that. She might as well flaunt what she had.

Back in the room Etta was sitting on a chair positioned in the light from the desk lamp, and Ruby was carefully dotting something on her forehead.

"What's going on?" Lizzie asked, walking over to her bureau and pulling out a pair of undies. A scarlet thong, to be precise.

"Ruby is making me beautiful," Etta said.

"You *are* beautiful," Lizzie said.

"Yeah, not beautiful parent-way, but world-way."

"You make no sense," Ruby intervened. "I deal with faces all the time. You aren't beautiful the way a model is beautiful, but you're going to knock people out even more."

"What's the makeup going to look like?" Lizzie asked, sitting down. "Bejeweled?"

"Only a few. I'm giving her world-weary teen who can't help being so hot." Ruby put down a slender brush and picked up a small bottle.

"Sounds perfect," Lizzie said, falling backward and looking up at the ceiling.

"You too tired to go?" Ruby asked.

"Nope." But she didn't get up. Letting her body rest on the surface of the earth while counting to ten was one of her favorite things to do.

"OK, then, almost done here and you're next."

Lizzie groaned. "I'm not up for a Cinderella scene. I've read those books. Suddenly my eyes will be subtly shadowed so I look like a manga wannabe, and . . . and whatever."

"Actually, I'm going to give you lipstick to match your underwear and call it a day. As Etta says, we've got a yacht waiting."

"Do you think it's vulgar to wear red undies with this dress? Can you see them?"

"Girls have to be vulgar to break through the patina of the patriarchy," Ruby said firmly. "Not sure who said that, but it's true."

"Cool," Etta said. "Come on, Lizzie!" By the time Ruby closed her lipstick, Etta was dancing in front of the door, then dashed down the stairs before them.

Chapter Nineteen

When Lizzie, Etta, and Ruby got downstairs, they found the three men waiting in the courtyard along with a good-looking guy in a tight blue-and-white-striped T-shirt. Dante got up and came to meet them, dropping a kiss on Etta's forehead, then one on Lizzie's mouth.

The stranger turned out to be from the yacht. *"Lei c'ha veramente 'na bella fami'a, signo',"* he said to Dante.

Lizzie had never been part of a beautiful family and she loved it, especially the part where Dante thanked him without clarifying anything.

They walked down the steps to the hotel's private dock, Etta in front, followed by Lizzie, Dante, and the rest, one by one.

"It's like magic!" Etta shouted because every time she put her foot down, three steps before her lit up.

"Pressure sensors," Rohan said, sounding as if the ground always flared to light whenever he stepped on it.

"Reggiti alla ringhiera," Dante ordered.

Etta grabbed the railing, and they followed her down. Not too far away a yacht floated on the surface of the dark water like a looming white city. A wide, open door spilled light at the waterline.

A small motorboat was waiting to take them to the yacht. Etta and Ruby sat in the very front, then Grey next to Rohan, whose thumbs flashed over the lit screen of his iPhone. Then Lizzie, with Dante's arm around her. "Augusto is managing the kitchen tonight?" she asked. "What's on the menu?"

"Red mullet with celery and caper sauce."

"Why do you smell like rosemary?"

"Starter—pomegranate cooked in cider with rosemary and lemon." He nuzzled her hair. "Unsuccessful. I had to add radicchio until the plate looked so pretty that people won't complain."

She giggled. "Not every dish the great Dante creates is perfect?"

In the dark, one of his hands curved around her left breast. "Ah, fuck me," he breathed into her ear.

"Other way around," Lizzie said primly and then burst into laughter.

"*Babbo, hai visto quanto è bella l'acqua intorno allo yacht?*" Etta cried from the prow.

"*Sì,*" Dante replied, his hand slipping down to Lizzie's waist.

"Did she say that the water was beautiful?" Lizzie asked, puzzling through the words.

"Where the blue lights meet the water," Dante said. "So whose yacht is this, and why are we going?"

"The man who owns this yacht might back *Romeo*."

"Interesting. This man is what? An arms dealer?"

"I don't think arms dealers care about Shakespeare."

"I hate men with yachts," Grey said moodily. "Especially wankers who think they need to have five decks to house their entourage."

"Sam's not a wanker," Rohan said, clicking his phone off just as they reached the blue light that spilled out around the yacht. "Wait till you meet him. The yacht only sleeps twelve."

"Twelve? And servants?"

"Not counting staff."

Dante elbowed Lizzie. "Stop giggling."

Once they climbed off the motorboat, a cheerful fellow led them to a huge room in the prow of the ship, fitted out with sofas in one area and a conference table in the other. There was only one man in the room, talking on the phone, but he put it away as they entered.

Samuel Stark had a shaved head and a pointed chin. The former seemed aggressively masculine, and the latter slightly feminine, so in the balance Lizzie thought it was likely that he wasn't going bald but just asserting his masculinity with a shaver and a humongous yacht.

Still, he had a good smile. He shook hands with all of them, even Etta, and then introduced them to his uncle Joseph, who wandered in, lean and shaggy, wearing a pink paisley shirt tucked into ancient tweed pants, never mind the summer heat.

"Joseph Nester Stark," he said, waving a glass at them rather than shaking hands. "Poet by trade."

Etta sat down next to Lizzie and looked about, eyes bright. Two staff members, wearing blue stripes, showed up and began offering mojitos to everyone, including Etta, before Dante intervened.

Lizzie accepted an icy glass crammed with green leaves, but she wasn't supposed to drink hard liquor, so she put it down on a table.

"Do you think we could explore the yacht?" Etta whispered.

"I need to be here to talk about *Romeo*," Lizzie whispered back. Grey was sitting opposite her, talking to the poet, who had read one of his novels.

"The current book's not working," Grey said. "I've tried mold spores and swarms of flies."

"Very biblical," Joseph said, not looking overly impressed.

"Now I'm trying anemones."

"Like the red ones I showed you?" Etta asked.

He nodded. "I could move the book to a submarine." His mouth twisted. "I know that's rot."

"That might be a bit exotic," Lizzie said diplomatically, the veteran of a million such conversations.

"Mold, I get," Joseph said. "The anemone would have to be the size of New Jersey and swallowing the Statue of Liberty, and even then I think it wouldn't work. It's got a sexual vibe that sounds more like that early Woody Allen movie. Or *Barbarella*."

"Kind of awesomely feminist, though," Ruby said.

"I think the scariest things are parents," Etta said. "Like the 'other mother' with button eyes in that book *Coraline*." There was a moment of silence, and then she said quickly, "Not that my babbo is scary, because he isn't."

"Huh," Grey said.

Lizzie knew that look. He needed to get away and think. "Sam," she said, leaning forward. "Do you suppose that Grey could take Etta for a stroll around your beautiful yacht? She's been so excited to see it."

"Of course," Sam said, and then promptly turned back to his conversation with Rohan. Neither of them were touching their drinks; they were deep in discussion of a film that went in turnaround—whatever that was—and had been bought by Universal.

"I'll take you," Joseph said, getting to his feet. "I've got nothing to say about Shakespeare."

"Neither do I," Ruby said, jumping up.

Next to her, Lizzie could feel Dante's risk assessment. It must be an automatic part of parenting. He trusted Grey and Ruby, so he sank back next to Lizzie as the little group headed out to the deck, Etta leading the way.

"I read about a yacht that had a marijuana grove," Lizzie said, feeling uncertain about whether she should have suggested the tour.

"Etta will think it's an herb garden," Dante said, and then to Sam: "Is this Cabo Uno? I like the hint of vanilla."

Sam looked surprised. "Most people can't distinguish tequilas."

"Dante is the owner-chef of the Principe Blu," Rohan said carelessly.

Sam's eyes lit up and, as it turned out, he had a reservation for the following night. Had had it for months, in fact. Was visiting this part of Elba for one reason, and it wasn't Rohan.

What followed was the sort of conversation that Lizzie had participated in before in English department meetings, where the stakes were low but the negotiations endless.

Sam turned out to be a tech guy who went to MIT but dropped out after a year and made apps—or something—and now he lived in San Francisco. He too had read Grey's books.

"I didn't know *Untimely Frost* had been optioned!" Lizzie put in a while later.

"Practically every book Grey has written," Rohan said with a flash of pride. "I have a feeling this one is going to be made because—"

He went into a monologue about break costs and packaging. Sam countered with talk of a priority agreement that had gone wrong in a movie he was financing. Rohan started talking elliptically about the new Avengers movie, which suddenly sounded as if it was about to go into production.

Dante put his mojito down, pulled her closer, and said in Lizzie's ear, "Do you think I was brought here on purpose?"

"Actually, I don't think so. Would you be bothered?" she whispered back.

"Not if you're here."

Some sort of primitive, silent link was forming between them. Lizzie fancied she could almost see it. A simple thing made of simple needs. And a complex thing that had seeped far below her skin.

She snuggled a bit closer, never mind how undignified it was.

Rohan moved smoothly on to Shakespeare, who was "pure money, cultural capital, of course."

Lizzie straightened up, because this was why Rohan was paying for her fancy hotel room.

"It's all about Romeo," Rohan said, fixing his eyes on Sam. "Timothée Chalamet would work, but I'd rather find someone new. Maybe just graduating from LaGuardia. An unknown."

Sam frowned. "I have to say that I've been looking for ideas springing from a woman's point of view."

"Disney is really interested in a *Romeo* that looks at masculinity in America," Rohan protested.

The energy was slipping out of the conversation, though, and Lizzie knew why. It was because Rohan couldn't find *his* Romeo in the actual play.

"What if you thought about the play as being about Juliet?" she asked.

Sam startled, as if he'd forgotten she was there.

"I'm a Shakespeare professor," she said, giving him a lavish smile. "Did you know that the balcony scene caused a huge scandal in the 1590s? For years after that, London heroines walked out onto balconies to announce that they wanted sex. In so many words."

"Did Juliet do that?" Sam asked, looking properly stunned.

"Not only. She proposed marriage," Lizzie pointed out.

"She did?"

That was from Rohan, so perhaps she should have checked to make sure he was understanding the language.

"Juliet asks Romeo if he plans to marry her and then says she'll send a servant to his house in the morning to figure out the time and date. She doesn't even let him send a servant to her."

"Huh," Sam said, looking impressed.

"In case you think he was into it, let me remind you that Romeo was in love with Rosaline five minutes before. And Rohan, you yourself said he had a preteen deficiency when it came to testosterone."

Rohan was scowling, but in a good way. "So you see the play as being about sex, not love?"

"No, love *and* sex, and mostly from a woman's point of view," she said, feeling Dante's silent chuckle next to her because they were back at the Dylan song "Po' Boy."

"I like it," Sam said decisively.

"There's Mercutio too," Rohan said. "I don't know if anyone's ever brought out what life would have been like for Romeo without him."

Sam twitched. "Is that too much?"

"Casting will be key," Rohan said, making a quick recovery.

A clatter of voices made them all turn their heads. One of Sam's staff members held open the big glass door leading to the deck. Another bald man, his head tanned to the color of a chocolate truffle, walked in, saying, "Think about eucalyptus tree fibers."

He waved and called, "Sam. One minute!"

As if the open door was a portal to another dimension, a stream of people followed the man into the room, girls—*women*—so tall that their necks resembled those of swans: alluring, beautiful females with exotic accents and slip dresses. A red-haired woman wearing a corset and skirt made from layers of pastel plaid tulle. A French man in a white linen shirt, smoking—his confidence so absolute that Lizzie fancied it shimmered around his head like a halo.

Sam got up and went to greet them, and four or five people swirled around him like a rock in a stream, while the others spread into the room, taking selfies and jabbing at their phones. They discovered Rohan was there, and like a second rock, an eddy of people formed around him.

Through the big glass windows she saw more people coming down the deck; they must have just climbed off a boat. The girl in front wore a short metallic overall that glittered so she looked like Joan of Arc, a small army of men in her wake.

"I think I should find Etta," Dante said, standing. "Would you like to come?"

She jumped up. "I didn't know there was going to be a party."

"I expect there's always a party," Dante said. He took her hand and they walked over to Sam, interrupting a conversation with a woman wearing a transparent pink raincoat belted over a black bikini.

Sam turned to them with his surprisingly charming smile. He raised his voice and said, "Judith?"

A voice spoke from the ether, pitched just right to be heard over the buzz of conversation. "Yes, Sam?"

"Where can we find Dante's daughter?"

A second's pause, and then: "In the cinema."

Lizzie frowned. Was the boat—?

Of course the boat must have cameras all over it. For theft protection, presumably. Privacy was hardly an issue. It was Sam's world, after all.

"Is Judith a real person or AI?" Lizzie asked.

"I'm a real person," the voice replied from a speaker in the ceiling.

"I apologize for suggesting otherwise."

"If I had an AI, I'd hope to have one who was just as efficient as Judith," Sam said. "You could get to the cinema through the kitchens," he said to Dante. "My chef is a great admirer. I'm bringing him to dinner tomorrow."

Lamps adorned with baskets of white geraniums were fixed to the walls of the yacht. Dante came to halt under a lamp, specks of light reflecting from white petals giving his skin a lacy overlay. "Sam doesn't look like an adventuresome eater."

"Don't be judgy."

"He'll want a latte after his meal tomorrow. If I offered a full menu, he would order soup and then pasta. He might even put parmesan on *spaghetti al mare*."

"He may not be fluent in Italian food," Lizzie said. "But I bet he won't ask for French fries the way I did, so give him a break."

"Etta wants me to put a Lizzie burger on the menu. You have single-handedly lost me at least one Michelin star."

"I'm your muse," Lizzie said, laughing. "The famous chef's trollop."

"Partner," he corrected her offhandedly, but his eyes were serious. What was she to say to that?

"If you were my trollop, you'd be less arty-looking," he added, amusement rumbling in his voice. "Around the feet, at least."

Lizzie looked down at her strawberry-striped slides. "Do you prefer women in four-inch heels?"

"Absolutely not. I only had one relationship in the last decade." He shrugged. "Other than Etta and two restaurants. I never stopped working long enough. Or maybe I was just waiting for you."

Behind his shoulder, four staff members burst out of a door, all carrying trays filled with mojitos. They walked into the party, fanning out like synchronized swimmers.

"If I were to apply for the position of floozy-to-a-chef," Lizzie said, turning back to Dante, "my sandals would be nonnegotiable. I just want you to know that."

"You already have the position," Dante said, his voice deep and happy.

Oh God, she should tell him.

She had to tell him.

Lizzie walked a few steps away and leaned on the rail. The water was pitch black, except directly around the yacht, where cobalt blue lights spread across the water in hard lines, like lasers.

A boat was arrowing through the dark water in their direction, coming from a yacht that was even larger than theirs.

"How do they know to come here?" Lizzie asked. All around them yachts were settled on the sea like vast birds drifting in their sleep.

"Instagram. You know those duck whistles that hunters use to scare up birds?"

Lizzie shook her head.

"They quack," Dante said. "Instagram quacks, and they all follow. That's why we don't allow photos at my restaurants. Instagrammers lured in by a photo won't accept no. Here in Elba, they crowd into the courtyard and take photos, even though they haven't got a reservation and aren't eating with us."

He moved behind her, curving his arms around hers and gripping the railing. "Can you swim?"

"Not really."

"What does that mean?"

"I'm afraid of water, but I waded in the ocean three times on this trip. I'm proud of myself."

"May I teach you to swim?"

Lizzie turned around and put her arm around Dante's neck. "You are such a protective alpha."

His dark eyebrows pulled together. "What does that mean?"

"Alpha. Man with testosterone."

"A definition that fits half the population," Dante pointed out.

"With *lots* of testosterone," Lizzie amended. "You expend that energy taking care of others. Teaching them to swim. Cooking for them."

He grimaced. "Have I just been emasculated? I'm pretty sure it's better to race around on a black stallion waving a lance."

"No, this is much better," she said, pulling his head down to hers.

They kissed until there was a burst of music from the room they'd left. Behind Dante, Lizzie saw two women dancing together, tangled like ivy, all luminous skin and red lipstick. They were laughing.

"Must find Etta."

She heard the rasp of Dante's voice with a jolt of dizzy pleasure. She wanted to tighten her arms and keep him, but she let go.

"Daughter," he rumbled, shaking himself. "Twelve-year-old daughter on a yacht with a possible marijuana jungle belowdecks."

"May I just say," Lizzie said, taking his hand, "that you are absolutely wrong if you think Etta wouldn't recognize a marijuana leaf?"

Dante frowned. "She's not old enough, and it's not legal in New York."

"I saw a vending machine in Rome selling sex toys and pot. My guess would be that Etta hasn't yet bought an edible, but I wouldn't underestimate her curiosity."

They went through the door ringed in blue light from which the waiters had emerged, down some stairs, and along a corridor—wide, lined with photographs in black and white of laughing people. Sam had a big family. Loads of sisters, all with the same pointed chin but bushy hair.

He also showed up in several photos with an arm draped around an extraordinarily beautiful woman—a different woman in each photograph.

"I must have been wrong about the way that Sam was looking at Rohan," Lizzie said, when they got to the end of the line of photos.

Dante shrugged. "No one's bothered by labels these days. Could be Sam's into Rohan, but he'd have to fight off Grey." He reached out and tugged at one of Lizzie's curls. "Grey would love to fight *me* off."

"Grey can't have everything he wants," Lizzie said.

They walked by a room where a woman was pulling white sheets out of a big dryer and two other women were manning ironing boards. The smell of verbena and heated linen drifted from the doorway.

"Ironed sheets," Lizzie said, when they were far enough away not to be heard. "Just like a hotel."

"My mother has her sheets ironed."

"I don't suppose judges have much time for laundry," Lizzie said.

"No." He gave her a crooked smile. "Etta loves the fact that her grandmother's linen is put away in sets tied with color-coordinated ribbons, but I refuse to pay someone to do that."

They walked by more closed doors that Lizzie would have loved to peek into. A thumping noise came from one, unmistakably the sound of a weight machine slapping to the floor and being hoisted back up.

Another open door.

"Hair salon," Dante said helpfully at her shoulder.

"I was thinking dentist's office."

"It could moonlight as that. Most big yachts have salons, with massage tables—over there, see? I bet that that wall folds out so a person could be massaged in the open air. We're just above sea level."

"Hanging off the side of a yacht? A person could roll right off into the water," Lizzie said, uneasily fascinated.

"Good reason to learn to swim."

"I doubt that I'll be offered a massage at sea level in the near future." They walked on, past more closed doors. Finally, they came to a neat sign: *Kitchens*.

"*Andiamo*," Dante said, pushing open the door.

The kitchens were enormous, with at least ten people at work who all glanced up and nodded, their hands moving.

"Is the chef here?" Dante inquired.

It turned out he was napping before the dinner service began.

"Please let him know that I will be happy to welcome him to the Principe Blu tomorrow."

There was a flurry of excitement as they all came over to shake hands. Dante and Lizzie were sent out through a different door, after hailing Judith to make sure Ruby and Etta were still in the cinema.

"Walk through the library," one of the sous-chefs explained. Then, with a smile: "There is a cookbook section, and your book can be found there, Chef Moretti."

"You wrote a book?" Lizzie asked once they were headed down another corridor.

Dante shrugged. "So to speak. A nice woman shadowed me in the kitchen for a month or so, and then the draft arrived in the mail."

"That kitchen is so *big*," Lizzie said.

"Three steam convection ovens, fryers, two ribbed griddles, salamander, heated—"

" 'Salamander'?" she repeated.

"A big toaster oven. One of my first head chef jobs was on a superyacht. We cooked like crazy, all day and night."

"Was it fun?"

He nodded. "Yeah. The yacht was owned by a Russian billionaire. He didn't mind what I cooked as long as it was interesting. Occasionally, he'd send me off in the helicopter to buy something he wanted—sea bass when all we had was grouper, or wild blueberries from the Apeninos, the mountains outside Florence."

Dante had a happily nostalgic look. "I developed a few signature dishes for him. Taught myself how to bake."

The library was the first room Lizzie had seen on the yacht that she might actually like to spend time in. The walls were fire-engine red between bookshelves that stood at right angles and created little nooks for overstuffed chairs. She saw a shelf of Agatha Christie, three shelves of Harlequin Presents, loads of YA.

Double doors on the far end opened to a shadowy room from which she heard a voice barking, "The police have been targeted. Two of our colleagues lost their lives today in the line of du—"

The sound cut and the image froze just as Lizzie and Dante got to the door.

"This was my first dead body, as an artist rather than assistant," Ruby said.

Dante wandered in, hands in his pockets. Lizzie stayed at the door.

The yacht's movie theater—a cinema, really—was designed in rows of round velvet chairs as big as kiddie wading pools. Ruby, Etta, and Grey were seated in the middle of the room. Grey was staring at the screen with a blank expression that meant he was thinking hard about his manuscript and ignoring the world around him.

"See that?" Ruby continued, waving the remote in her hand. A red bead bounced across the screen and paused on the dead man's cheek. "I used Aquacolor water-based makeup. They use it in mortuaries as well."

"Babbo!" Etta cried. "This is so cool—Ruby is showing me her dead bodies!"

Dante headed over to sit beside her.

Ruby waved at Lizzie. "You see that tattoo showing under his shirt?" she said, turning to Etta. "My first solo tattoo."

Ruby hit play again, and another image flashed on the screen. Lizzie backed out of the doorway, aware she was shaking.

There was no Aquacolor in her future, for God's sake.

She'd already paid for cremation.

Chapter Twenty

Lizzie walked straight until she couldn't hear anything, then turned to a bookshelf and stared at it blindly until the raw feeling passed, and her heart stopped thudding against her ribs.

Ready to face the world again, she noticed three bookshelves over her right shoulder. They shaped a little nook containing a curved lavender sofa and a chair—and Joseph, the poet.

He was leaning back in the corner of the sofa, eyes closed, an open book across his knees. At first Lizzie thought that he was asleep.

But then she realized that his fist was clenched, and he was gasping for air. His skin had turned violet under his eyes, and his cheeks were a sickly color.

Lizzie froze and then lurched forward. "Joseph!"

She grabbed his hand, and he opened his eyes and squinted at her.

"Oh my God," she cried, and then remembered. "Judith!" When no one replied from the ceiling, she shrieked, "Judith!"

"Not here," Joseph wheezed.

"I'll get help," Lizzie said, patting his hand idiotically. "You just relax, OK? I'll be back—"

"Don't."

She had dropped his hand and was poised to run. "What are you saying? I have to get help," she cried. "You need a doctor."

"No. Regular."

Did he mean this was normal? His eyes squeezed shut again, and he thumped his chest with his fist.

"I have to get help," Lizzie said, her voice shaking. "You're having a heart attack." Dying, maybe. Her mind skittered around the word, and she could feel herself starting to hyperventilate, as if taking in more air would make his breathing ease.

Joseph's eyes opened. "Betting . . . better." He reached toward her. Surprisingly strong fingers curled around her hand and tugged.

Betting?

Getting. He meant *getting better.*

Knees weak, Lizzie sank down beside him on the couch. He wasn't gasping as hard as he had been. Still, if his fingers loosened around hers, she would run for the door. If his breathing stopped or halted, or if . . .

Instead, color came back into his cheeks. Finally, he dropped her hand and pushed himself higher on the cushions.

"That was *not good,*" Lizzie said, her voice still shaky. "I'll go tell Judith to find a doctor. I'm sure they have a hospital on Elba."

"No," Joseph said. Eyes closed, but he said it.

"I think you had a heart attack, Joseph."

"Would you mind pulling that cord?" He gestured toward a purple velvet cord that she hadn't noticed.

Lizzie lunged at it and yanked.

"I need a cocktail," Joseph said, his voice still thready. "That was a rough one."

"A rough what? You can't have a drink!"

"Persistent atrial fibrillation," he said.

"Don't they have medication for that?"

He took a deep breath. "I take some. But my heart is damaged. Stiff, they say. Stiffened by life, I say." His voice was wry and he started rubbing his chest.

Lizzie gave him a long look. Lean, fuzzy-haired, old but not that old. "Isn't that what they use pacemakers for?"

"Sometimes."

"Why didn't Judith answer when I called?"

"I made Sam turn off the audio system in the library. What if I want to have raunchy sex in here?"

Lizzie didn't think that was the sort of question that needed answering, at least not by her. "Do you spent a lot of time in here?" she asked, clearing her throat and looking around. Books everywhere.

"I spend most days here," he said. "I want friends around me. Books."

"When dying, you mean," Lizzie said flatly.

"And living."

She leaned back against the sofa and tried to calm herself down. Joseph wasn't dead, not this time. She took a deep breath.

"Will Judith herself answer that bell?"

"No, likely the butler, Walnut."

"But you won't tell Walnut or Sam what just happened."

"Neither will you," Joseph said, giving her a look. "My nephew worries."

"I don't . . ."

"You won't be complicit, if that's what you're worried about. He couldn't get me to put in a pacemaker, and no one in the Elba hospital—if it exists—would be able to either."

"Ah," Lizzie said.

It wasn't her business.

It was his life and his death, even if the irony was glaringly obvious. She cast around for something to say. "There's a party going on upstairs."

"Generally is," Joseph said, catching his breath. "Alas, my dancing days are over."

"So, Walnut is a butler just like in a Trollope novel?" Lizzie asked, flailing around for a subject of conversation.

"Will you be horribly disappointed if he's not an elderly, loyal Englishman in livery? Walnut's first name is Buddy; he hails from Rhode Island; and he wears the same white-and-blue vaguely French navy outfit as the rest of them."

Joseph was sitting up again now and didn't look much different than he had upstairs. The blue shadows under his eyes hadn't gone away, but he'd stopped rubbing his chest.

"I will take any sort of butler," she said. "What are you reading?"

"An old friend." He turned the spine toward her. "James Wright."

"I don't know— Oh, wait, perhaps I do? A poem about lying in a hammock."

He waggled overgrown eyebrows at her. " 'Lying in a Hammock at William Duffy's Farm.' I believe you're the first person I've met in some five years of living intermittently on this yacht who knew a single poem by Wright, let alone that particular one. One of his best."

"I don't know his work well," Lizzie confessed. "I vaguely remember that poem from grad school."

"Must have been a good program," Joseph said. "Don't tell me where, because I don't want to have to judge you. I have spent so much time in English departments that I formed virulent dislikes of any number of them."

"Do you dislike professors as well?" Lizzie inquired. "I teach Shakespeare."

"Shakespeareans are better than most because they don't teach creative writing. I suppose you get along with everyone. You have a straight nose, which must be very helpful in department meetings."

Lizzie almost laughed, but she was still too frightened. Her stomach was in a hard knot. "What has my nose to do with it?"

"My nose was no help when I wanted to look serious," Joseph said. "I was never sure if I wanted to *be* serious, which didn't help. I used to aim at being as lugubrious as Wright in poetry, but I wasn't any good at it."

"Your better poems were cheerful?" That made her smile. "Kittens, rainbows, happy department meetings?"

"The last would involve an alternate reality," Joseph said. "I used to veer madly between joy and sorrow; in fact, I could scarcely keep the two of them separate in my own mind. After my daughter died, I stopped writing."

Lizzie stopped herself from saying she was sorry, because he was giving her a hard look that said not to. "What do poets who aren't writing do?" she asked instead.

"Teach," Joseph said. "Unfortunately, close contact with students leads to more writing blocks. We either die before we ought to, like Wright, or we last forever, ever more salacious, longing, ugly, hairy."

"Don't stop," Lizzie said when he ran out of breath. "I'm learning so much."

His brows jerked up. "You have something to learn? A beautiful woman like you in red underpants?"

She winced.

"That wasn't meant as harassment," he said quickly. "Merely an observation. I'm a sexist old man, I'll just say it so that you needn't bother."

As a feminist, she should have marched out of the room. But she liked Joseph. And he had almost died.

"You are Wright's bronze butterfly, an exquisite gift to the world," he said. "*A bronze butterfly sleeps on a black tree trunk, and cowbells follow each other into the distance of the afternoon.* Not word for word, but that's the gist of it."

"Do you think poets are more observant than normal people?" she asked.

He hesitated. "If you are hoping that no one else noticed your undergarments, I'd have to lie, because my guess is that every man on the yacht did. Well, most of the men."

Lizzie thought about it and shrugged.

"I'm learning not to lie," Joseph said. "A project I've come to late in life but still worth doing."

Words spilled out of her before she planned them. "I'm learning how to die. Because I'm Stage Three, cancer. I'm deciding how to say goodbye—well, that or whether I should keep fighting the inevitable." She managed a smile. "Not telling feels like a lie, but it's not simple."

He looked at her silently for a moment, his eyes kind. "You may have noticed that I've taken on that particular challenge as well. But you're what, late twenties?" He paused, and then, concisely: "That sucks."

"Early thirties. What a dismal subject for conversation." She found herself smiling, because it was nice talking to someone who was matter-of-fact about it. Her therapist's tears had put her off for days. The department secretary—whom she honestly didn't talk to more than to complain about the copier—had sobbed when she heard the news.

"There's a lot to talk about," Joseph said. "A dying Shakespearean ought to have more fluency in the subject than the rest of us. So much wisdom trapped in iambic pentameter, like flies in amber."

"Lizzie?" Dante called from the other side of the room.

"He doesn't know my diagnosis," she told Joseph.

He nodded. "You don't find secrecy exhausting?"

Rather than answer she got up, poked her head around the bookshelf, and waved Dante over. He sat down next to Lizzie, followed by Walnut, who went off with a frown to get mojitos.

"Does Walnut disapprove of you in general, or just your drinking?" Lizzie asked Joseph.

"Oh, me. I specialize in irritating butlers. So what were you watching?" Joseph asked Dante. "I heard gunfire at some point."

"Ruby was illustrating how she uses makeup to create dead people."

Joseph's eyes caught Lizzie's for a moment. "A profoundly uninteresting topic," he said. And then to Lizzie, "An Italian is a good choice. Much less prone to depression than Minnesota poets."

"Are you a Minnesota poet?" Dante asked, as Lizzie noted with secret delight that he appeared unperturbed at the idea of being "her choice." In fact, he put an arm on the back of the sofa as if he were claiming her.

"We've been discussing James Wright." Joseph tapped his book. "A Minnesota poet with a fondness for farm life. I've found your Lizzie in a line of poetry: *A bronze butterfly sleeps on a black tree trunk, and cowbells follow each other into the distance of the afternoon.*"

"Wasn't there a line about cowbells that blaze up like golden stones?" Lizzie asked, rescuing the image from some forgotten part of her brain.

"No. Wright says that horse droppings blaze up like golden stones. Idealized, but that's his point, I fancy. The end is my favorite: *A chicken hawk floats over, looking for home.*" Joseph paused, raised a finger. "Last line: *I have wasted my life.*"

"How could he complain of wasting his life, when he had written something so beautiful?" Lizzie said a bit crossly.

She hadn't wasted her life, but she had the sudden thought that perhaps she'd spent it "looking for home." She wasn't a butterfly, then, but a chicken hawk. She started grinning. Who'd want to be a butterfly? Beautiful, short-lived.

It made sense in her gut that she'd spent her life floating, looking for home. That line summed up her thirty-two years.

"From idealistic to grandiose," Dante commented.

"Poets are." Joseph shrugged. "God knows I am. Here, take a look. Wright was the opposite of grandiose, actually. Lavish only in his praise of horse droppings."

He handed the book to Dante, who opened it with a reasonable semblance of interest.

Walnut showed up with mojitos.

"These poems are dark," Dante said after Walnut left. "Here's one talking about the starved shadow of a crow." He flipped to another page.

"Wright was good at talking about difficult stuff," Joseph said. "What we need from poetry, what we *require,* is a way of talking about the impossible."

Dante nodded, and Lizzie felt a rush of affection because of the respect and interest in his face.

"I don't think I want to be a bronze butterfly," she said. "Don't they live only one day?"

Joseph grinned at her, even though no one who knew of her cancer ever smiled if she mentioned death.

"I don't think so," Dante said. "Monarchs migrate across the U.S. They couldn't do that in twenty-four hours."

"You don't want to be a butterfly," Joseph said, spitting out a fibrous piece of mint leaf. "I refuse to be a blazing piece of horse-shit, even though at seventy-three I do spend a good deal of time feeling like crap."

"Maybe Wright was talking about metaphorical halos," Lizzie said. "Blazing gold, like saints in medieval churches."

"Horseshit halos? A comment on Lutherans? Naw. Jim wasn't the sort."

"You actually knew him?" Lizzie asked.

"I told you I did. Not well, but I did." He swirled his finger in a circle. "This is the poetry alcove."

"I haven't wasted my life," Lizzie said firmly. "Even though I haven't written any poetry about sacred horse droppings."

"We can't all be geniuses." Joseph put down his glass. "It's taken me a long time to learn that we can only use what we've got. Nobody gave me any hammocks to lie in. When the shit got kicked out of me, I couldn't put it into words."

"James Wright did?" Dante asked.

"Yup. But some of us just spend our life circling around, looking for home."

"Nice," Lizzie said.

"Yeah, I have the poetic touch." And Joseph's voice was so sourly wry that she burst into laughter.

"We were wondering where you were!" Etta exclaimed, rounding the corner of the bookshelf, followed by Ruby. "Grey went back upstairs to hang out with Roh."

"Come sit down," Dante said, moving to the far end of the sofa.

"Do you live on this yacht full-time, Mr. Stark?" Etta asked, sitting down so that her slim hip pressed against Lizzie's leg. "You can fit here too, Ruby."

"I'm good," Ruby said. She was poking about, looking at poetry books.

"I do not live on the yacht," Joseph said. "I come and go."

"I didn't think so," Etta said, satisfied.

"Why not? Don't I look like yacht fodder?"

"Not unless you've sworn off using the hair salon."

"Etta," her father said in the warning tone of parents everywhere.

"Sorry," Etta said, sounding extremely un-sorry. "He's got an Einstein look going."

"I tried locs, but I'd need my own hair salon," Ruby said. She came back and sat on the floor.

"A yacht is the devil's stomping ground," Joseph said, winking at Etta. "Only the foolish bother with their hair." He picked up Lizzie's untouched mojito. "I gather you're not interested in poisoning yourself?"

"Trying not to."

He tipped it up and drank whatever liquid made its way around the wads of mint leaves crammed into the glass. "You ladies are not our usual yacht fare, I don't mind telling you. My nephew's money emits a mating call to uninteresting women."

That made Lizzie realize that if they waited downstairs too long, they might have to stay for dinner. She uncurled her legs and stood.

Dante straightened as well, with a speed that suggested he was taught to rise whenever a lady did. The judge must have been fierce. *Ironed sheets,* Lizzie reminded herself. *Tied up with ribbons.*

"Time to go home," Lizzie said when Ruby looked up at her, eyebrow raised.

"I want to stay for dinner," Etta objected. "The sous-chef said he would make hamburgers with French fries." She shot a look at her dad. "He has *hot dogs.*"

Dante shook his head. "You got to see a big yacht. That's enough excitement for one day."

"Can we eat at the Bonaparte? I bet they have hot dogs there," Etta insisted.

Joseph didn't get up, as much as slowly extend like a folding ruler. "Staying at the Bonaparte? I always meant to take a room there someday."

"Why would you stay in a hotel when you could stay on a yacht?" Etta asked.

"I might find a wife," Joseph said, rather surprisingly.

"If I was your age, I might marry you," Etta said generously.

"I appreciate that, kid. Forgive me for saying that if you were my age, you'd be a little high maintenance for me, given the jewels you have glued to your face. I don't think I could afford you."

"I wouldn't wear so many jewels if I was ninety-five," Etta pointed out.

"I'm a young seventy-three," Joseph said. "Let's get upstairs."

"Up the stairs?" Lizzie asked, frowning at him.

"Naw, there's an elevator," Joseph said.

"You should have told us," Ruby said to him. "You seemed pretty tired out on the way down."

"Exercise is good for me," Joseph said without looking at Lizzie.

Back upstairs, Etta's eyes grew large, because the party had grown again.

"It's fun to watch," Joseph said to her. "Let's go up there." He pointed at a small elevated deck.

"For a few minutes, and then we're going home," Dante declared. Joseph ushered them through a fingerprint-protected door that led to a winding stair kitted out with a moving seat.

Joseph seated himself and grinned at Etta. "Watch this, kid." Pushing a button sent him zooming up and around the curve, Etta running after him.

Upstairs, the deck overlooked the party, and on the other side a couple of sofas were tucked under a roof. Etta went straight to the railing, so they all followed her.

Joseph lit a cigarette. The tobacco fought the salty ocean and made the boat smell like Lizzie's childhood. Mrs. Bedrosian had smoked, and even though it made her growl in a low alto, she never stopped.

"I like this song!" Etta exclaimed.

Joseph cocked his head to hear the lyrics. "What's he complaining about?"

"Being on the edge of poverty and about to have a meltdown," Lizzie told him.

"Me too. My bank account is empty."

"My babbo gives me hardly any allowance," Etta said. "Have you tried selling your poetry?"

Dante tugged a lock of Etta's hair. "Joseph may not be ready for your particular brand of honesty, *carina*."

"I'm too much for some people. *Shallow* people," Etta said to Joseph, patently unoffended.

He barked with laughter. "Kid, I'm the original gladiator when it comes to overwhelming people. Guess how many wives I've had?"

"Five," Etta guessed.

"Four. This is my favorite time of day. The air still holds heat, but there's a promise of *la dolce vita*."

"No talking about sex," Ruby ordered, poking his shoulder. "Etta is only twelve."

"Twelve-year-olds know everything," Joseph stated as if he were an expert in adolescents. "*La dolce vita* is the time just before dinner when it's cool enough to open the shutters. So what are you good at?" he asked Etta.

"Not much," she replied.

"I like you better already. I can't stand accomplished people."

"I'm going to be accomplished," Etta said, putting her elbows on the railing to prop up her chin. "Like Babbo. But I'm not sure where to focus yet."

"I planned to be brilliant at something," Joseph announced, waving his cigarette so it looked as if a firefly was bobbing around his head. "It didn't happen."

Dante pulled Lizzie off to the side and dropped a kiss on her mouth.

"Maybe you didn't try hard enough," Etta suggested. "My nonna says that I could be a judge if I try harder in school."

"God, no," Joseph said, obviously appalled.

Dante backed up a few more steps. "I take one look at you," he whispered, "and I want to throw you on a bed. *Dolce vita,* indeed."

"Is it my red underwear?" Lizzie asked, unable to stop smiling. She linked her arms around the back of his neck.

"Yes. Though when you set Rohan straight about Romeo, it put me into a frenzy."

"Frenzy?" Lizzie said, grinning because nothing she did had ever put anyone into a frenzy. Well, as long as she didn't sing. But Dante wasn't talking about her voice.

He moved away again, far enough so that the rumble of the poet's voice was lost to music and the thumping of dancing feet.

"A fucking frenzy," he said in a low voice, his thumbs drawing little circles on her cheeks. "I was one ache from head to foot. I wanted to pick you up and take you away. Some primitive part of my brain kept pointing out that we would just have to go far enough away that we couldn't be seen, and then I could yank up that dress and take you against the wall of this damn boat."

His mouth slid down her neck. "You're extravagant," he whispered. "I'm so grateful for your red underwear. And that you went to the public beach so that Lulu found you."

Life is a weird thing. It's possible to be blissfully in the moment and yet terrified, running in mental circles, shrieking. Lizzie smiled so widely that the corners of her mouth hurt and, all the same, her heart thumped with panic.

"I don't want to fall in love with you," she said, the words slipping out easily. Less easy were the words she didn't say: *I don't want to hurt you. I don't want to break your heart when I leave.*

"Too late for me," Dante said matter-of-factly, dotting her collarbone with kisses. "And no, it wasn't because you sang to me."

Lizzie blinked, because that had been her first thought.

"Dinner under the flowery arch," he said, kissing her between words. "Your joy in life, your giddy love of pea soup."

The sky behind his head was dark purple. Bats—or seagulls—were circling, wildly diving down and back up.

He kissed her mouth. "Etta has Dr. Seuss on her door. The youness of you," he whispered. "Seuss with a difference."

She could tell him. She had to tell him.

Dante straightened. "I have an uneasy parental feeling. That old poet didn't proposition you, did he?"

"No." She hesitated. "He did mention my underwear, though."

"Damn it." Dante took Lizzie's hand.

But when they got back to the others, Joseph was leaning against the railing, giving a lecture about the horrors of the judicial system. "Anger is an explanation, but never an excuse," he said, waving his cigarette. "Sit in a courtroom for long enough, and you'll hear people offer up the fact that they were angry, as if that would satisfy the gods."

"Where do gods come into it?" Ruby asked.

"Did you know there was no concept of punishment until architecture came into being?" Joseph said. "Except that which came from the gods, of course."

"Why?" Etta asked.

"Until people could build a permanent building with four walls, they couldn't lock people away, could they? So they told stories about how the gods would come along with a handy bolt of lightning. Think about that before you become a judge, kid. You don't want to be responsible for locking someone up."

"I don't think I'd mind," Etta said. "If I was a cave person, I'd just stick a bad guy in a cave and put a rock in front of it. What do walls have to do with it?"

"Starve 'em to death, would you?" Joseph asked.

"No!" Etta said. She turned. "Babbo, you need to defend Nonna for being a judge."

Dante shook his head. "I stopped doing that long ago, *topolino*."

"*Topolino?*" Ruby asked. "Little something, right? Little top hat? Little toadstool?"

"Little mouse!" Etta cried.

"Ten-minute warning," Dante told Etta.

"Do you think I could take some photos?" Etta asked. "Like, nobody at home would believe this."

"Sure," Joseph said. He looked at Lizzie. "Come sit with me?"

Lizzie and Ruby followed Joseph across the deck to the sofas. "Check this out," he said, when they were seated. He pushed something and glass walls rose from the floor to meet the roof.

Ruby raised an eyebrow. "Are we trapped in here?"

"Door over there," Joseph said, pointing with the bright end of his cigarette. "My nephew can have endless phone conversations without important people knowing that he's lazing around the Mediterranean. Soundproofed."

Sure enough, the music had turned to a vibration under their feet.

They sat there silently for a few minutes. Under moonlight the water looked like an alien landscape shaded in grey.

"He's not your husband, and she's not your daughter," Joseph said finally.

"Surprise!" Ruby said.

"Merely a summer romance," Lizzie offered.

He snorted. "I don't think so."

"I have that problem I told you about," she said.

"Death? Death is a problem we *all* have."

"You told him? Girl, you need to tell Dante before you go telling strange men on yachts," Ruby said.

"I just blurted it out," Lizzie said. "We were talking about lying, and it's started to feel as if I'm lying to Dante by not telling him."

"So, tell him," Ruby said. "But just that you're sick. No need to talk about death. It ain't over till it's over."

"In my case," Joseph said, "the immediacy of the problem has presented itself in a hundred small ways." Then, glancing at Lizzie, "And large ways too."

"And still you smoke?" Lizzie asked, keeping her tone even.

"I court the Grim Reaper. I woo him, and why the hell not?" A red spark flew from his cigarette and blinked out.

"I would like to live to seventy-three," Lizzie said, and despite herself, her voice broke. "Sorry. I'm still getting my head around it."

"So am I," Joseph said. "So am I."

Ruby's shoulder brushed Lizzie's. Neither of them said they were sorry, which was such a gift that Lizzie felt a surge of affection. "Let's talk of something else," she said.

"The president?" Joseph offered. "Always a lively topic."

"No."

"The state of the world in general?"

"No."

"We've already discussed literature."

"Let's talk about Lizzie's voice," Ruby said. She switched seats and sat down opposite Lizzie.

"I don't like to sing in public," Lizzie said.

"Neither do I," Joseph put in.

"Yeah, but you probably have a voice like a foghorn," Ruby said to him. "She sounds like Etta James. Or freaking Ella herself."

"I quit singing a while ago," Lizzie said.

"Because of the cancer?" Ruby asked.

"Before that."

"What day?" Joseph asked.

"What do you mean?"

"What day did you quit singing? Was there a moment in which you said, 'The fuck with it, I'm done with song'?"

"I had my heart broken, and after that I was too angry and sad to sing." She glanced at Joseph. "Like the way you stopped writing poetry, except of course it's worse to lose a child. After a while I realized that no one had asked me to sing 'Ave Maria' at their wedding. No one had mentioned *American Idol* in ages; instead we talked about *Top Chef*."

"Can you cook *too*?" Ruby demanded. She threw out her arms. "More evidence of the unfairness of the universe!"

"Oh, the universe is unfair, all right," Joseph growled.

"I can't cook," Lizzie said. "I don't even like Dante's food."

"A chef, is he?" Joseph asked. "I missed that."

"Brought along to make your nephew happy," Lizzie said.

"Comes with the territory," Joseph said. "People are always trying to make Sam happy. It's the reason I spend summers with him: I need to hammer his ego back in shape after nine months of flattery and gorgeous women."

"I could do that for Rohan," Ruby said. "I knew him back when he had spots and three hairs on his chin that he called a soul patch."

"I didn't recognize his name at first, but then I don't have a TV," Joseph said.

"Don't tell him that," Ruby advised.

"Why not? I don't need anything from him. I don't want to be his friend."

"It's not about you," Ruby said. "I'm around actors all the time. He's trying to hang on to this vision of himself as the great artist, right? He told me that Shakespeare was in his DNA." She lifted a palm to Lizzie. "You don't need to say it."

Lizzie kept her mouth shut.

"Underneath, he's afraid that people only like him because he's famous. If someone doesn't know he's famous, then they might question whether—well, whether Shakespeare is in his DNA."

"So?" Joseph lit another cigarette from the one in his mouth and then dropped the old one and stamped it out.

"Pick that up," Lizzie said.

"Jesus. You and I aren't going to be around when the world is buried by a huge tsunami of trash," Joseph said to her.

"I, for one, am trying to leave a light imprint," Lizzie said, leaning over to pick it up. "You know, on people and things." She dropped it on the table.

Ruby shook her head. "It's too late for that."

"That's why you're pretending Dante's a summer romance?" Joseph said.

"Yeah, let's hear some wisdom from the old white man bank," Ruby said.

"I've had more years than the two of you added together," Joseph said. "My point is that once a duckling imprints on a broom, it's over. No feathered bird will do."

"Are you talking about Etta?" Lizzie asked.

"Yes," Joseph said. "The broom can't warn off the ducklings, in case you're wondering."

"I'm a broomstick?" Lizzie said, glancing down at her breasts.

"I told you I was a bad poet. But I know that if there's someone to love, the heart insists on doing it. My daughter's been gone for more years than she was alive, but I love her anyway. My heart won't give her up."

"I'm not giving up," Lizzie said, even though she hadn't quite made up her mind about treatment.

"Because you have so many people to love," Joseph said.

Chapter Twenty-one

Etta Moretti's bedroom door,
from *Peter Pan:*

"You won't forget me, will you?"
"Me? Forget? Never."

Etta woke with a terrible feeling that took a few minutes to figure out.

She hadn't even thought about the paper she was supposed to rewrite this summer: her biology paper, the best thing she'd written all year. It was going in her portfolio for high school, and it had to be done by the time she went home.

Which was coming up in a few weeks.

Unless, of course, she tried out for LaGuardia, in which case she'd have to do an audition, whereas Beacon meant an interview and portfolio.

She lay in bed for a while and listened to the silence. She could ask Lizzie for help with the paper, obviously.

But it didn't answer the question: Did she want to go to LaGuardia and end up an actor working with people like Rohan? He was OK. A bit scary when he was howling on the phone, but overall decent.

Or she could be a novelist, like Grey.

She suspected writers didn't make much money, though. Just look at that old poet from the yacht.

If she tried for LaGuardia, she'd have to have an audition piece, and it went without saying that Miss Hallburton wouldn't help her. Deep inside, Etta suspected that she wasn't rubbish at acting. She could do it if she tried.

Rohan was right: Anne Frank wasn't the right part. If they'd let her do Hermione, she could be great.

She sat straight up.

Or Juliet, obviously.

She grinned at the wall. She could get Rohan to help her, then she'd try out for the film, be the best Juliet ever, and she'd get an Oscar.

She hopped out of bed, her bare feet slipping a little on the cool tiles. She pulled on clothes and ran downstairs shouting "Babbo!" But of course he wasn't there. Signora Pietra was in the kitchen, ironing shirts. When she wasn't running Babbo's restaurant, she did everything else.

She gave Etta the evil eye. *"Lui è al mercato."*

"Vado al Bonaparte a cercare Lulu," Etta cried. She ran back up the stairs, into the closet, grabbed her backpack with her paper in it, and slammed out the door, pretending not to hear Signora grumbling.

When she got there, they were all sitting around in the courtyard. Rohan was talking on his cell. Grey was listening silently to Lizzie; he did that a lot. After that day when they went to the black beach, Etta had the idea that he was in love with Rohan and everything, but maybe he loved Lizzie as much.

Ruby saw her and waved, and Lizzie smiled at her. Lulu jumped off Ruby's lap and ran over to paw Etta's thigh, then dropped down and dashed back under Lizzie's chair.

Etta walked over slowly, because there hadn't been all that many times in life when she *belonged*. But she belonged at that table on the far side of the courtyard.

She had thought she would find a group in middle school, like girls did in novels. Misfits who would end up in love, or mean girls who had to learn to be nice. Honestly, she didn't care.

But instead she'd been through the two years of middle school and hardly anyone paid attention to her at all. She could go through a whole day without a kid saying a word to her outside of class. She had hoped the drama club would present her with a group of friends, but that didn't work out, obviously.

When she got desperate, she thought about joining the after-school cooking club, but that would be totally lame.

So she slowed down on her way to where the coolest group was. Lizzie was *it*. White curls, great boobs, the way she laughed.

Lizzie's laughter was deeper than most anyone's, much deeper than Etta's giggle.

"Hey, you," Ruby called, pushing out the chair next to her.

Ruby was all that too. This morning her curls were pulled up on top of her head, corkscrews going in all directions. Kind of like an anemone, but not red.

Grey raised his chin at the waiter and said, "Breakfast," pointing to Etta. Rohan was on the phone, but he nodded hello.

Etta sat down and beamed at everyone. Today she was going to giggle, no matter how silly her voice sounded. It wouldn't matter because she belonged here, at this table, with a famous actor.

Lizzie leaned over and kissed her cheek.

"Hey, sweetie."

The waiter showed up and put down a tray with brioche and fresh orange juice.

"Romeo just wants to write poetry, but Juliet wants to marry him," Lizzie said to Rohan after he put down his cell. "He poeticizes his pain and anguish because he can't say anything about Rosaline. He didn't know her and didn't care to know her. He talks about *himself*, not her."

"I get it. But I can't direct a whiny boy."

"Romeo's a virgin," Lizzie added.

"I didn't read anything about that," Rohan said, scowling for real.

"Juliet mentions a 'pair of stainless maidenhoods' when she's talking about their wedding night."

Etta couldn't remember reading that either, but her English teacher would definitely have ignored the whole virginity thing. The boys would have gone nuts with disgusting comments.

"Do you want a frittata, Etta?" Lizzie asked. "They made me a great one."

Etta said yes, even though she didn't, because hey: mom vibes.

"We should have asked that poet about Romeo," Rohan said. "Sam's uncle. But the yacht pulled anchor this morning."

"Joseph smoked too much," Ruby said. "I'm coming up on my five-year cancer anniversary, and I'm not planning on getting cancer again from secondhand smoke."

"You had cancer?" Etta asked. Ruby looked so healthy. "What kind? My mom had liver cancer." She'd decided long ago that it was better than saying cirrhosis. People always got sad if they knew, as if she would care that her mother drank herself to death.

Well, she did care, but not all that much.

"Breast, though FYI, people generally don't like to be asked."

"Your mother died of cancer, Etta?" Grey asked, looking appalled.

Etta liked that. All the same, it wouldn't be fair to make a big deal of it. "I didn't know her," she said, shrugging.

"Etta," Lizzie said.

Etta eyeballed her. "OK, not cancer exactly. Cirrhosis. She drank too much."

Grey nodded. "Mine too, E."

E?

That was cool.

"Your mom had cirrhosis too?" Etta asked.

"She died when I was six," Grey said. "I'd better go upstairs. I have to get in some pages."

"My mother is alive and kicking," Ruby said after Grey left. "She hangs out with Rohan's mom now and then. Runs the Brighton and Hove newspaper. Prays for me."

"Because of the cancer?" Etta asked.

"Her greatest fear—almost certainly likely to come true—is that I'll kick it without being saved first. She thought that cancer would do it. She kept waiting for Jesus to whack me over the head and welcome me to his arms, but it never happened."

Lizzie began laughing so Etta started laughing too. The Roman waiter showed up with frittatas and frowned at them, but Etta just laughed harder. She didn't even care that her giggles sounded high and silly.

When everybody stopped laughing and started eating, Etta remembered her paper and pulled it out of her backpack. She flattened it out on the table. "I need some help."

"I can help," Lizzie said, picking up the paper. "I've taught freshmen comp for years."

"This paper has to be super good so I can get into Beacon," Etta said. "Unless you think that I could do a monologue from *Romeo and Juliet* and get into LaGuardia."

"Are you any good at acting?" Ruby asked.

"Yes," Etta said, because if you said something, it was likely true. It *was* likely true. "My acting teacher didn't think so, but she was really mean, and Rohan said that maybe Anne Frank wasn't a good role for me."

Rohan was back on his phone, but he nodded.

"Could you apply to LaGuardia, and also work on this paper?" Lizzie asked.

"Do you think I'm a crap actor?" Etta asked.

"I have no idea," Lizzie replied. She reached over and tapped Etta's nose, just the way her babbo did. "You want to act something for us?"

"I wouldn't know what to act," Etta said. "I've never been in a play."

"Why would you want to?" Ruby asked. "I work around actors all the time, and most of them are complete peens. And that's putting it nicely."

"Rohan is an actor," Etta pointed out.

"This isn't a bad paper," Lizzie said, looking up. "I like your intro paragraph. Mating habits of birds are interesting. Do you want to be a scientist?"

"Nope." Etta shook her head. "But my school counselor said that was my best paper."

"Did you write any papers for English class?" Lizzie asked. "Besides the Shakespeare one that got a B."

"Yeah, on *Siddhartha*. I said that Hesse was a sexist pig and the book was boring, and my teacher gave me a D. Totally unfair, and only because he thinks *Siddhartha* is the best thing ever."

"I'll have to teach you the art of getting an A," Lizzie said.

Etta loved that because . . . future.

Mom vibes.

Tea arrived and more toast.

Lizzie had turned a page. "I didn't know that birds couldn't sing while they fly." She looked up. "I don't suppose chicken hawks ever sing."

"What's that got to do with it?" Ruby asked. "I was OK in English, but biology?" She snorted.

"I failed all the bio tests," Etta said, choosing honesty, the way you're supposed to. "But that paper was good plus it has eight foot-notes, so I did OK in the end. I think he gave me a B in the class or something like that."

"How did you pick the topic?" Lizzie asked.

"We had to pick between mating habits of birds, polar bears, or black widow spiders," Etta said. "All the boys went for the spiders, obviously."

"I like this part about flamingos turning pink because they eat shrimp," Lizzie said. She had to be skimming because no one read that fast. "Did your teacher give you any suggestions on how to revise?"

"You mean, like comments? No."

"I think you could do more with the singing part," Lizzie said, putting down the paper. "Make that the center of your argument. Right now you have mating songs, then pink feathers, and then there's this great bit about the bird who created a cave and deco-rated it with dung."

"Ugh," Ruby said.

"Believe it or not, Joseph and I talked about a poem about dung yesterday," Lizzie said. "It described horse droppings blazing up in the sun like golden stones."

Ruby snorted, which was pretty much what Etta thought too. No wonder Joseph didn't have any money if that was the kind of poem he liked.

"I saw the bird on this nature show," Etta said. "He thought black dung was beautiful so he decorated his cave with it, trying to get a mate. And then it sprouted, and he got upset and started pull-ing the sprouts out, but the lady bird didn't wait for him. She went off to a guy bird who had decorated his cave with flowers."

"Maybe that's my problem," Ruby muttered. "I'm flinging dung at guys and they want flowers."

"Other way around," Lizzie said, grinning at her. "You're run-ning into guys who decorate their nests with dung."

"No kidding," Ruby said. "I need a guy with a house like Dante's. They told me in the hotel that it's the biggest in the village."

"My babbo didn't buy our house," Etta said. "It was my great-grandmother's, that's why it's so big." Lizzie looked a little uncomfortable, so Etta added, "Our apartment in New York is regular-sized."

Lizzie picked up the paper. "Why don't I read this more slowly later, Etta, and we can talk about it then?"

"I can do better," Etta said, feeling kind of nervous. "I expect it's pretty bad. Maybe I should—"

"It's great," Lizzie interrupted. "I love the rejected bird and the songbirds who never sing while flying." She tucked it under her arm and stood up. "Want to go to the beach, the hotel one so we can bring Rohan along?"

"Yes!"

Ruby got up too. "Sounds good to me."

Etta picked up her backpack. "I forgot my swimsuit."

"Great, because I want to see Dante's palace," Ruby said. "Show me the flowery bower that your babbo waved in front of Lizzie. I have the feeling that she was no pushover."

"Do you want to go to the beach?" Lizzie called to Rohan, who was still talking on his cell.

He nodded and got off the call, which was kind of surprising. Lizzie walked over and tucked her arm into his. "Let's go snag a couple of pink umbrellas." Her laughter followed Etta and Ruby into the street.

"You feeling like a lucky girl?" Ruby asked. "Because you are."

"Sure," Etta said. There was nothing worse than people who asked you if you felt lucky.

Ruby elbowed her. "Listen."

"Yeah?"

"Nostalgia is underrated as an emotion. I think this summer is going to be that for you, and it's OK."

Etta said, to be polite, "Nostalgia is when you miss something, right?"

"It's like a yearning for something that happened before."

"You're supposed to live in the moment," Etta said, feeling a little sorry for Ruby.

"Yeah, that's what children do," Ruby said. "But grown-ups don't. You're on the edge of being grown up."

Etta bit back a smile because she *was* almost a grown-up, even though Babbo didn't realize it half the time.

"When you're a kid—or at least when I was a kid—time wasn't a *thing*," Ruby said. "It wasn't a bunch of moments that followed each other in order and never stopped moving. You had a day and then another day, but my summers turned into a blur of swimming and tennis camp. My mom is big on tennis."

"Cool," Etta said. She, for one, was pretty much always aware when the end of summer was coming, and school would start.

"But then things happen," Ruby said. "They turn into the ways we measure time."

"Like going back to school," Etta said. "This is home, by the way."

"Shit," Ruby said. "This is some sort of fever dream. Like I dreamed of a house on Elba and here it is."

Etta looked up at her house, trying to see it like a dream. It was wide open, with arches and tiled floors. The sea air blew in, and sometimes a seagull as well. "I just remembered that I left my swimsuit on the floor, and Signora Pietra might have taken it away."

They walked through the big doors into the living room and then up the marble stairs that swept up around the first floor, or the second, as they called it in America. Etta's room was at the far end of the house.

Ruby went about halfway and then stopped, looking down over the side of the railing that ran along the living room.

"I'll just be a minute!" Etta called, running into her room. Sure enough, her swimsuit was gone. She pulled open her top drawer and started rifling around, looking for her faded one-piece, but she hadn't seen it in a while. Her red bottom was there, but Lizzie didn't like it when she didn't wear a top.

"E!" Ruby said a minute later, from the doorway. "You're making a mess."

"I can't find a swimsuit," Etta said, her voice going high, as she burrowed through another drawer. "I can't go without a swimsuit."

"Here's one," Ruby said, picking up the one Etta used to wear two years ago.

"That's gone transparent," Etta said, feeling as if she might cry. She was missing time on the beach with Lizzie. She picked up a bunch of clothes and stuffed them back into her drawer.

"Is this yours?" Ruby asked.

Etta looked over. Ruby was holding up an orange-striped bathing suit covered in glittery pineapples. "Yeah, when I was about seven."

"You kept it?"

"It was my favorite!"

"Yeah, I see that," Ruby said. "These pineapples are great."

Etta suddenly remembered that her old one-piece was hanging on the shower rod, so she darted into her bathroom. Yes! She pulled off her shorts and underwear.

Back in her room, Ruby said, "Fuck, it's like a whole childhood in one room."

"It's not that bad," Etta said, hopping out of the bathroom with one flip-flop, as she untwisted the straps over her shoulders. "My baby stuff is in the attic."

"You know what I was saying earlier? About time?"

"Yeah?" Etta was totally uninterested, every bit of her wanting to run down to the beach and drop onto the sunbed next to Lizzie.

"Lizzie's there," Ruby said, "and even if we walk slowly, she'll still be there."

"OK," Etta said. She found the other flip-flop and toed it on.

"I'm trying to say that time isn't a river, OK? This day, this week, this summer, they'll all be there for you when you want them, just the way the blinged-out pineapples are still here. You may decide you're better off without this day, but never think that it's gone."

"I guess," Etta said.

"Can I brush your hair? We have time and there's a big knot on one side that's driving me crazy."

Etta pressed her lips together. She couldn't remember combing her hair. "I could just jump in the ocean," she suggested.

"Remember that girl down at the beach who was hiding a life-form under her turban?" Ruby asked. She picked up Etta's brush and waved it around.

"It's not *that* bad," Etta protested. "I just have—I have Italian hair, you know? There's a lot of it."

"Uh-huh," Ruby said. "This'll just take a few minutes. I'll do a fishtail braid, which is miles better than a turban."

Etta hesitated.

"Very expensive, yacht look," Ruby added.

"Oh, all right," Etta said, dropping onto the chair in front of her desk.

Ruby went around behind her and started brushing from the bottom up. "Got a tangle or two here, kiddo."

"I do brush it, mostly."

"So you have to apply for high school in New York?" Ruby asked.

"Some of them. Maybe all. Were you good in school?"

"Nope," Ruby said cheerfully. "Not my cup of tea. I used to say that I was specializing in disappointing my mother. Now I think it was just that she and I are so different."

Etta picked at some of the little fuzz balls hanging off her bathing suit. Everything that came to mind about her mother was a lie. "Lizzie's not the right age to be my mom. Like, my friends' moms are older."

"Motherhood is a state of mind," Ruby said, dividing Etta's hair into sections. "Not one I'm in, mind you. I'm more the big-sister type."

"Do you . . . do you ever come to New York?"

"All the time," Ruby said. "There! You can't see, but your hair looks great."

Etta had no interest in looking. She jumped up. "Can we go now?"

"Yeah, of course."

She turned around and gave Ruby a hug before she thought better of it.

"Is this because I'm so great with hair?" Ruby asked, hugging her back. "Or a good big sister?"

"Whatever. You're Ruby."

Chapter Twenty-two

Lizzie had made many friends over the years. She had friends at work with whom she gossiped and occasionally squabbled. She kept in touch with three foster sibs through Facebook—though now that she thought of it, she hadn't opened the app in months.

Ruby had inserted herself into Lizzie's life as neatly as if she had advertised a position: *Friend Needed*. She rampaged about, saying the things that people were afraid to say, making cancer into a joke—although one that was still a secret from Dante and Etta.

Grey had settled down, though he still had a haunted look now and then. Etta had appeared every morning for breakfast. Rohan got her interested in solving the *Times* crossword puzzle.

And then there was Dante.

He had become her sun, the still center around which everything else circled. Was that a poem? She felt as if *this* falling in love was fashioned from poetry, because her emotions were too big for ordinary words.

I love you.

If she could say what she felt for him—if she could put it into words—it would be a song, so she sang it.

Which led to her singing all the time.

"Like a lark," Dante said from the bed, after a second bout of lovemaking.

Lizzie wrinkled her nose at him, but she was—for the first time in her life—working at singing with the same diligence with which she had worked at her study of the pluperfect in graduate school.

All the lessons Mrs. Bedrosian taught her had come back. Mrs. Bedrosian had been an opera singer before she found God, and while Lizzie had no interest in opera, she could put her hand on her diaphragm and feel the rumble of operatic song.

It felt like life.

She discovered that while singing she could ignore pain, at least a certain amount of it. She stopped napping for quite so many hours in the afternoon.

Oh, she didn't fool herself that she could sing herself into remission, the way desperate patients talked about prayer and Mexican herbalists and weird injections.

Song was a form of prayer, directed not at the heavens, but at the world.

She sat on the sill of Dante's window, back to the piazza, and sang.

The songs she knew by heart were mostly Episcopal hymns. *"Praise God from whom all blessings flow,"* she sang now. Whenever she sang, out in the piazza—or so she'd been told—the town stopped to listen. Tourists were shushed, waiters leaned against the wall.

Even so, she stopped singing long enough to tell Dante that orgasms were included in blessings. Then she grinned and put her fingertips on her diaphragm, feeling life course through her. *"Praise him above, ye heav'nly host; Praise Father, Son, and Holy Ghost."*

Dante wound his arms behind his head, and she took a moment to admire his chest. It was very fine. Muscled, strong. A few hairs.

"Would you have liked it more if I was completely hairless?" she asked, leaving the sill because the song had tired her out.

Or maybe all the sex tired her out.

She snuggled next to him, head on his shoulder.

"No," he said, sounding sleepy and hot. "A bald pussy isn't really . . ."

She fell asleep on that thought, dropping suddenly into darkness the way cancer had taught her to do. When she woke hours later, Dante had gone off to the restaurant. He had left a heart in sugar, which ants had discovered.

They were tiny brown ants, and their scurrying bodies seemed to show joy along with a businesslike fervor. She dropped into a chair and watched as they organized an assembly line that went down one table leg. It would take them all day to carry away that sugar.

They weren't disassembling the heart yet. They had begun on the far edge, which was a Sahara of sandy sugar away from the heart at the center.

Dante was lavish, in sugar and love.

She showered at his house, having learned that to waltz into the Bonaparte with sex hair was to welcome mockery from Ruby, applause from Rohan (who was now holding out hope that her extraordinary skills in bed would woo Dante into opening a restaurant in L.A.), and silence from Grey.

That evening after they all sat down at their table in front of the kitchen window at the Principe Blu, Dante came out to say hello. When the table next door figured out he was the famous chef and started clapping, he pulled Lizzie up, bent her in his arms, and gave her a leisurely kiss that tasted . . .

"Moroccan," she said, when he set her down, her knees weak. "The spice road, with a bit of ocean."

"Monkfish with white asparagus," Dante told Rohan, tousling Etta's hair.

"And the *primi piatti?*" Rohan asked, vibrating slightly.

"*Gnocchi di latte cagliato con cozze e coniglio,*" Dante said. "Gnocchi made with curdled milk, the sauce of mussels and rabbit." He laughed. "For the heathen at the table, *gnocchi di patate burro e salvia*. Plain gnocchi with sage butter."

The wooden floors that covered the courtyard were weatherbeaten, painted deep blue at some point in the past but now worn to the color of skim milk. Cicadas sang behind the kitchen, spending their whole short life in song.

A large group was arriving, listening to Signora Pietra's admonishments. They were all Italian, in pale linen and simple jewelry.

"A branch of the Missoni family," Rohan said, waving back at one of them.

"*Salvia* is sage," Etta said to Ruby. "But you should have the main dish, because Babbo's rabbit is phenomenal."

"I can't join you right away," Dante said, his hand curving around Lizzie's neck. "Most of the restaurant is booked at the same time, from the Missoni yacht."

"I could help," Rohan said diffidently. True, he had been going to the kitchen every morning, chopping celery while furthering his idea of opening a Principe Blu in L.A.

"Watch out," Grey drawled. "He's going to be plating our takeout when we're back in New York."

Dante nodded. "Sure, we could use a hand."

"Babbo, you never let people into your kitchen!" Etta crowed.

"People change." His voice was low, with laughter in it.

The warmth of his fingers felt like a permanent imprint on Lizzie's skin, a tattoo shared by lovers without ink or pain. She bent her head back to see: Dante was smiling at his daughter, a crooked, unguarded smile.

Rohan took off, looking happy, stopping at one table to sign autographs and another to say hello before he disappeared into the kitchen. After that, he was just one of the people moving quickly, his fame hidden in a white coat and white hat.

"Do you suppose that he will open his own restaurant?" Lizzie asked Grey.

"No, but I think one of the superheroes in that Disney series he's developing is going to be a chef."

"Cooking in his spare time, when he's not leaping tall buildings?"

Grey nodded.

"That sounds as if it wouldn't leave much time for plating."

Lizzie turned back to Ruby and Etta. "I don't think you're old enough to read it," Ruby was saying.

"What are you talking about?" Lizzie asked.

"*Call Me by Your Name*," Etta answered. "It's my favorite movie, but Ruby says that I shouldn't read the book because it's got too much sex stuff."

"The movie's pretty," Grey said. "But the book's about the kind of desire that roars in the belly. A feeling that will hit you around age seventeen or perhaps earlier, because girls are smarter than boys."

"I can read about desire," Etta said stoutly. "It's not such a big deal."

"The book is a fierce thing," Grey said, "ridiculous sometimes, powerful though. It's about male bodies that are almost the same, interchangeable instruments that play the same tune."

"I get that it's about ferocity and ownership," Lizzie said, leaning forward. "But the guy, Oliver, the older one . . . from the beginning, he's just a 'later' kind of guy. Pausing on his way to somewhere else."

"Elio tries to hold him back by taking his body," Grey said, swigging Elba wine. "It doesn't work, it never works. In the end, sex is just a path on the way to something else. Of course, it's a hell of a path."

"That sounds like something smart," Etta said, scowling, "but I don't think it really is."

Lizzie burst into laughter. "She's got you there, Grey."

"My point is that sex is good, but it's the journey that matters."

Dusty Springfield was drifting out of the open window of the kitchen.

"It doesn't have anything to do with Elio and Oliver being both male," Grey added.

Signora Pietra was on the other side of the courtyard, but she had caught sight of one of the Missonis lighting a cigarette. She whipped between the tables like a small tornado.

The offending diner stood up and offered her his cigarette.

She narrowed her eyes until they looked like little raisins and snatched it from his hand. Italian cracked in the air like a whip, as every table in the restaurant watched, awed. The man picked up her hand—the one not holding the cigarette—and kissed it.

She marched away with a final reprimand, holding the cigarette aloft with triumphant disdain.

"Was she calling him a cabbage?" Lizzie asked Etta.

"Yeah, that's her favorite," Etta said. "*Cavolo* is like saying 'ferk.' It's not as bad as *cazzo*."

"I'm pretty sure she called him that too."

Augusto emerged from the kitchen and plunked down a huge platter of gnocchi, and a small plate in front of Lizzie. The big platter smelled marvelous, rabbit and mussels harmonizing with a slight sour twinge.

But Lizzie smiled at her plate, which held a small mound of perfectly shaped gnocchi sitting in a puddle of browned butter with a few leaves of wilted sage. It was like a song that had no trumpet in the background.

Dante complained that she only liked the food that one served to children. Pale chicken broth with tiny pasta that looked like rice.

Spaghetti with butter—except the butter was a high-fat version that she'd never tasted before. Dusted with pink salt.

Why wouldn't she want that food?

This was the food that was made with the fiercest love of all.

Made by people who would never say "later" to the ones they love.

Chapter Twenty-three

In the following week, Lizzie had many orgasms—each of which she was blindingly grateful for. Rohan was on a rampage, refusing to talk about *Romeo*. He'd added another yoga class to his schedule, teaching it just as the sun was going down.

He haunted Dante's restaurant, going every morning to chop, having graduated from celery to tomatoes. At night, he gave every bite ferocious attention. One evening, he said he'd like to go to the market, so the next morning Lizzie, Dante, and Etta went to the hotel to pick up Rohan.

Etta ran back to the Fiat and threw herself in the back seat, but Rohan stopped short. "That's an antique," he said, staring. "Does it have seatbelts?"

Etta poked her head out of the window. "I want Babbo to get a Maserati."

"It's a perfectly good car," Dante said. "I can't remember the last accident I heard about on Elba. Maybe three years ago."

Rohan's jaw was tight. "My contract says that I can't go skydiving or mountain climbing. That includes this car."

"We can get a hotel car," Lizzie said, slipping her arm around Dante's.

Etta whooped as she jumped back out of the Fiat. "Air-conditioning!"

When they walked back into the courtyard, Ruby was sitting under the trees, reading a book and drinking tea. Etta went inside with Dante and Rohan, and Lizzie walked over to say good morning.

"Any interest in going to the market?" she asked. "Rohan wants to see farm-to-table Italian-style." She perched on the arm of Ruby's chair. She was tired, but not in a sickly way. Just the way that happens when two people sleep together, and every time they roll together in the night they wake up just enough to make love again.

Ruby shook her head. "I'm reading this pathetic play about pathetic teenagers." She thumped the worn copy of *Romeo and Juliet*. "I've got as far as the ball. I agree with Rohan that Juliet would rock some jewelry."

Lizzie tapped Ruby on the cheek. "The 'pathetic' play has survived four hundred years of bad acting and worse costumes, and still has something to say."

Ruby grinned. "I'm not allowed to throw shade at the big S?"

" 'Pathetic' is shade without substance," Lizzie told her.

"The professor is in!" Ruby crowed.

Dante, Etta, and Rohan came back out of the hotel, followed by a Roman with keys to one of the black cars. It seemed the market was in a different place every day, and today it was only a few villages away.

The road climbed until they were far above the sea. Whitecaps caught the light and glinted like bits of ice floating in blue water. When the car started coming down again, a town grew around the road, hotels clinging to the hills like barnacles, each with its own patch of umbrellas.

The road filled up with cars parked haphazardly to the sides. The black car crawled along slowly until it hit a barricade.

Lizzie climbed out, the air so hot it took her breath after the chilly car. Etta followed, hopping around like a five-year-old. She hadn't brushed her hair and it bounced on her shoulders.

"Come on!" she shouted and grabbed Lizzie's hand.

Dante saw that and a smile glinted in his eyes before he turned and walked off with Rohan. Lizzie and Etta followed until they all emerged through a narrow archway into a crowded piazza.

Lizzie had imagined a market from a French movie, each stall arranged with a glistening pyramid of apples manned by a red-cheeked, serious farmer, his waxed mustache trembling with gastronomic passion.

Instead, the market was made up of rows of white canvas roofs, long tables underneath, and people of all nationalities hawking everything from radios to underwear. Lizzie stopped at a tent selling curtains. Long transparent panels dusted with embroidered flowers hung from the roof and billowed in the slight wind.

"Nonna would never," Etta said, seeing what Lizzie was looking at.

"Why not?"

She dropped Lizzie's hand to pick up the fabric. "Machine-made. Not cotton or linen." Her voice wasn't disdainful; she was simply factual.

"But so pretty."

Etta dropped it and shook her head. Apparently in the judge's world, inconsequential fabrics didn't exist. "They should be linen, with white-on-white flowers, if any."

Lizzie remembered just in time that she was no longer interested in possessions, not even Pratchett books. That decision felt as if it had been made in a different lifetime.

After shoes and bags—"Made in China, most of them," Etta reported—they reached tables of food crowded with plastic bins full of disorderly vegetables. They were not arranged for visual effect.

Green beans were in piles looking like skinny green fingers. Mounds of limes came next. Balls, if Lizzie had to choose a body part. Green ones.

The cartons of raspberries didn't have the plumped-up look of fruit from Westside Market back home. They were different sizes, lumpy, but with an enticing peppery smell.

Did American raspberries even have a smell?

"Don't touch!" Etta squealed, pulling back Lizzie's hand a second before she picked up a berry. "Signore Berti will scream if you touch the fruit in front of Babbo, because he wants to sell his to the restaurant. Bragging points for the week."

"I thought—"

"See?" She pointed to Dante at the other end of the stall. The man behind the table was carefully choosing a tomato, which he handed over. Dante ate it like an apple, nodding. "He likes it," Etta said. "So Signore Berti will drop crates of tomatoes at the restaurant later today."

Signore Berti was giving Rohan a tomato too.

"Babbo will be here forever," Etta said. "He has to do the cheeses, and see—the sausages are over there. The honey guy is here today, and that guy with the big mustache usually has mushrooms. You only hunt truffles until December but he keeps good ones for Babbo. Farther down is the goat guy—he sells a *capra* cheese that Babbo really likes. Plus fish is down there, and my friend's babbo who farms sheep. Remember the lambs' tongues?"

"I forgot that." Maybe she should go back, commandeer the black car and driver, and go home for a nap.

"You refrigerate your tomatoes, don't you?" Etta asked, grinning at her.

"Sometimes," Lizzie said cautiously.

"Don't ever tell Babbo that. Come on." Etta dragged her briskly between two tents and over to a café where they sat down under a swath of canvas and ate Italian yogurt. "Yomo," Etta said, waving her spoon. "Italian milk. It's the best. Like, that's why gelato is good."

Lizzie and Etta talked about the mating habits of birds for a while until Rohan showed up. He was in disguise, more or less, in a hat and dark glasses. All the same, people kept squinting at him, trying to figure out if they knew that chin.

"It was great for a half hour," he told them. "But Dante is having an endless conversation about squid, and I couldn't understand anything they said."

"I'll go see how long he's going to be," Etta said, jumping up. "We could take the car and go home, and he'll still be at the fish when they come back for him."

A waiter brought Rohan a tiny, thick coffee.

"*Grazie,*" Rohan said, with a plausible accent, to Lizzie's ear. He threw back the coffee, shuddered, and looked at Lizzie. "So the London *Times* is calling to interview me this morning, and I don't know what to say."

Lizzie blinked. "The London *Times*? And you're here, in the market?"

"If the interview isn't going well, I'll say that I can't hear them over the fishmongers and then hang up."

"Are you supposed to talk about *Romeo*?"

He nodded. "My PR people sent around a thing about Juliet as the heart of the play, and apparently it went viral. I thought I had a few weeks to figure everything out, but they asked to talk now, and Disney wants to keep the excitement going."

"What is the *Times* expecting to hear?"

"How I will make that play mine. Fast and big," he explained. "It has to move and have a great soundtrack, and make you want to cry."

"You've got that last part covered. The end, remember?"

"Yeah, but you know: the construction of masculinity too. Performance of it. That's my thing, even if the film is about Juliet."

"Is that why you pose every year in your underwear for *People*?" Lizzie asked with a sudden flare of interest.

He blinked. "No. That's just one of those things that happened. It's a pain in the ass, but if I give it up . . ." His voice trailed off.

Obviously, it wasn't easy being forty and living in Hollywood. According to Grey, Rohan would be destroyed if *People* didn't call months before the Beautiful issue and start setting up the shoot.

"I need help," Rohan said.

Lizzie put her empty yogurt container to the side. "OK," she said.

"What am I going to say other than that Juliet proposes marriage?"

"You're going to talk about how the characters think about death. Mercutio laughs at death, Juliet fears it, Romeo chooses it. There's your nontoxic masculinity right there."

"Oh," Rohan said, getting it. "Damn, you're so good, Lizzie."

"How do the young think about life? What does it mean to waste one's life, for example? Is a life wasted if it's short?"

The words were ordering themselves in her head, coming out without conscious thought.

Rohan had that look that students get sometimes, excited and freaked at the same time. "I don't know how to do that in a production."

"Death is a huge topic of conversation. The reporter will grab it and be interested. Just ask what *she* thinks of love and death."

"What does it mean to waste a life?" Rohan said. Then he turned to her, eyes sharp and narrow. "You're not thinking that you wasted yours, are you?"

She shook her head. "No. Juliet didn't waste hers either, or Romeo, or even Mercutio. If someone told them, *You're only able to love for two days, for half a day, for the space of one poem, and then you'll be gone,* they would have grabbed it."

Rohan looked at her, and then he pushed back the brim of his hat, even though he risked being seen.

Lizzie leaned forward. "He's not in love with me, Rohan."

"What?"

"Grey. He's not in love with me. He loves me, and I'm dying. He's in love with you."

"Oh God," Rohan said, "is this the scene where the dying girl tells me to take care of the man she loves?"

She poked him. "Shut up. I'm telling you something important."

"I know that. Why do you think I'm with him?"

"Well, he's Grey. Beautiful and smart."

"The world is full of beautiful men. But ones like Grey? Loyal in their bones, and loving with everything they've got? I told my agent I wasn't going to be secret anymore."

"That's big," Lizzie said.

"Except Grey says no, so it hardly matters."

"He's trying to protect your career," she suggested, feeling awkward.

Rohan snorted. "I'd rather have him than be on the beautiful people list, but he won't listen to me. What's more, I think fans would love a gay Captain Britain. It's not like the whole franchise isn't queer as fuck."

His phone buzzed and he turned it over. "The London *Times*." He thumbed it off. "Grey said you were thinking of not having some operation that might make a difference."

She looked down at the scuffed metal table. "I'm not entirely certain, but I think I will do it."

"Look at me."

Rohan's voice was as beautiful as her own, she thought dimly.

"You have to fight, Lizzie. You can't do that to Grey."

Her smile wobbled. "Cancer is happening to me, not to him."

"If the cancer takes you, then it does. But if you don't fight it, Lizzie, you're saying he's not worth fighting for. Dante and Etta are up to you. But Grey is worth fighting for."

She went still. "I'm—"

"It's all right. He's mine too. But you could break him, Lizzie."

"I'm afraid."

He took her hand. "You're the bravest person I know."

"You don't know me very well." She managed a lopsided smile.

"You gave up Grey. You charged into life-after-Grey. I can't . . . I can't imagine it. I'm not making Grey out to be Jesus Christ or something. I'm just saying that for you and me, for the two of us, he's all that."

Lizzie drew in a deep breath. "Yeah," she said, letting the air go. "He is."

"You are too."

It felt as if they sat there for an hour, holding hands, not looking at each other. Then someone darted over, having gotten their courage up, and asked if he was *really* Rohan Das.

He admitted he was.

A *chicken hawk* floats over, looking for home.
I have wasted my life.

Chapter Twenty-four

The next morning Lizzie put on her bathing suit and went down to the public beach and spread out her little kingdom under the umbrella.

She was reading Pratchett's *Men at Arms,* because she and Dante had decided to reread the police series and he had bagged the first one, *Guards! Guards!*

Lulu arrived first, followed by Etta, who proceeded to winkle the history of Lizzie's first period out of her. That hadn't been a good time, given that Mrs. Bedrosian was nurturing but disorganized.

"It could have been worse," Etta said.

"Yeah," Lizzie agreed. "Could have been much worse."

"In fact, we're both pretty lucky," Etta said. She kept trying to solidify whatever this thing was that was happening between Dante and Lizzie. And Lizzie kept trying to push her away by sounding careless and non-motherly.

"What do you think of my hair this morning? I forgot to use conditioner," Etta asked.

Don't sound maternal, Lizzie told herself. "It has some resemblance to a hedge," she said truthfully. Then they spent the next hour making up similes.

"Grey's nose is like an arrowhead," Lizzie said.

"It's like David's nose. You know, the statue," Etta contributed.

"One more. We need three."

"I can't think of anything."

"Grey's nose is like—"

"The problem is that I don't care about his nose," Etta announced.

"It's a nice nose," Lizzie said, defending him.

"I don't think you should have gone out with him."

"Why not?"

"Because he was gay, obviously."

"He wasn't, back then. Life's more complicated than that, Etta."

"People always say stuff like that. I don't see anything complicated about doing a guy instead of a girl. Or dying because you drank too much vodka."

She marched off, and Lizzie let her go because a mother would try to do something about the acrid ring in Etta's voice. A bystander like herself would shut up or make a face that resembled pity. An alcoholic mother was hard to get over.

Something unfurled in her heart when Dante came wandering along the beach later. She told him the truth. "Etta is brooding about her mother."

"I noticed this morning when she asked me if I ever drank Bloody Marys for breakfast. Her mother and I wooed each other over vodka," Dante said, nudging her over on the sunbed so that he could lie down and kiss her. After a while he picked up where he'd left off. "Chefs generally drink too much. I had to stop because Etta needed warm milk at night, and a babbo who wasn't hungover."

He knifed to his feet. "Not enough room here." He dropped his towel on the sand at her feet and lay down, arms behind his head, not having any idea that she loved to ogle him under the shade of her hat. "Like Etta, you rank above vodka. And you are starting to rank above the restaurant." Dante's voice was brisk and matter-of-fact.

Lizzie lost her breath and didn't say anything.

Lulu gave a sigh and pushed hard into Lizzie's belly, before she dozed off. Dante went to sleep too, his breath evening out and the creases between his brow smoothing until he looked young, like a man without a restaurant or a daughter.

The sun crept closer to the edge of his cheek, so Lizzie got up and struggled with the umbrella until it covered his face. Then she lay back down and watched him some more.

When she told Dr. Weir that she was leaving the country, and she was thinking of not taking more treatment after the current chemo failed, her doctor obviously thought she was trying a desperate alternative medicine, horse guts in Mexico or Tibet.

But no. She had just been trying to decide whether to *be absolute for death*, as Shakespeare had it.

"Death" was a wonderfully calming word. It meant she never had to develop a backbone and confront her demons. She'd freecycled all her books, even the Pratchetts. She'd pared her possessions down to the bone.

Getting rid of the residue of those bones? Surprisingly difficult.

She'd finally signed up with the Cremation Society, and paid extra to have them drop her ashes off with the Episcopal church down the street from her apartment for their prayer garden.

The priest was a pigeon-toed woman named Sally Dempsey. She seemed taken aback, but after Lizzie explained that she didn't want to be scattered in the national forest because of mercury residue, and that she figured the prayer garden would have to be declared poisoned land at some point and cleaned, Ms. Dempsey capitulated. Or perhaps that should be Reverend Dempsey? Sally?

"Are you Episcopalian?" Ms. Dempsey had asked hopefully.

"I'm a Shakespearean," Lizzie had said, giving her a smile—the one with joy behind it. The one she saved for moments when she really wanted her own way.

"A Shakespearean may be just what we need in the prayer garden," Sally had said, giving in. Kindly people have few defenses against sad stories. "Lately, it's been all irascible elders."

"I plan to be a very soothing ghost. I'd love it if you said a prayer for me," Lizzie had added, untruthfully.

Sally had seen through her, but she nodded.

It would be fine to have tiny shards of Lizzie floating around Sally's prayer garden.

Except now she was losing that dandelion sense of having shed everything. Life thrummed in her veins with reckless speed every time she looked at Dante's muscles. Scarred hands. Surprisingly thick eyelashes. Beautiful eyes.

She was screwed.

Bob Dylan's song went through her head over and over. *All I know is that I'm thrilled by your kiss. I don't know any more than this.*

Dante woke up the way his daughter did, without opening his eyes. Lizzie couldn't imagine that. She always jerked awake, her eyelids flying open fast, fast.

She reckoned he had been awake a good minute before his eyelashes opened and he looked at her. "Do you smell the sea?"

Lizzie nodded.

He got up and leaned over her sunbed. "Can I take you back to your room and ravish you? Because you smell better than the sea, all sweaty. You don't wear sunblock, do you?"

Lizzie shook her head.

"Never?"

"No."

"Why—" He opened his mouth, and shut it, and then sat down hard on the side of her sunbed.

She watched as it all went through his head: that she wouldn't have children, that she had scars, that Grey sometimes looked as if he'd been crying. . . .

In the end, she didn't have to say the speech she'd planned. He worked it out on his own. After a moment of watching him stare into the sand at their feet, she reached out and covered his right hand with her left.

She was pretty sure that dying women in movies were always gripping someone's hand and looking soulful. Lizzie didn't feel soulful. She felt hot and sweaty and as if wrinkles would leap onto her face right now because she wasn't wearing sunblock.

"That's what you meant about lucky/unlucky," he said a good five minutes later. "About Etta."

"Yeah." Shame was pressing on her eyelids. She shouldn't have slept with him. She shouldn't have napped with Etta. She shouldn't . . .

Dante didn't have much of an expression. Not that she wanted him to be awash with pity. She would hate that. Or anguish, which would be gut-wrenching. Anger, anxiety, energetic wish to help—each emotion was worse than the last, frankly.

They were all bad.

Dante shoved her over a little and then lay down at her back and pulled her against his stomach.

Romantic moment, Lizzie's brain informed her. *Stop thinking about how sweaty you are and the way your leg itches.* She felt like a Precious Moments figurine that couldn't figure out how to be precious.

Sometimes silence feels like eternity, especially when you don't have an eternity.

She felt oddly empty, because now another person—maybe the most important person, Dante—knew that she wasn't going to be in the world for long. And that made her feel as if she was unraveling around the edges.

"You're lucky/unlucky too," she offered a while later. She reached down to scratch her leg because she couldn't stand the itching any longer, even though she was in the midst of the most romantic moment of her life.

"I'm only lucky," Dante said. His voice had dropped and was more Italian than it had ever been.

The sound of it brushed the back of her neck like a kiss.

Chapter Twenty-five

Etta Moretti's bedroom door,
from Pinterest:

TEENAGERS
Tired of being harassed by your parents?
ACT NOW!!!
Move out, get a job,
Pay your own way,
QUICK,
While you still know everything!!

High school was a big deal in New York City. Everyone had to apply, just like going to college. You had to get in, even if you just wanted to go around the corner from your apartment. Etta was hopeful, though: LaGuardia was hard, but since she was eating dinner every night with a famous actor, she figured it ought to be easy for her.

Tonight Babbo cooked right up until Lizzie, Grey, and Rohan

showed up. Then he sat down next to Lizzie for the whole meal, leaving Ricardo in charge of the kitchen.

He didn't move even when a whole yacht-load of royal people showed up. They had to make do with Ricardo's cooking, not that they knew. They didn't recognize Rohan either, because he had a hat pulled down to his ears.

Etta had to keep an eye on her babbo to make sure that he didn't start boring anyone by going on about food. She didn't think that Lizzie would dump him if Grey and Rohan got bored . . . but maybe?

Every time Babbo started to talk about food, Etta cut him off and made Rohan talk about his movie, because that man was a big talker. If she were *his* daughter, she'd tell him to pinch himself every time he said, "Disney thinks." Disney wasn't a person.

Like right now, he was going on about Romeo. Boring.

She was sitting next to Lizzie—she *always* sat next to Lizzie, because she wasn't stupid. If her babbo messed things up, she was going to keep in touch with Lizzie anyway, on her own. She'd go to Fordham.

Maybe Lizzie would give her the key to her office and she could chill there before classes. Or hack into Lizzie's computer and change her grades for better ones, because a girl should have ambition.

Lizzie was battling with Rohan about whether it was important that Romeo was a virgin. If she'd had the nerve, Etta would have pointed out that virgins were just like everybody else, except they'd kept themselves out of embarrassing situations.

She nudged Lizzie in the ribs until Lizzie looked back, eyebrow raised. It was a good look, because Lizzie had a mop of white-blond curls and dark eyebrows.

"Rohan's a huge poodle, one of those expensive ones that don't fit in New York apartments," Etta whispered.

Lizzie glanced at him across the table and shook her head. "Too hairy." She waited a second. Rohan kept monologuing about teenage sex. Then she whispered back, "He's a Ken doll: no body hair, and I'm pretty sure that Ken always thinks he's right."

Rohan seemed to be deciding that teenage virginity could sell.

"Virginity is just a state of mind," Etta said, speaking up.

Her father had been holding Lizzie's hand under the table and staring into space, but he snapped awake.

To head off anything embarrassing that he might say, she added quickly, "The problem is that Romeo isn't interested in sex, and Juliet *is*. American boys aren't supposed to be like that."

"Great point," Lizzie said.

Etta felt that this was a moment that should be noted, so she leaned forward and reached across Lizzie to poke her babbo. "Did you hear that? Mrs. Gardish said that I didn't pay attention in class, but a *Shakespeare professor* doesn't agree!"

"The way I heard it, you kept leaving class, going to the bathroom, and not coming out until the bell rang," her babbo said.

"What do you mean, Romeo isn't interested in sleeping with Juliet?" Rohan asked, turning back to Etta. "It's the greatest love story ever told. There's the freaking balcony scene. He doesn't want to leave, remember?"

On the other side of Lizzie, Babbo muttered something. She could see that he had a hand on Lizzie's thigh. It was tight, so tight that Lizzie's warm brown tan disappeared in white marks around his fingers.

Lizzie rubbed her head against his shoulder the way a pet cat would, if Babbo had a pet cat. His fingers relaxed and Etta took a breath.

What in the heck was that about?

"Romeo is undersexed and Juliet is oversexed," Rohan said.

"Let up with the patriarchal crap," Ruby said, pointing at Rohan.

Etta looked around and saw Grey stealing shrimp from Ruby's plate, because Ruby was arguing with Rohan and wouldn't notice. Her babbo was kissing Lizzie's nose and whispering to her. Etta really liked that mad grin of Lizzie's.

It was almost like having a family.

No: It *was* a family.

Something swelled in her chest, maybe joy, because she'd finally grown old enough to have gotten the thing she'd prayed for when Nonna took her to church. It felt like the world had grown bigger, after she shoved wishes at it.

Dessert hadn't even arrived, but Babbo tugged Lizzie to her feet. "Enough Shakespeare. Let's go for a walk on the beach."

She watched them go. At the archway, Lizzie turned around and sent a kiss back to Etta.

This summer was bananas.

Ruby squeezed her hand. "Remember that old bathing suit of yours?"

"You're so weird," Etta said.

"Yeah, I know. But tonight is covered with shiny pineapples, don't you think?"

Etta started smiling. "Yeah. Yeah, it totally is."

Chapter Twenty-six

The whole Stage Three thing had a way of distancing life that was good—and bad. Right now, for instance, Lizzie was walking along a beach in the night with an Italian who was really good in bed and who liked her.

No: who loved her.

He had said that he loved her, that he was in love with her. He said it more than once.

And yet she felt as if she were telling a story about her life rather than living it. As if the moment the doctor said the word "cancer," she started narrating a fictional version of her own life.

Authentic Lizzie had gone missing, replaced by this one who had fuck-all luck right up until the moment when a fuzzy dog jumped up and licked her.

She'd been performing plucky, unlucky Lizzie for two years, so maybe that was why she couldn't quite get herself back into the before-cancer Lizzie, a Shakespeare professor who mostly spent her time reading and drinking with friends.

It had been a half-assed life, no doubt. No saving lives or fighting for the environment.

Just doing what she wanted to, most of the time, with the justification that a fucked-up childhood meant you could give yourself a break on the Mother Teresa stuff.

Sometimes, like now, she felt such a desperate longing for pre-cancerous Lizzie that her whole stomach twisted. Lizzie 1.0 would have been ecstatic to walk on the beach. Perhaps she'd be planning to text Grey and boast about it . . . but she would be *there*. Adoring every moment. Clinging to Dante's arm, probably.

Dragging him down on the sand, maybe. They could make love with their toes in the surf, like that old black-and-white movie.

Except that the seawater was cold when it sloshed against her feet.

For his part, Dante seemed perfectly happy to stroll along the beach, his hands jammed into baggy linen pants, the kind that American men could rarely pull off. She reached out and slid her hand through the crook of his elbow and down his ropy forearm, fingers bumping over a scar and finally curling around his wrist and pulling his hand free.

"What are you thinking about?" she asked.

"My daughter," he said. "Sometimes Etta is intolerable." He flashed a look at her and then back out to sea. "Moody, snide, hot-tempered. She's been in principals' offices in every school I've had her in and she's not even a teenager."

"I expect she blames her Russian blood," Lizzie said, amused.

"Actually, she tells me that it's my fault. My mother has a penchant for shouting."

"Etta doesn't want to blame her mother," Lizzie realized. "That just goes to show how nice she is, Dante. You're there, and you're alive. You can take it."

His hand tightened on hers for a second, then he dropped it and stuck it back in his pocket.

God, she had to stop analyzing her life from the outside. So what if the handsome Italian wanted to walk along with his fists in his pockets? Perhaps it was a sign of secret pain.

It turned out it wasn't, because a bit farther down the beach, when Lizzie had stopped thinking about Dante's hands—harder than you might think, because she loved big, scarred hands—he stopped and pulled them out of his pockets.

What he had in his right hand caught moonlight.

She made a strangled noise.

He was looking down at her, warm eyes. The warmest. "Please marry me."

Her pulse thumped in her ears. "I . . ." She had no idea what to say. It was as if he'd somehow forgotten that she lived on a different planet than he did. The planet of the dying.

"I love you. I am in love with you."

Lizzie finally managed to say something. "I'm *ill*."

"One of the things I love about you is that you have two voices." He had her hand now, her left hand, and his thumb was rubbing circles in her palm. "There's the shocked, indignant voice that I don't hear very often. And then there's the velvety contralto who talks of Shakespeare and Bob Dylan."

"I can't," Lizzie whispered.

He kept going. "I love the way you are counting minutes and letting them go. You live fiercely, more than anyone I know."

It wasn't true. She was a coward, floating above the world, circling, wasting her life. Tears started to burn the back of her throat.

Dante read her eyes, and laughter burbled out of him like Elba wine. "You don't know what you are. You hide what you are. But everyone crowds to be near you, Lizzie. Not just Etta. Ruby. Grey. Rohan."

His smile cracked. "Me. Me most of all."

"I'm not—" Lizzie said, and stopped. She was floundering, and she knew it. "I'm dying, Dante. Dying. You can't marry me. I shouldn't have let you love me." Anxiety rose in her throat and pressed against her heart. "I shouldn't have said hello to Etta. Especially Etta. No, you too." She stopped with a gasp.

"I thought you'd say that," Dante said, casually almost. Still smiling.

"I *am* saying that," Lizzie said, trying to summon up insulted pride. He was discounting a genuine feeling, one that had anguished her for night after night.

Dante took out his phone, which gave her a flash of anger. But he stabbed the screen in the clumsy way he did, not noticing that she was scowling, and then the music broke out, a bit tinny.

It was almost too much, but she let him stick the phone in his pocket and they swayed together to Bob Dylan's raspy voice, a little muffled by Dante's linen shirt.

"I'm like Desdemona in that Dylan song, don't you see? I gave you poisoned wine and you drank it," she told him.

Dante shook his head, even though his cheek was tight on the top of her head. She realized that he'd planned the evening to end with a couple swaying, like that boy in the song, *'neath the stars that shine.*

She swallowed hard and rubbed away a tear, commanding herself not to cry.

"I couldn't bear being poison wine," she said, trying again. "For you, for Etta. If I—married or not, if we saw each other in New York, if we were together, it wouldn't always be summer."

"No, it wouldn't."

"You gave me so much." Damn it, her voice was trembling. "I've never been so happy. Ever. I even . . . I even sang. I am singing every day. For you."

She looked up: not even a glimmer of a smile in his eyes.

"I would give anything to wake up with you, and sleep with you, and give you a thousand kisses and more."

"Then do it." His right hand was curled tightly around the ring he still held.

"I don't have time."

He made a sudden movement, sharp. "We can discuss the ins

and outs of time later, Lizzie. Right now: I want the time you have. Please. *Please.*"

"I can't protect you," Lizzie said, tears welling up. "You don't have any idea. Your life is so lovely, and death is like . . . Death smells and it's horrible, mortifying, painful. It's night after night, and the pain doesn't go away. It's—no. Don't you see, Dante? Please, can't you let me have you and Etta and this summer as a perfect memory? For me?"

"For you?" His eyes were too dark to read.

"For me." She nodded. "Because if we—if we part now, then I have this, this perfectness in my head. It's your smile, and Etta's giggle. It's all those orgasms and sunsets and Elba wine. It's sea glass. It's even Grey shouting at me. It's perfect.

"But if I take that ring, then the perfect memory will turn to doctors' visits, bleach, pills, fear, smells. Etta crying and maybe you too. I've seen people on the chemo wards: husbands, and children, and friends."

Tears dripped off Lizzie's chin, but she kept looking at him, willing him to turn and walk away, or better, to enfold her in his arms and say he understood.

"It would be unbearable to drag Etta into all that," she whispered, her voice rasping. "She deserves so much better. I know you're protective, but you can't caretake me through this. You can't. It's not the right thing to do, because someday there will be nothing but caretaking left."

Silence came between them, and all she could hear was the slushing of water breaking against the pebbled shore.

When he finally spoke, his voice was so gentle that she almost confused it with the sea. "No."

She used her dress to mop up her tears.

"I'm sorry," she said finally. "It's my decision, and *my* no. You don't get to refuse to listen to me. It's my death, and if I choose not to do it in the company of an Italian chef and his twelve-year-old daughter, then I shall do so."

His eyes moved past her, up on the beach, and then he said, "May I?"

"May you what?" She sniffed.

Dante took a step, and then he picked her up. He fell back a step because—guess what—he wasn't a navy officer, and this wasn't an old movie, and she weighed more than any dying woman had the right to weigh.

But she kept her mouth shut because he had the right to stage his own movie, and he walked sturdily back up the slope of the beach and turned and sat down. Someone had deserted a beach chair, one of the rickety ones made of striped fabric and easily bent metal.

It groaned but didn't break under their weight.

Lizzie curled up her legs and nestled her cheek against his chest.

"So you think it's time for goodbye?" he asked a while later, when her heartbeat had slowed, and her world had contracted to the large warm body that closed around her like a seashell.

"Almost," she whispered.

"My heart will never say goodbye," he said. "Not to you."

"But I will have to."

"Mine will still be loving you on that night." His voice was steady, and he was putting kisses on her hair. "I have roads left to travel, my Lizzie. Promises to keep. And so do you."

"Your promises are to Etta."

"Is it better to have had a mother for a week or a month or whatever time you can give us—or never at all?"

Lizzie swallowed because it would be rude to suggest that he find a better woman to love, one with years instead of months, and decades instead of years. One who could pick out a wedding dress for Etta and rock her baby on the day it was born.

If there was one thing she'd learned in life, it was that longing doesn't make things come true.

Maybe that was because she hadn't known how to long for Dante and Etta. She'd spent her time longing for a mother who cared, or a father who existed.

She never longed for a haphazard family. She had wanted a daughter so much, and the world had given her Etta, and there was no better daughter to be imagined.

"My love goes where you go," Dante said. "Etta already loves you. You didn't think Grey's love for you would disappear, would it? When you got sick, or when you die?"

She shook her head. "I tried to leave him."

Dante made a little sound, like a chuckle but not. "There are knots that cannot be untied, and love makes them."

"I don't *want*—"

"I know." His voice was as level as the sea. "I know. But your love is something to rejoice about, no matter whether Etta and I have you for five minutes or fifty years."

"I'm going to cry again." Her voice wavered and she drew in a breath. "It's just so awful. You don't—"

"I remember what you said. Mortifying, smelly, horrible in every way. I would weigh all that against one thing."

She sniffled. "Love?"

"Not love, though that's part of it. *You*, Lizzie. All of that on one side and you in the balance, and I'd choose you and whatever years you have every time. Always."

Lizzie shifted so she could wind her right arm around his neck and kissed him in the hollow of his neck, where his pulse beat. "Thank you for not pointing out that you might be hit by a taxi tomorrow. Usually people try to persuade me that they might die any moment."

"I forgot that," he said, a rumble of laughter in his voice. "May I—"

She put a hand over his mouth. "No!"

He nipped at one of her fingers, and she moved her hand.

"Please marry me, Lizzie. Please give me the time you have left. I know how selfish I am. I understand that I'm tying you down, when you were giving away your books. I get it. But please . . . please don't give me away."

Time crumpled as they lay together. Lizzie could hear Dante's heart beating under her ear. She had never been very good at changing her mind. She had loved Grey and she kept loving Grey, even when he . . . even given all that happened.

Taking Dante's ring meant the operation, for one thing. More experimental stuff that Grey wanted her to try.

"I spent so much time visualizing my death," she said, trying to explain. "So that I wouldn't be afraid, and I wouldn't be a burden. I knew Grey would cry, but . . ."

"Grief is a gift," Dante said. "Grief means that you threw your heart into life and lived it fiercely. Suffering is a gift."

"But hope is no gift," Lizzie said, trying to explain it a different way. "I see it on people's faces when they come to visit the wards. I didn't want anyone to *hope,* because it's so corrosive when it fails."

"Is that why you thought about not having that operation?" At her sudden movement, he said, "Yes, Grey told me. He found me this afternoon, and basically told me that I had one reason to live, and it was to give *you* a reason to live."

"Was the ring?" She sat up, twisting free. "Is that why you—"

He snatched her back. "I've been carrying the ring for days. Before I asked you about sunblock, before Grey mentioned an operation. I knew I would be getting that ring out of the safe after the second time I met you on the beach, when you came to the restaurant."

"You cooked for me," she said, hearing the wonder in her own voice.

"After you sang for me, for me and the monks, I took it out of the safe, but I was already in love with you."

This smile came from her heart. She *had* sung for him. Birds couldn't sing in flight, a chicken hawk didn't sing, but she had stopped circling, stopped looking for a home, sat on a branch and filled the air with song.

So she *had* known, even then.

She turned around, put her knees on either side of Dante's legs and wiped the last tears away. "I suppose it's not quite time for goodbye," she said, her voice cracking. "But I would like you . . . I would like to say goodbye to you when that time comes."

He leaned forward and made his words into small kisses. "May I put this ring on your finger, Lizzie? May I bring you home with me—or go to your home, if you wish?" She could hear him hold his breath.

She held up her left hand, grinning madly, and Dante Moretti slipped a ring over her finger.

There had been enough tears for the night.

She was wrong, though.

It turned out that if two people make love under the stars, and one of them is trying to turn every kiss into a link that can't be undone, that person might—to his surprise—find tears on his face.

Later Lizzie tugged Dante to his feet and dragged him over to where the sand was packed underfoot, where the water had been swept away as the tide went out.

"Dance with me again."

Tears left glistening trails on his cheeks that the moonlight caught.

"Dylan?" He kept one hand on her waist and fumbled with his phone.

She shook her head. "I'll sing."

Dante cupped his hands on her cheeks. "I don't want you to ever feel you have to sing for me."

She laughed. "I feel like singing for you. I feel as if I can sing and the world—who cares about the world? I have you, and Etta. I have a family."

His smile wavered but it was there.

Then he pulled her hard against him. Nonsense felt like the right thing, so she did Lear. They swayed back and forth, and she could feel semen going down her leg, because the world is always with us, right?

Hand in hand, on the edge of the sand,
They danced by the light of the moon.

Chapter Twenty-seven

Etta Moretti's bedroom door,
from J. K. Rowling:

Erised stra ehru oyt ube cafru oyt on wohsi.
I show not your face but your heart's desire.

When Etta woke up in the morning, she ran down the stairs think-ing that she would go over to the Bonaparte and have breakfast with everyone. But she glanced into the kitchen out of the corner of her eye—knowing that her babbo would be at the market—and saw . . .

Lizzie.

Lizzie, sitting there with her hands wrapped around a mug, smiling as if she was waiting for Etta to come down the stairs. Lulu was there too, lying on her faded pillow in the corner.

The feeling was weird.

If she was writing a novel about a girl without a mother, it would be a new chapter, maybe. But then maybe not. What did a mother's smile look like, anyway? Was Lizzie smiling a maternal smile?

It looked like a Lizzie smile: laughter crinkles around her eyes, tan like you're not supposed to get, no makeup.

"Are you giving me a motherly smile?" she burst out, plopping down onto a stool opposite Lizzie.

Lizzie blinked.

"Because that's the contessa's diamond ring," Etta squealed, unable to keep her face from breaking into a smile so huge that it probably threatened the permanent arrangement of her teeth.

Lizzie was looking at Etta's face in that way that novelists call "searching," but she turned her eyes down to the ring.

"He didn't tell you?" Etta asked, rolling her eyes. "He's so . . . Anyway, that ring belonged to the contessa, my great-grandmother. She was really rich and haughty and stuff, but I never met her because, obvs, I'm illegitimate."

The smile dropped from Lizzie's mouth, and her eyes narrowed. "The contessa refused to meet you?" She looked as if she might throw the ring to the floor.

"Oh, no," Etta said hastily. "Not like that. At least, I don't think so. Babbo was probably waiting until I could talk in order to bring me over so I could charm her, but she died before I could do my magic. Which I did do," she added punctiliously, "to my grandmother, who wasn't too happy about the idea of me either, but now she likes me a lot."

"I see," Lizzie said. "When I was in foster care, there were kids who knew how to charm people into loving them. I wasn't good at it myself." That was definitely a mom look. "You already have me, Etta."

Etta sat with that a moment and then she said, "OK."

She was feeling a hideous wash of self-consciousness. Obviously, Lizzie loved her babbo, but she was getting Etta too. Etta looked under her lashes across the table, which was scarred with a million knife cuts because Babbo thought that cutting boards were for meat only. Lizzie was tracing the marks with a toothpick.

"I will try to be a decent teenager," she said, making a stab at it. "I can't promise anything, though. Sometimes I feel very bad-tempered, and I'm only twelve. I get in trouble in class a lot. I don't have my period, and my friend Annabel said it made her bi-polar and it's a symbol of everything that's wrong with being a woman."

Lizzie's laugh . . .

Lizzie's laugh was everything. It made you feel OK with the world. Her whole face lit up, and she got wrinkles, the good kind. Her voice was deep anyway, but her laugh was velvety and joyful. It would be good to laugh with her, but Etta's stomach was still clenched, nervous.

"She's not wrong," Lizzie said, when she stopped laughing.

"About being bipolar or it being a symbol?"

"About periods being hellish. Once Mrs. Bedrosian sent me to Bible camp on a bus in white jeans, and I got my period, but I didn't tell any of the counselors. I sat in the back of the bus and I had to walk past the kids all the way up the aisle. All the way."

"Big yikes," Etta said, shivering. She felt suddenly shy, so she traced a few of the cuts with a finger. "I guess this means you're going to live with us?"

"We haven't talked about it," Lizzie said. "Would that be all right with you?"

"Yes," Etta said, not looking up.

Lizzie reached over and caught Etta's hand. She had a big hand for a person who wasn't very tall. Etta was definitely going to be taller than her. "I know I won't make up for not having a mother."

Etta moved her shoulders, staring at their hands together. "It's OK."

"It's not OK for me," Lizzie said. "It's never been OK, and I had good foster moms."

"No sending me to Bible camp, no matter what color pants I'm wearing," Etta said. Lizzie's smile made her duck her head and stare at their hands again.

Who would have thought this would be so embarrassing? She'd been planning for this moment since the very first time Lizzie looked at Babbo's food and wrinkled her nose.

"Maybe we should make up some stepmom ground rules," Lizzie said. "Because if it's all right with you—and I really mean that, Etta—I'm going to be your stepmom. Number One: no Bible camp."

Lizzie was looking at her with affection. Etta could feel it, like the protection that Harry Potter had as a baby, except no, that was—

She threw away the thought.

"I guess you know this, because I did the *Parent Trap* thing, but I'll help," she said. "I know Babbo gets annoying, but I can help."

Lizzie's laughter rolled around the kitchen. "I might take you up on that."

"He's a fanatic about doing the dishes before bed," Etta said. "He can be really uptight about stupid stuff, not like grades, because I get that. But wearing a coat outside when it's perfectly warm! He's always sure I'm going to get a *frescata*."

"A cold?"

Lizzie's hand still held hers, which was getting a little embarrassing, in Etta's opinion, but she couldn't take hers away.

"I thought maybe we could do something together this morning," Lizzie said, looking as embarrassed as Etta felt.

And maybe a little desperate?

Of course, Lizzie hadn't been a mom before.

"Brilliant!" That was idiotic. Etta sounded like a geek being asked on her first date. She cleared her throat. "What would you like to do?"

Lizzie chewed on her bottom lip. "Go to the sea?"

Etta couldn't help feeling a little disappointed. Shouldn't there be more ceremony to the first day a mother and daughter spent together? Or maybe this would all be way more casual. Like, she was the cool stepmom who would smoke pot—

No, Lizzie wasn't lame like that.

Right now, she looked kind of terrified.

"You already did some mom stuff," Etta told her. "Remember? You told me to mind my manners. You got this!"

Lizzie didn't look any calmer.

"OK, Rule Number Two," Etta said. "First off, I'm going to take my hand away, OK? I'm starting to feel as if we're starring in a Hallmark movie, one of those sad ones."

Etta wouldn't have seen it if she wasn't looking right across the table, but Lizzie's eyes got tight, and she looked sick. "I don't mind holding your hand!" Etta exclaimed. She reached out and grabbed it back. "I totally don't mind holding hands in public either. It's not like you're an evil stepmother."

"I hope not," Lizzie said. "I don't know, though. . . ." Her eyes had a twinkle again, so Etta eased out a breath. "I didn't ever have a mom or a stepmom. It strikes me that neither of us has the faintest idea how we're supposed to behave. Maybe this *is* Hallmark movie territory."

"Rule Number Two," Etta proclaimed. "No curfew."

Lizzie laughed. "Try again, Etta. That's a nonstarter and you know it."

"You could be on my side," Etta argued. "You could be the voice of reason in the household, and I need one. Babbo has ridiculously old-fashioned ideas, more than just that I can't go outside without wearing a coat."

"To the beach without your swimsuit top?"

"He didn't know," Etta had to admit.

"Your babbo is going to have to set the rules, Etta."

"No, call me E. I like it."

Lizzie gave her a lopsided smile. "E. Your babbo is your babbo and he's in charge."

"Once you're married, you'll share that."

"We won't share you."

Etta's heart sank like a heavy stone.

"I didn't mean that," Lizzie said quickly. "I want half of you, E. But the safety stuff? I can't overrule your babbo."

"What if he's being ridiculous? Like, he says, 'Are you going out dressed like that?' I should be able to wear whatever I want, what other kids are wearing."

"Bra showing or boob showing?"

"I don't have any boobs," Etta pointed out, taking away her hand so she could pull her T-shirt flat against her chest. "Or bras. I haven't asked, but if I did, I know what he'd say. I have a white T-shirt that would look great with a red bra under. Like, they have a bra at Urban Outfitters that's red, with crosses in the front. He wouldn't buy it."

"Oh God, I suppose Dante has been going shopping with you?"

"Of course he has! Who else would?"

Lizzie cleared her throat. "His girlfriend?"

"I don't want to make you feel like a unicorn," Etta said, "but you are. I can see your twinkly horn from here. He hasn't had a girlfriend, not for years. You can take me shopping for red bras, so that's Rule Number Two. Shopping for stuff like that."

"All right," Lizzie said. "But what happens when your babbo says, 'Are you going out like that?'"

"You overrule him and say that we bought it yesterday and it's fabulous."

She shook her head. "Nope. I get you on bras that are for display. I have a couple. But I'm not buying them for a twelve-year-old."

"You'd buy one for yourself and not for me? Mean!"

"Alas, Urban Outfitters doesn't make bras in my size."

Etta frowned. Lizzie's boobalicious look had some drawbacks. "You're not old enough," Lizzie said.

"How about when I *am* old enough?"

A weird look went over Lizzie's face, but she nodded. "If I'm shopping with you when you're old enough, then I will buy you a red bra. And if I don't happen to be there . . . The day when you know that I would think you're old enough, then you get that red bra and wear it."

Of course she wouldn't want to go shopping too often. She was a professor. "I won't plague you about shopping," Etta said. "It's just that I see moms all the time, like, with girls my age."

"I know," Lizzie said. And she did, Etta could tell. "Hanging out in the dressing room or outside the curtain. Daughters being snarky or whiny because they don't know what they have."

"Yeah," Etta said. "We were in Paris last year, and there was this mom in the dressing room next to me. Her daughter was trying on stuff—a skirt maybe."

"Do you speak French?"

"Nope, but it's pretty close to Italian. Anyway, the Mom just kept crying, 'Ooo, la-la!' Just like that, like a movie. 'Ooo, la-la, Marie. Ooo, la-la.' "

Lizzie laughed, and Etta felt as if she'd never been so happy.

"Maybe she was trying on a red bra?" Lizzie suggested.

"A skirt or dress, because the mom said it was so short it was up to her eyebrows."

"I can do that," Lizzie said. She looked pretty happy. "What's Rule Number Three?"

"If I ever get a boyfriend, you have to stop Babbo from embarrassing me."

Lizzie's eyes laughed, even when she didn't. "Oh? And how would I do that, Miss E?"

"Just stop him," Etta ordered. "He's going to ask the wrong

questions, and probably wear one of those sweaters I hate that make him look like a pensioner."

"He seems pretty elegant for a chef," Lizzie observed.

Etta sighed. Lizzie was wearing a really nice dress, but anyone could tell that she saw it in the market for thirty euros and bought it without trying it on. Maybe a French market, because they sold all those linen dresses in the street. But still.

Fashionable she wasn't.

"I know," Lizzie said sympathetically. "I *am* a professor, you know. A Shakespeare one, yet. I'm not even teaching pop culture. If you point out the most offending sweater, I might be able to do something about it."

"There's more than one. They're cashmere. He buys them at this store in Firenze that's about a million years old, and they know about the contessa, and they always called him Cavalier Moretti."

Lizzie looked startled. "Knight?"

"Yeah, that. It's embarrassing. The sweaters are awful—the wrong size of V-neck and terrible colors. They last forever so he never gets rid of them. You don't want to know how many maroon sweaters he has."

"Maroon is not a good color," Lizzie said, nodding. "Rule Number Three: Don't ever buy a maroon sweater for Dante's birthday."

"*And* take a scissors to the ones in the closet," Etta said. "You could do it during a fight and get away with it, which I could not."

"I would never cut up Dante's belongings! Or yours," Lizzie added, looking shocked.

Etta shook her head, putting on a properly pitying expression. "You haven't had an argument with Babbo, have you?"

"Not yet."

"He's not bad, but he's *loud*." All of a sudden, she felt a pang of worry. "That's not a deal breaker, is it? Because he's Italian. It's like in his DNA. He doesn't mean it, not the way an American would."

"I can survive it," Lizzie said, very relaxed.

Etta's heart stopped thumping.

"But I'm not cutting up any garments in a rage or a pretend rage," Lizzie said, "and if Dante eyes my clothes, he'll be very, very sorry."

"He won't," Etta said. "He would never. He actually doesn't yell that much. He's getting old, you know."

Then she blinked, wanting to take that back.

"Not a deal breaker," Lizzie said, smiling. She had her elbows folded on the table. "I need some coffee. Want to go to the Bonaparte?"

Etta shook her head. "They're all there. Grey, Rohan, Ruby."

Lizzie said, very carefully, "Do you not care for—for them, Etta?"

"I do," Etta said. "It's just that today is the *first* day. So maybe— how about if we go to Napoleon's house? Just you and me."

"I'd love to." But she was looking hard at Etta, as if she could stare into her brain. *A mom look,* Etta thought proudly. *Someone's giving* me *that look.* "Did anyone say something to you that you disliked?"

"Mom tone," Etta said, letting delight leak into her voice. "Not the first time, because you did it on the yacht too, and that's when I knew that you'd decided to marry Babbo."

Lizzie's mouth fell open, the way you read about in books but never see in person. *"What?"*

"You mom'd me," Etta said. She rapped on the table. "I knew it right then! Babbo had bewitched you, even if not with his food." She started laughing because Lizzie's face was appalled.

"Anyway," Etta said, catching her breath, "I like Rohan. He thinks I could be an actress if I get the right role, and I should go to LaGuardia. Grey is nice too, maybe a little salty because my babbo took you away."

Lizzie's brows drew together. "Grey does like Dante."

"He'll live with it," Etta said. "Ruby, I love her. That's your fam, I get it." She stopped.

"Your fam too," Lizzie said.

Etta let that one sink in while Lizzie kept talking. "Grey and Rohan live part of the time in L.A., but they have an apartment a block from the restaurant, and Rohan is going to work on *Romeo* there. Ruby is coming to New York to design the makeup for the new film."

"A family." Etta whispered it.

Lizzie had an odd look on her face, almost like she was lonely, which didn't make any sense. But then she reached over and squeezed Etta's hand.

"Family."

Chapter Twenty-eight

Lizzie and Etta arrived at Napoleon's villa in style, transported in one of the hotel's black limousines, driven by a Roman named Mauro.

Lizzie kept thinking how nice it was to be driven around by a man who didn't say anything and didn't expect a tip.

"I could get used to this," Etta said, scrambling out of the car.

"Used to what?" Lizzie asked.

"A car with air-conditioning," Etta said. "You know Babbo's car. It's about one hundred years old, and he says that it works, so why get another? I've tried to say things about airbags." She gave Lizzie a crafty look. "He would listen to *you*."

Lizzie raised an eyebrow. "Do you think that I'm the type to champion a new car?"

Etta eyed her. "A Prius?"

"Sundress doesn't mean Prius," Lizzie told her.

"Maybe not a sundress," Etta said, "but you don't wear lipstick."

"I don't have a car at all in New York, and I like it that way." They began meandering down a dusty road lined with tall trees and souvenir stands, Lizzie walking slowly because she had to tell Etta the truth. She had to say that the mom look had a time limit.

Maybe bad news should be revealed in the presence of Etta's father. She wasn't a real mother. She didn't know how to tell bad news to a child the right way. Whatever that was.

Probably someone had put advice on the web. Or perhaps Dante should tell Etta in private. He was her real parent.

Looking at Etta, walking beside her, arms swinging, Lizzie was in the grip of a yearning so strong that she felt it in her loins. In every cell.

I would do anything for you, she said silently.

Etta started humming tunelessly. Lizzie managed to recognize Dusty, but it was difficult.

"If I really was your daughter, I'd have your voice, and I could be in musical theater," Etta said.

Lizzie's heart thumped. "You really are my daughter." It was rash and stupid and optimistic. It was not true either. Except it was a bit true, or mostly true, or perhaps all the way true.

Etta's smile wavered, and then she skipped a little. "The house is just up there," she said, louder than she needed to.

So Lizzie knew that she'd said the wrong thing, or the right thing at the wrong time. The trees opened up, and there was a house. A mansion, really, with formal gardens.

"Ugly, isn't it?" Etta said with satisfaction, the way a New Yorker agrees that the subway is dreadful, full of rats, and always breaking down.

Horrible, but hers to complain about.

"It's surprisingly small," Lizzie said. "He'd been an emperor, after all."

"He had another place, in Portoferraio. This was his love nest. For the summers, you know."

"Marie Louise?" Lizzie asked, not sure. "Josephine?"

"No idea," Etta said, not interested. "Come on around here." They climbed up a path shaded from the sun and arrived at the side of the building.

The villa was incredibly small: eight rooms in all.

"I can't get over how trifling this house must have felt to Napoleon," Lizzie said when they reached his bedroom.

"His bed is tiny," Etta said. "See?" It was a sleigh bed, done up in blue sheets. She dropped on the ground beside it. "I'm practically taller than the emperor of all France, and I'm only twelve."

"Just think, he had lived in the castle of Fontainebleau," Lizzie said.

"That's the big place with the Hall of Mirrors, right?"

"No, Versailles has the Hall of Mirrors." Mostly she remembered drifting with Grey in a boat before the palace, pretending to be a stoned aristocrat. But she thought that the walls had been papered in silk. Here the walls were painted with pale green curtains that didn't even try to fool the eye.

It was like the Sears of wall decoration.

Etta was skipping again. They went through all the small rooms, and she pointed out bees in every one.

"He was still an emperor," a British man with a strident upperclass accent told his wife. "He was the emperor of Elba, that's all."

"You have to see the bathroom," Etta said.

Over a stone tub was a cheerful naked lady.

People were wandering the terrace, taking photos of the countryside. "Are you hungry?" Lizzie asked.

"I could eat," Etta said. She brightened. "I know where we can go!" She danced down the path, waving madly at Mauro, who was leaning against the car looking hot and broody.

A half hour later they were seated in a small trattoria in the mountains. There was one small window and ratty strings of plastic beads at the door to keep flies out.

"The food's good," Etta promised, as Lizzie decided not to rub the plastic tablecloth and see whether it would peel under her finger. "Signora Maria is famous, not the way Babbo is, but on Elba, with Italians. She's really old, like one hundred, and Babbo always comes here the first night we're in Elba."

"Does Signora Maria come to his restaurant?"

"She's too old." Etta hesitated. "Also, she probably wouldn't like his food."

"Is there a menu?" Lizzie asked. A taciturn fellow had plunked down Elba wine and water, and a basket of bread, and gone back into the kitchen.

"Nope. We eat what Signora Maria cooks. It's like Babbo's Elba restaurant but one step further because she doesn't pay attention to vegetarians, allergies, none of that. She's not mean, but she doesn't have the energy."

The first plate arrived.

On it was one yellow flower, deep fried. Lizzie ate hers in two bites and Etta in one. Lizzie managed not to groan. "That was amazing."

"Right? Now we have to wait while she makes the next course. She doesn't have a sous-chef or anything. Just think," Etta said brightly, "someday we can go shopping for prom dresses together! If someone asks me, I mean."

Lizzie's heart sank. It was so unfair.

"Also wedding dresses. Have you seen *Say Yes to the Dress*? Once when I was sick, I watched two seasons, and afterward I made Babbo promise to find a wife before I need a wedding dress. I was seven," she explained with a huge smile.

Lizzie couldn't sit here and let this conversation happen. She couldn't pretend, because it was like a lie. Lizzie didn't remember much about her mother, but she remembered the lies. She had lied so easily and often that Lizzie had promised herself that she wouldn't even tell fibs to her children.

Etta was hers. She felt it in the depth of her bones. She couldn't push the unpleasant task off on Dante, or expect him to take over and soothe everyone's feelings.

She couldn't run away.

She made herself plow forward. "Etta, I'm sick."

Etta's head swung up.

"Remember all that medicine on my bureau? I have cancer, a bad kind. I've been through chemo once, and it didn't work as well as it might have. Now I'm on a new one and I'm better, but . . ."

Etta stared into her eyes as if she could read them, and more than anything in the world, Lizzie wanted to take the words back. But no one ever said "I'm kidding" about something like that. It wasn't funny.

Did she understand?

"I may be dying," Lizzie said, tasting the words as if they were *bitterest gall*, to be Shakespearean about it. "Not right now, but—" She caught her breath.

There was a long pause, so long that Lizzie had to start breathing again. A fly had made its way through the tired strings of plastic beads. It buzzed around the room.

"I'm sorry," Lizzie whispered finally. "I didn't mean to fall in love with your dad. With you."

"Babbo," Etta said. "Not dad."

Lizzie bent her head, unable to meet those clear eyes any longer without crying.

The fly buzzed some more. Lizzie's mind rocketed around in her skull. Girls at this age weren't supposed to think before they spoke. They had gut reactions.

What if Etta wanted her to leave? Said that she didn't want Dante to go through her death? Said it wasn't fair, Lizzie wasn't enough, it wasn't—

She almost stood up, except she couldn't preempt what Etta wanted to say. If she wanted to protect her babbo, she had that right. Lizzie couldn't diminish it.

Swallowing hard helped. Digging her fingernails into her thigh helped. No crying. There would be no crying because she was the grown-up here.

Etta took a deep breath, and Lizzie looked up, despite herself.

"How much time?" Etta whispered.

Inside Lizzie shrieked. What was the right answer? Would she not pass muster if she only had six months? Because she didn't know. She'd carefully not asked.

And so far . . . this summer, the last kind of chemo seemed to be impeding growth. The pain hadn't gotten worse. Maybe it was better.

"I don't know," she said finally. "Months for sure, but perhaps a few years. There's a new operation I can try. That I *will* try. And more chemo after that. I'm going to fight it, Etta. I promise."

Etta pushed back her chair. Lizzie watched, hoping desperation didn't show on her face, memorizing Etta's pointed chin and quirky, intelligent face. She got up, walked around the table, and stood beside Lizzie.

Overwhelmed, Lizzie stared up at her.

"Push back," Etta said, not sounding angry.

She did.

Without a word, Etta folded her lanky, thin body onto Lizzie's lap, putting an arm around her neck and leaning her head against her shoulder.

Lizzie's arms went around her as if they'd always curved around the same girl. As if her grip had started small, with an infant, and grown with that baby. Etta's hair wasn't perfectly brushed in the back. She smelled like girl sweat and sea salt and toothpaste.

This wasn't the moment to feel as if she couldn't breathe. Somehow, she managed to draw a breath. Etta didn't say anything, and neither did Lizzie. Time passed. Through the open door to the kitchen, she heard quiet noises, as if mice were preparing their meal. Another fly made it through the barricade at the door and zoomed about their table, noticed the bread, and stopped for lunch.

Lizzie had the feeling that Etta's weight was holding her to the earth. Which must be how mothers felt. She'd been in the oncology ward once, a week into a stay, when her roommate refused morphine and managed to not sleep all night.

The woman had wanted to see her daughters one more time. So Lizzie stayed up with her as she sweated and shook, fighting pain, fighting sleep. Fighting death.

At the time, Lizzie swore to be different when it was her turn, to let go, to ask for more painkillers rather than less.

But now she understood.

Her roommate hadn't died that night. She was awake when her husband brought the children into her room, holding his hand, letting go so they could dash to her bed and climb up. They were experienced with hospital beds, those girls. They crawled around wires and tubes to snuggle next to a body that was still warm.

Finally, Etta straightened, her weight shifting so she was directly on Lizzie's thighs. She was heavier than she looked.

"I think we ought to sing something," she said, rather surprisingly.

"We should do what?"

"It's my first time being hugged by a mother, and your first time hugging—"

She paused.

"No, I've never had a daughter," Lizzie managed.

"You're kind of young to have me—I mean, a twelve-year-old," Etta said. "We should make up for all the stuff we missed." She was dry-eyed, almost cheerful. But it sounded as if the air was being forced out of her lungs to shape words.

"Why sing?" Lizzie asked, tightening her arms again because she could. It seemed that she wasn't being thrown out for having the temerity to be dying. For being the poison wine that would take down Othello.

"You love singing," Etta said. "I will try to keep the tune."

Lizzie had a sob rising in her chest, but she couldn't cry when a twelve-year-old girl was being so brave. "What would you like to sing?"

Etta's smile was uncertain. "This is going to sound stupid."

Lizzie shook her head.

"Rock-a-bye Baby?" Etta's face contorted, and Lizzie realized that Etta was as good as—maybe even better than—she was at keeping her expressions hidden.

Lizzie pulled her against her chest again and lifted her chin from Etta's hair just enough to sing. "*Rock-a-bye baby, on the treetop. When the wind blows, the cradle will rock.*"

Behind them, the kitchen went silent. When she sang, her hearing sharpened. The sounds of mice preparing a meal stopped. "*When the bough breaks, the cradle will fall. Down will come baby, cradle and all.*"

"Not very cheerful, now I actually hear it," Etta said thickly.

"Someone told me another two lines and years ago I made up a couple more to rhyme with them," Lizzie said. "Back when Mrs. Bedrosian, one of my foster moms, had taken in young children." She had meant to sing it to her own child, someday.

And now she was.

"*Mama will catch you, give you a squeeze, send you back up to play in the trees.*" Her voice strengthened, and love rang under every word.

Etta made a sound that could have been a chuckle. Lizzie realized that people had come out of the kitchen and were standing against the wall, but she didn't let it bother her.

Actually, it *didn't* bother her.

Her own lines, the ones she had written:

"*When twilight falls, and birds seek their nest,*" she sang, hold-ing Etta tight. "*Come home to the one who loves you the best.*" She sang that verse twice because it was the most important of all. "*When twilight falls, and birds seek their nest, come home to the one who loves you the best.*"

Etta took a deep, shuddery breath, and they sat until the waiter appeared, still grim-looking, and put down plates of pasta before each of their chairs, along with a stream of incomprehensible Ital-ian.

Lizzie nodded at him and smiled. He walked away, returning to the kitchen. The fly had risen in honor of his arrival, but it settled back down.

"All right," Etta said, getting to her feet and walking back around the table. Then she sat down and said, busily unfolding her napkin, "I won't thank you, because babies never do."

Lizzie laughed.

"I should add that *they* thank you, back in the kitchen, and also that this is wild boar sauce, from an animal shot by the butcher's son."

The boar sauce was salty and somehow ferocious, as if the spirit of the wild animal had made its way into the sauce.

"He was an acorn-eater," Etta said.

"How do you know?"

"It's in there. Can you taste a woody taste, a little sweet?"

Lizzie took another bite. Flavor exploded in her mouth, but what did "woody" mean when it was a flavor? "I don't think your palate is as bad as you claim."

"I don't want Babbo to think that I might go to culinary school," Etta said, shoveling pasta into her mouth and talking right through it.

Lizzie thought about table manners and rejected the idea. She was borrowing Etta, but Dante was raising her.

At least Etta was using her napkin.

But then she saw that Etta was using her napkin to wipe away tears that were sliding down her cheek and making their salty way onto her plate. Lizzie got up and they ended up eating together, with Etta on Lizzie's lap.

Lizzie's legs went numb, but she ate half a plate and Etta ate a plate and a half.

At the end of the meal, Signora appeared. She was old, going bald, with what hair she had gathered on top of her head like a twist of whitish silk. She spoke so quickly that Lizzie hadn't a chance of understanding.

"She'd like you to sing something," Etta said, getting up. "I can tell her no."

"It's all right," Lizzie said, standing and bowing slightly to Signora. "Does she have a preference?"

"No, because everything she might want would be in Italian," Etta pointed out.

"Prayers do not need a language," Lizzie said, quoting Mrs. Bedrosian. "This one is in Latin."

She sang "Ave Maria."

Just like Mrs. Bedrosian would have, Signora Maria cried.

Etta cheered up, though.

"Your singing is a bit of a downer," she said, giggling.

Lizzie smacked her on the bottom as they went out through the dingy plastic strings of beads into the sunshine, where Mauro leaned against the car, checking his cellphone.

Chapter Twenty-nine

That night, Lizzie walked down the stairs and into the courtyard feeling rather self-conscious. She hadn't seen Grey or Rohan all day; the yacht had come back, so they'd gone off to negotiate with Sam. It looked as if he was going to be the main backer and Disney the distributor.

Grey hadn't seen her ring. What did one wear with a ring that size? In the end, she put on the raspberry linen dress that she wore the first night.

Rohan was nowhere to be seen, but Grey was drinking a glass of wine and reading a book. She walked over and sat down. He glanced up, smiled, closed his book.

Good enough.

She said, "I'm getting married, Grey."

Blunt and to the point.

To her surprise, pure joy spread over his face. Grey was normally so reserved that happiness was easy to identify. "Fuck me, that man *rocks*," he said, his accent thick as mud.

"I'm gathering you don't mind."

"I've been sweating like a crawdaddy in a pot waiting for him to make his move." He leaned forward and took her hand. "Nice."

Then he looked up. "I've got an appointment for you next week, right after we get home."

"What?"

"With the head of immunotherapy at Sloan. He's doing trials on hypercalcemic small cell ovarian carcinoma, Lizzie, and he's having success with a combo of the operation and chemo."

And when she didn't say anything, he added, "That's your type."

"I know that!"

He looked so incredibly happy—triumphant, even. Her eyes narrowed. "Why do you look like that?"

"Like what?"

"Like you baked the canaries and ate them before anyone else got a chance!" she retorted. "How long have you had that appointment?"

"Since I read the article in the *Times* about immunotherapy being surprisingly successful."

"Before Elba." Lizzie's fingers linked with his and squeezed. "Did you already know that I was thinking of not doing the operation or any more chemo?"

"Last time I visited, there wasn't any soap under the sink, and you shrugged. You gave away your books. I was praying."

He meant that.

Ruby came by and admired the ring. "Maybe Dante can introduce me to a chef. All the ones I've met have had too much month at the end of their money."

Rohan shook off a few fans and fell into a chair. He whooped, and said the ring was worth a few million, and that Halle Berry had worn one like that to the Oscars last year, which made Lizzie gulp.

"Where are we with all the telling that needs doing?" Ruby asked. "Not to be grim at a happy moment, but you've got more than that ring to talk about."

"Everybody knows everything," Lizzie said, feeling happy. "Etta too. I even talked about treatment with Dante."

"There's the operation where they bake in the chemo," Ruby said, showing that they had discussed it behind Lizzie's back. Before, Lizzie would have bridled. But now?

That's what family did. They schemed and threatened and worried.

The Roman waiter appeared with a tray of Elba wine. "Our last night," Ruby said. "I can't believe it."

"Neither can I," Rohan said.

"Did Dante say you could cook with him?" Ruby asked.

Rohan nodded. "Yeah. Apparently half the village will be there, and Augusto and the others will be at the tables. Dante and I will cook."

"Better you than me," Ruby said cheerfully. "I like a world where men do all the cooking."

Lizzie went off into a little haze, wordlessly staring at her ring and thinking about moving into an apartment with Dante. Living with him. Etta's room would be a mess. She'd be damned if she was going to start doing loads of housework, the way women in marriages did.

"I've never cooked for Dante," she said, breaking into the conversation.

"And . . . that's a good thing," Grey said. "We want him to get to the altar with the lining of his gut mostly intact."

She wrinkled her nose at him. "It's time to go to the restaurant."

"We have to have champagne tonight. This is big," Grey said, his voice happy. "Lizzie came to Elba, fell in love, and now she's shelved her harp and halo."

"There was more to it than that," Lizzie protested.

"Yeah, the magic Italian penis," Rohan said, grinning madly. "We should all have one around, ready to stop us from deciding to die and other mistakes like that."

Lizzie groaned, and Ruby reached over and gave her a pinch. "Dante must be pretty damn good in bed, considering that you're taking on a near-teenage girl. I don't know about you at thirteen, but I was a nightmare."

"Adolescent foster care kids either go nuts, or they polish the halo," Grey said. "Lizzie was all about being loved."

"No, I was about being unnoticed," she corrected. "Even as a teenager."

"Teenagers get familiar with their bodies," Rohan said. "Sex changes that for the better."

Ruby finished her glass. "I'll give you that. My boobs were just uncomfortable attachments until Caleb Connor Williams convinced me otherwise."

Lizzie's phone burred against her hip, and she turned it over. "Etta is wondering where we are."

Rohan rose, pulling Grey to his feet. "Another reason for champagne. Guess what?" he said, his voice not so casual. "*People* is putting me on the cover and not for being beautiful."

"Fabulous!" Ruby cried.

"For *Romeo*?" Lizzie asked.

Rohan put his arm around Grey, right there in the hotel, where anyone could see them. "Because I'm in love with a man, that's why."

"Bravo!" Lizzie cried.

Rohan's grin covered his whole face. "That man finally said I could tell the world. You're not the only one getting married, Lizzie."

In the midst of hugs and hurrahs, Lizzie realized something. Joseph was right. She would have to go on living, not because of sex, but because of all the love that was tying her to the ground, to Elba, to people. Her people.

"Come on," Ruby said a while later. "That magic Italian penis is going to get lonely over there, being a famous chef but with no one to kiss."

Chapter Thirty

The last dinner of the summer was a ritual, as important as having his first meal on Elba cooked by old Maria up the mountain.

Dante closed the restaurant to anyone from the yachts, and he cooked dinner for all the waiters, for Signora Pietra, Augusto, and everyone else who mattered. Carlo, whose mozzarella resisted the teeth just the right amount. Orazio, who took off in his *peschereccio* every morning and saved the best anchovies for Principe Blu, sending the rest to market. Vera, who baked bread with crust that was better than anything Dante could find in New York, and attributed it all to spit, which he hoped was a joke.

"*Leccaculo!*" rocketed across the courtyard, the howl of an enraged husband. Vera was patently unfaithful to her husband. Yesterday she had supposedly done a personal service for an American who wandered into her bakery. Worse: He had been from a yacht.

"*Basta!*" Dante shouted. "*Quest'anno c'è qui la mia famiglia.*"

"*Cagacazzo!*" Vera shouted, not at Dante but at her husband, who was sitting at a different table.

The courtyard was full of Elba folk, drifting from table to table to gossip. Francesca's cousin, the ninety-three-year-old one, had fallen and broken her hip. Her son sent her to the hospital in an ambulance alone. Why? Because his show was on, and she'd been there before. It's not as if she didn't know the way.

That sort of thing.

It was always the same, year after year. And still, this year was different.

His family had grown. Someone was cooking with him. Rohan wasn't bad either. Dante had to keep an eye on him, but the famous actor had learned to make gnocchi this afternoon, and even if they weren't all precisely the right size, they were good.

Tonight they were having "Lizzie food."

The meals she loved were simple. The *salsa rosa* his grandmother liked, made with tomato, garlic, and not much else. Rabbit cooked with crispy skin and shreds of basil.

He was paying Fabrizio's waiters to pass it out on big platters. No plating.

Etta was sitting next to Lizzie, a hand on her chair. He had the feeling that soon he might find his daughter clutching Lizzie's shirt-tail, like a toddler in a mall.

Lizzie wouldn't care.

No, she would care. She would love it. He could see that every time she tilted her head toward Etta.

Rohan wiped his forearm over his face the way Dante had taught him, gave his patent winking smile, and wandered out into the twilight.

The sky—the air—was that pure blue color that would turn cobalt in ten minutes but was holding its breath, keeping light in reserve. Dante stayed by his window, watching as Rohan sauntered into the courtyard.

Strings of lights swung in the sea breeze. Rohan waved as people cheered; Orazio's wife had told Dante, privately, that her son had bought her a DVD with the brown actor's show on it.

"Not as good as *ER*," she told him. "But good."

No matter where he looked, Dante kept turning back to Lizzie. Her hair sprang out around her head, and the strings of lights made it look like butter, sweet spring butter made from new milk.

If only he could have all the Lizzies who might have been—from this Lizzie all the way to a woman as old as Signora Pietra, her tart replies being translated to English for Grey's benefit.

For a moment he gripped the counter and let the pain of it rip at his gut. Then he straightened, took a breath, and went out. Only a stupid man would mourn a moment when he was still living it.

Like all men, he was stupid sometimes but not always.

He went around to each table and thanked everyone. The summer was a success; the restaurant thrived. It wasn't their fault that he no longer cared. They toasted him over and over, for finding a woman, a songbird, *una professoressa*!

"Too good for you!" his cheese-maker shouted. "I'll take her!" His wife leaned over and slapped him on the shoulder.

"You?" his brother joked. "She'd never take you. You are like a lemon tree that never ripens, just little stones hanging down where there should be sweet juice."

Dante moved on. He made it around the courtyard and finally sat down beside Lizzie. She grabbed his hand.

"I think you're going to have problems with an overly desirous Juliet," she said to Rohan.

"That makes her real," Etta said, from the other side of Lizzie. "Girls are way more interested in boys than boys are in girls."

That made Dante a little nauseated. Of course Etta was interested in boys. The idea made him feel like a gnarled old olive tree.

But then he looked down at Lizzie's hand holding his, and got an erection. This summer he was plagued with them, all these years after adolescence.

"I beg to differ," Grey put in. "Look at your favorite, Elio from

Call Me by Your Name, Etta. That boy can't get his head out of the gutter—or someone's private parts—for more than a minute or two."

"Elio's old," Etta said more or less patiently. "*Old.* Elio is *seventeen.*"

"Take that," Dante said to Grey, who was on his right.

"Romeo was only thirteen," his daughter said. This new daughter, the one whom the English teacher discounted, was confidently dissecting Shakespeare. "Fourteen at the most," Etta continued. "He's my age, almost."

Dante pulled Lizzie's hand closer and said to her quietly, "You've turned my daughter into an English scholar."

Lizzie grinned at him and rubbed white-gold curls against his shoulder. "More like a critic."

Ruby came back out of the bathroom and dropped into the seat beside Etta. "What are we talking about?"

"Shakespeare."

"As one does," Ruby said, grinning.

"Think about Etta's biology paper, the one talking about songbirds," Grey said, leaning forward. "Birds don't sing on the wing. They settle on a branch and fill the air around them just like a peacock splays out his feathers—to attract a mate. Think balcony. That's Juliet."

Dante murmured in Lizzie's ear. "Is that what you did to me?"

"Yes," Grey said, overhearing. He waved his wineglass. "American songbird shows up here, sings a few measures, snags the best chef in Italy."

"Dante walked into the restaurant when Grey and I were singing Monty Python, about sacred sperm," Lizzie said, laughing.

"I want to hear that!" Ruby said.

"Yeah," Etta chimed in.

Dante thought she didn't know who Monty Python was, but

he'd have to accept that she knew what sperm was. Not personally, though. Not yet.

"So the sperm song was a mating call," Dante said, kissing Lizzie's ear. "I love it. So subtle too."

Even Grey laughed, and Rohan was fairly bellowing.

"I had no idea that you were lurking in the doorway," Lizzie said, impish and happy. "Plus, the first thing you heard me sing was a hymn, remember?"

"I'll never forget," Dante said.

"A toast!" Ruby called. "To all the women who've flattered men into thinking their sperm was sanctified!"

Dante raised his glass with everyone else, noticing that their laughter was contagious. All the tables were laughing more than he remembered from other years. Vera's husband had made his way over to her and was hanging over her shoulder.

Rumor had it that her skills in fellatio were as incredible as her bread.

"A toast to Juliet, up on the balcony, singing poetry," Grey suggested.

"Asking Romeo to marry her!" Etta shouted.

Dante squinted at her glass. She was supposed to drink only *vino-acqua,* but that looked like straight Elba wine with no water added.

"She's only had a glass," Lizzie murmured. He yanked her chair closer so he could pull her weight against him.

"Yeah, she's up on that balcony like a songbird on a branch," Rohan said. "She fills the air with poetry. *What's in a name* and *a rose by any other name,* et cetera. Romeo can't help himself. He doesn't have a chance." He tipped up his glass.

"Juliet took all that airy poetry of Romeo's and grounded it in a song about desire," Lizzie said.

"To cut to the chase: sacred sperm," Ruby said, chortling.

"If you want a thirteen-year-old Juliet," Etta announced, "I'm available. I have all the qualifications. I'm not a great actor yet, but you could teach me that. I'll be exactly thirteen by the time you're casting."

Dante stiffened, but Lizzie rubbed his leg.

Rohan put down his book. "I never hire members of my family, kid."

Dante watched his daughter absorb not the rejection but the word.

Family.

My Family.

Rohan was talking on, oblivious. He probably had brothers and sisters, all the extra people that Dante and Lizzie and Grey hadn't had until this summer.

"I got a nephew who is doing pretty well for himself in a Netflix series, but I wouldn't hire him. It's been done, but it shouldn't be done—if you see what I mean."

Etta didn't say anything, but Dante saw her lips shape the word "family."

"My daughter is so happy," he said in Lizzie's ear. "Because of you."

She shook her head and soft curls brushed his cheek. "I never knew how much the heart can expand."

He tightened his arm around her and leaned forward to fill her glass and his.

Big platters of meat were being put down at every table. Dante kept an eye on things, but he'd paid Fabrizio a small fortune to close his doors and help out. Fabrizio was over in the corner, and one of his waiters was threading through the tables, refilling pitchers with wine.

Ruby pointed at Dante. "Talking of songbirds, Lizzie told me all about *you,* giving her a hamburger and fries, the best she'd ever had. Singing, dude. You were singing with everything you had."

Dante nodded.

"I think I really understand that play now," Rohan said, stowing his notebook away in his vest pocket. "Basically, it's about language and sex."

"Like sexting," Etta said.

"You're *good*," Rohan said to Etta before taking out his notebook again.

Etta's eyes looked like fireflies, shining with internal light that had nothing to do with the courtyard.

"Did you see that?" Lizzie whispered.

Dante nodded.

"Mrs. Bedrosian did that for me," Lizzie said. "What Rohan just did for Etta."

"But you stopped singing."

"It didn't feel good. Safe. But now—"

"Now it is."

Funny how different people's ideas of "safe" were. To Dante, Lizzie was standing on the edge of a cliff, and his arms were holding her so the wind couldn't blow her away. But to her, his arms meant she could sing.

"We're singing for you tonight," he said in her ear. "I just want you to know that it wasn't my idea. I suck at singing, but my daughter is even worse."

Lizzie straightened up, and he let his hands fall away.

That moment—seeing her face—made up for the growling embarrassment he felt at the idea of it. "Not until the rest clear out," he told her, nodding at the tables. He hesitated. "The crowd may ask you to sing."

She shrugged, happy. "Grey planned for that. He's got a gorgeous alto, and he loves a concert."

"Yet he's a novelist?"

"He's good with words. But he hated it when I stopped singing. Singing bound the two of us together back when we were kids."

Dante wrapped his arms around her again and watched over her head as Rohan scribbled more things in his book, and Grey let the word "fuck" slip out, even though Etta was there. Ruby swatted him, and Grey pulled one of her curls, and she swatted him again.

After big pans of tiramisu hit the tables, a kind of anticipatory hum swept the courtyard.

"Time?" Grey said to Lizzie.

Dante reluctantly let her go. Sharing had never been his forte.

Grey and Lizzie walked up in front of the big window, and Fabrizio's waiters scurried out the side door and sat down.

Lizzie glanced at him, happy eyes, and then she and Grey launched into Dylan's "Po' Boy." Hardly any Italians would understand the words, but they didn't care. Grey's Deep South accent rolled even deeper than in speech. Perfect for the song, with its beatnik jazz, minstrel-show roots.

Dante never thought much about God, though he'd been praying lately and knew there was more of it in his future. To him, Lizzie's voice was proof of God's existence.

Etta scooted across the empty seat between them and curled herself against Dante's shoulder. Lizzie and Grey sang some hymns. They sang Monty Python when Ruby called for it. A Taylor Swift song about Romeo and Juliet that had Rohan scribbling in his notebook again.

Finally, Lizzie blew kisses, and Grey said this would be their last song.

The courtyard was utterly silent. Lizzie opened her mouth and sang the first two lines alone, *"All praise to you, my God, this night, for all the blessings of the light."*

Grey joined in, deep and calm, with the next two. *"Keep me, O keep me, King of kings, beneath the shelter of Your wings."*

Two verses would be followed by the third verse, the verse Lizzie always skipped, the one she said she hated. Dante had looked it up after they were at the abbey, trying to figure out why she skipped it, but it hadn't made sense to him then.

She didn't skip it this time. Grey wrapped an arm around her shoulders, and she looked straight at Dante. And sang.

Lord, may I be at rest in You
And sweetly sleep the whole night thro'.
Refresh my strength, for Your own sake,
So I may serve You when I wake.

Chapter Thirty-one

The Elba people began leaving around midnight, shouting about next summer. Two elderly gentlemen kissed Lizzie's hand. One said in broken English that he wanted to live until next summer so he could hear her sing.

She caught back words that he didn't want to hear.

That traitor, hope, had made its way under her skin, and there was nothing she could do about it. So she smiled and promised to come again.

The big round column candles were slanting sideways and guttering now. Insects danced in the small lights above their heads.

"Want to go for a walk?" Grey held out a hand.

Lizzie squinted at him. "No more talk of the operation. I'll do it. I'll go to the appointment."

Dante got up. "I'm going to pay Fabrizio and make sure my kitchen is intact."

She and Grey walked through the courtyard arch and turned left toward the village.

"I've been an ass," Grey said. "I kept thinking that if I . . . if things had been different, you would have fought more. For me."

"Oh, Grey," she said, stopping and winding her arms around his middle. "I wasn't not fighting for you."

His chin came down on her hair. "I know. But I keep thinking about that poem you told me about, the one about a chicken hawk circling, looking for home. I didn't make a home for you."

Her arms tightened in silent protest.

"Just because of the way things are," he said. "I'm not blaming myself. Just saying it."

"I love you," Lizzie whispered. "I love you so much."

"Back at you," he said, his voice raspy in the quiet night air.

"I'll fight," she promised. "I will do it all. Everything. Chemo with heat and all the rest of it. And if . . . if it doesn't work, it won't be because I didn't try to stay here, Grey. I promise. No more playing chicken."

"I knew that as soon as I heard you start singing again," he said, and this time his voice broke. "I was so angry that it wasn't me, but that wasn't fair."

"This time in Elba is the best present that anyone has ever given me," Lizzie said, raising her head and kissing him on the chin. "You and Rohan gave me this, Grey. You gave me what I most wanted in the world, and I'll never forget it. Not if I live another fifty years."

His arms tightened around her, and she caught the gleam of tears in his eyes, so she buried her face in his chest. But she didn't feel guilt this time. Just love.

She'd learned a lot about love in the last weeks. It wasn't passive. It was a charge to delight in what was here and now.

The moment had an awkward, fragile delicacy about it. They stood together until the silence was broken by a shout of laughter inside the courtyard.

"I'm going to marry Rohan," Grey said, "because I mixed up loving and being in love."

She grinned at that.

"Oh, and, Joseph? He said to say hi to you. And that he'll see you at the opening of Roh's film."

Back inside, they found Dante going around pouring small glasses of saffron-colored liqueur. "For courage," he said, plunking one down before her.

For a moment, she thought he was talking to her, to her wish to avoid bedpans and pain, but no. She'd forgotten the concert he'd promised.

"They'll get married under the arch!" shouted Etta to Ruby.

That did it.

Lizzie had to live at least twelve more months and get married behind the restaurant. She let plans flutter around the courtyard, talk of the arch and more. Plans for Rohan and Grey's wedding too, which might take place in Paris and would certainly be outrageously elegant. "What is this stuff?" she asked, holding up the glass.

"Mortella," Dante said. "Elba's own liqueur."

She sipped cautiously, having decided Limoncello was raw alcohol with a lemon waved over it. "It's herby."

"Mint," Ruby said, wrinkling her nose. "And other stuff."

"Fennel," Dante said, sitting back down beside her. "But the main flavor is myrtle."

"What's myrtle?"

"A scrub plant with black berries," Rohan said. He had his iPhone out and was reading about the liqueur rather than drinking it.

Mortella slipped down Lizzie's throat and burned its way into her stomach, like something a medieval nun might distill from beets and rosemary, hoping to ward off disease.

"I learned, in Elba, to cook with every part of the animal," Dante said. "Mortella is like that. No one else in the world makes anything from myrtle. But here, on the island, we use it."

"The flower of the gods, sacred to Aphrodite," Rohan read aloud, a deep thread of amusement in his voice. "Considered a symbol of love." He glanced up. "And immortality."

Dante's eyes filled with certainty, and he leaned over and kissed Lizzie on the mouth. "I choose love over immortality," he whispered, "every time."

Lizzie kissed him back, tasting the conviction in his voice. "I would give up immortality every time, to go home with you."

For a moment they just stared at each other, and then Dante gave himself a shake and turned to the others. "It's time."

Lizzie grinned. "I've been waiting all night for this."

Ruby threw back the rest of her Mortella. "Not as good as brandy, but it will do."

Dante, Rohan, Grey, Ruby, and Etta got up.

"All of you?" Lizzie gaped. She had thought it would be only Dante and Etta.

"You sing for us," Ruby said, "so we figured we'd sing for you."

"The quality of some of our voices leaves a lot to be desired," Rohan added.

Grey was smiling so widely that she almost didn't recognize him, pinned between Etta and Rohan. Perhaps his voice could lead the two of them to the right notes.

Lizzie started laughing so hard that she almost couldn't catch her breath. They were so *dear*, standing together, looking somewhere between tipsy and drunk. Though Grey was sober, of course. And Dante too.

"OK, everybody, remember how we practiced it," Grey said.

"You even practiced!" Lizzie cried.

"It's a Beatles concert," Grey said, giving her a rueful grin. "It was the only music we had in common."

"Not true!" Etta said. "Everybody knew Justin Bieber's 'Baby,' even Grey."

"Shameful," Grey muttered. "OK, stand tall, people."

No one had ever sung for Lizzie before; generally people asked her to sing, if they knew about her voice. One time she was even asked to solo "Happy Birthday" for her own birthday.

"We each got to pick one song," Dante said, looking ferociously embarrassed. "Then we argued and ended up with three."

"Yeah, 'cause Grey wanted that totally weird 'Paperback Writer,' " Etta shouted and then dodged as he tugged her hair.

"My choice first," Ruby said.

She waved her hand. They sang, *"Something in the way she moves."* Ruby shimmied to the music, and Rohan missed all the high notes.

"Perfect!" Lizzie cried at the end, laughing and clapping.

"Dante chose the next one," Ruby said. "We all want you to know that we think it's pulverizingly overdone—"

"Disgustingly sweet," Rohan put in.

"But we said he could ask you to dance rather than sing," Etta finished, beaming.

Dante was walking toward her, looking happy.

"I heard you growling along," she whispered. "You're not bad!"

"Not true," he said. "You must dance with me, because it got me out of singing this one. Actually Etta's idea, by the way."

They swayed around the courtyard to a not-bad rendition of "And I Love Her," with Lulu running around their feet.

"Lots of argument about the third one," Grey said. "There were those who wanted another love song, and one person held out for 'Norwegian Wood.' "

"Pure genius!" Ruby interjected.

"But we ended up with 'In My Life.' Come on, Dante, we need you back here."

Lizzie came along, hand in hand, so all of them ended up singing together.

In the years after her first trip to Elba, whenever Lizzie thought about the island, to the side of her mind was a glimmering photo, though no one picked up a camera that night.

A family, singing about places they'd remember, about friends and lovers, and memories that lose their meaning.

And those that don't.

Epilogue

ETTA

Lizzie wanted some of her ashes in the Episcopal prayer garden in New York "so you can visit me, if you want, E." She wanted the rest of her ashes in the sea where it touched the shore of Elba.

Part of Etta never wanted to go back to the island, even though she had spent most of her childhood there. She suspected Lizzie had guessed how she would feel, and that was one of the reasons Lizzie wanted her ashes brought there.

"Brought home," she'd said.

So they all went back the summer she died, five years after her first visit to the island. Etta and Dante, Rohan and Grey and their two kids, Ruby and her partner, Elijah, and their baby. Plus Sally, the Episcopal priest, because she and Lizzie had become such good friends in the last year.

They scattered Lizzie's ashes into the sea just as the sky darkened, in that moment Lizzie called *la dolce vita*.

The sweet life.

Then they went to the restaurant. They had dragged restaurant chairs around to the back and set up in the herb garden.

Etta and Ruby had spent the afternoon threading white myrtle flowers into the wedding arch. At twelve years old, she'd done a pretty messy job. But now she had a helper, and she and Ruby had added more and more myrtle until the arch looked like a puffy white cloud.

"It would make Lizzie laugh," she'd told Ruby, when they were done.

"Everything made Lizzie laugh," Ruby said, blinking away tears.

Sally was the first person to get up and stand under the arch. She had bristly white hair and kind eyes. She had pulled her black gown on over shorts, and her bare ankles and Birkenstocks stuck out from the bottom. She talked about the joy that Lizzie brought to the church by singing. She said that even people who were lacking a god found one in Lizzie's voice.

"The thing about her voice," Sally said, "was that it crowded out fear and worry. Everyone listened—the air, the light, even the stained glass, listened to her sing, because she poured soul into it. Her singing told people that anger and hatred aren't as big as God's love." Then she gave a wry smile and said, "Though Lizzie didn't believe in God. One of the last things she said to me was that once she'd fled this mortal coil—I think that's Shakespeare—she had no expectation of meeting a white guy crowned with thorns, but that if she did, she'd say hi from me."

They had all agreed to sing a song for Lizzie, because she loved being sung to. Even in the last few months, when she could barely talk, she would still smile if someone sang for her.

Sally raked her hands through her hair so it stood up straight, and sang a couple verses of "All Things Bright and Beautiful" in a husky voice that avoided the high notes.

Ruby was the next to get up. She had on an orange linen dress and scarlet lipstick that should have clashed but didn't. It looked as if she was dressed for dinner at the Principe Blu, except that a couple of years ago Babbo had gotten sick of plating, sold Principe, and opened Lizzie's, which had the best hamburgers and French fries in New York, but was never given a Michelin star and never wanted one.

"Lizzie was everything," Ruby said. Then she stopped, and everybody could tell that she was crying. "You guys knew, or maybe you didn't, that I wasn't actually doing all that well when I showed up in Elba. This isn't about me, though. It's just to say that Lizzie taught me that life is about more than makeup, that it's actually better without it." Then she paused and said, "But, Lizzie, you have to forgive me, because I couldn't do this without lipstick. After I got cancer, I told myself that I was fine. Lizzie always said that she'd been a bird circling around, looking for home, 'member?"

Etta nodded, and then glanced to her side and saw that a tear was running down her babbo's cheek, so she curled her hand around his and held on tight.

"*I* wasn't," Ruby said. "I was just flying from place to place, telling myself that I wasn't afraid. Being brave. Ignoring the whole idea of 'home.' Then Lizzie came along: falling in love in the face of cancer and death, holding on to life with everything she had. I didn't know what courage looked like until I met her.

"Without her, I'd still be running away. No makeup line, for sure. I was going to buy sperm off the internet, but instead I found Elijah, and we have Noah. She taught me to trust enough to stop running. So I'm going to sing a song by Nina Simone that Lizzie and I sang together sometimes." She cleared her throat and gave herself a little shake, and then she started low, *"Birds flying high, you know how I feel . . ."*

She kept going all the way but when she got to the last verse, she thumbed her phone and Lizzie's voice joined hers, *"Dragonfly out in the sun . . ."* The last two lines, Ruby went silent, so Lizzie's huge joyful voice rose into the air, *"And this old world is a new world, and a bold world, for me."*

Tears were all over her face, so Ruby waved her hand around, and sat down without saying any more. Elijah handed over their baby, Noah, and she buried her face in his hair.

Rohan got up next. He talked a bit about *Romeo and Juliet,* and the fact that Lizzie made him understand Juliet, turning the film into a success, which was a pretty mild way of talking about three Oscars. But weirdly, the more famous Rohan got, the less celebrity-ish he was. "Most important: I don't think I'd be a married man except that Lizzie told my beloved to grow a pair and marry me.

"I know we're all supposed to sing, but Lizzie once told me that I sounded like a bullfrog, so I'm not going to. Back then, nobody ever insulted me. I was so tired of thinking that I'd used up—outgrown—my chances to be loved, and I had to be perfect. I had to be deep and literary, and inside I knew I wasn't equal to the task. Lizzie was about the truth, even if a famous actor wanted to make Romeo deep instead of silly. Because that famous actor was silly instead of deep."

His smile wavered, so Grey went up there and gave him a hug, and Rohan went back to sit down.

Grey looked a lot older than he had that summer five years ago, when he'd come to Elba for the first time. To Etta's mind, he was even more handsome. Less perfect, more real.

He shoved his hands in the pockets of his pants and looked at everyone. "The day I met Lizzie, I was terrified. My mom was long gone, and my dad had just died. A social worker took me to a group home, and left me there just long enough so that the kids could terrorize me with foster care stories before she sent me to Mrs. Bedrosian."

He grimaced. "I almost peed in my pants walking into the house, I was that afraid. I never told Lizzie, but I reckon she's listening now and knows. She looked like good people, you know? Even in my panic, I could tell."

He stopped and swallowed hard and then cleared his throat. "She always knew how afraid I was. I was afraid to lose her, afraid to be gay, afraid to marry—" He gave Rohan a tiny smile.

"God, we're all such cowards," Ruby muttered, her voice deep from tears.

"I used to tell Lizzie that she was a runner, that she ran away from me and from life," Grey said. "But the truth was that *I* was the one running, and she was my place, my heart, because life was bearable with her. If she hadn't kicked me out, I wouldn't have found my way to Rohan."

Rohan had a hiccupping kind of laugh at that.

"I was going to try to be Hemingway. She told me to take all that fear and put it into a horror novel, and she was right. So I guess I owe my marriage and my children and my career to her." He swallowed. "I owe her everything I hold dear."

He was the only one of them who could actually sing, so he straightened up, even though there were tears on his cheeks, and he sang a hymn that Lizzie liked, about God being a shelter from the storm. Then, when he got to a line about time bearing all its sons away, *"They fly forgotten, as a dream dies at the opening day,"* he stopped and said, "but Lizzie will never be forgotten."

Etta was thinking about time bearing away "sons" and not daughters, but she got it.

Then it was her turn.

She stood up feeling self-conscious, which was stupid because these were her people. She got herself under the arch and then turned around. "The last week, I did this thing in the prayer garden," she said, holding up her phone. "I put the list on random, and I let Lizzie choose the music, so I'm going to play something before I say anything."

" 'Tis a gift to be simple" started playing a bit too loud, so she thumbed down the sound. "See? Maybe Lizzie does pick the music

for me. I don't believe it," she said, sobs catching the back of her throat. "I wish I hadn't been so shitty for a couple of years there."

"*Cara,*" Babbo said. He got up and gave her a hug. "It's OK," he said, rocking her. "You were never shitty, just defiant. Splendidly defiant. Lizzie loved the puzzle of you. You still have her, you know. Not the same, but she'll be there." Then everyone started crying again, and it took a long time to stop. All the way through "'Tis a gift" and into the Beatles.

"There's so much I want," Etta said, wiping her eyes. Her babbo moved to the side. "I want to find a man with a voice like Lizzie's, so we can have a daughter who can keep a tune, and I'll name her Lizzie."

She was wearing an old linen vest over a white T-shirt, and she pulled it off. "You see this red bra?"

"Yes!" Rohan and Grey's older kid shouted. He was ten, adopted a year ago.

"Lizzie promised me, the first day when she told me she had cancer, that when I was old enough she'd take me shopping for a red bra, the kind that shows under a shirt. And Lizzie taught me that the most important thing is to keep your promises.

"So last year when I turned sixteen, we went to Urban Outfitters, and we bought a crimson-colored bra, like a stop sign. She said it was a signal to boys that I wasn't to be messed with. She gave me the mom look, you know? I loved that look."

Etta stopped, took a breath, and clicked off her phone.

"I'm going to sing the lullaby that Lizzie sang for me our first day as mom and daughter, which is wicked sentimental, but Ruby told me once that nostalgia is a good thing. Lizzie wrote the last two lines herself." She took a breath, the way Lizzie taught her. "*Rock-a-bye baby, on the treetop . . .*" Right through to the lines that Lizzie made up, and Etta considered to be *her* special present, from her mom. "*When twilight falls, and birds seek their nest, come home to the one who loves you the best.*"

Then she went over and sat down, which left Dante standing under the arch, looking tired but peaceful. He hadn't cried much, maybe because there'd been so many tears in the last few months.

"I'm not good at talking," he said. "Lizzie said I talk with my food, and so I'll tell you the menu. Roh and I are making gnocchi with sage, Lizzie's favorite, and tiramisu."

Tears were dripping salty into Etta's mouth, so she pulled out another Kleenex.

"Lizzie wasn't just sweet and good, the way people say about their dead spouses. She was so much more than a nightingale. I learned so much from her. Not about singing, but about working. She had wanted to let go when she first came to Elba. She wanted to float away. But after she fell in love with us, with me and Etta, Ruby, Rohan, and Grey—you know how much she already loved you—she started working to live. I never saw anyone work so hard at such a rotten job, and I never will again. She endured the vomiting and the colostomy bag—she hated that—and the bone pain. But all that pigheaded devotion she had to life—to *us*—gave us five years, and I'm grateful for every smelly, emotional moment I had with her.

"Probably most people think that what she did best was teach Shakespeare, or if they knew, if they heard her, they thought it was singing.

"But it wasn't. I'm not saying this with pride or as if we were worth it, but what she did best was love us. I said she worked at living, but what she was really doing was working at loving. Every breath, even the ones that hurt so much at the end, every single one was her gift. She was extravagant, Lizzie: in her voice, her soul, her love.

"You can say that a person kicks the bucket, but you can also say that she hops the twig. That's what our Lizzie did. She settled on that twig for us, and then she hopped. Lizzie had the heart of a lark, and she's singing somewhere," Dante said. "I can't hear her now, but I live . . . well, I live to hear her again, because I will."

Everyone was sobbing, and he held out his arms. "Come on up here. Lizzie and I planned this last song together, and she promised that she'll sing with us."

Etta blew her nose again and stood up, feeling light-headed with grief. They all crowded up there, even Elijah with the sleeping baby.

Dante handed out the lyrics, and Grey beat on his thigh, and started them off. When they got to the third verse, Grey took a deep breath and said, "Go soft, on this one."

So Etta opened the back of her throat, the way Lizzie had taught her.

Lord, may I be at rest in You
And sweetly sleep the whole night thro'.
Refresh my strength, for Your own sake,
So I may serve You when I wake.

Acknowledgments

This novel is dedicated to its many editors.

My agent, Kim Witherspoon, read three years of drafts, always plunging in with joy.

My second editor was my dear friend Meg Tilly, who knows Hollywood and its foibles. She understood Rohan, and I learned to love him through her.

My third editor was the marvelous YA author Marie Rutkowski, who brought her deft, clear understanding of twelve-year-olds to Etta's journey.

My fourth editor, Susan Kamil, adored Lizzie and Dante and Etta. Her joy in Lizzie's happiness reflected her love of life and its fictions. She made the novel infinitely better, as she did the world.

My fifth and sixth editors brought me face-to-face with my own limitations; I particularly want to thank the reader who understood who Ruby could be, and my friend Lisa Gill for her advice.

My final editor, Whitney Frick, brought the book an incalculable burst of youth. She *saw* the secondary characters as no one had, and deepened their stories to sing in tune with Lizzie and Dante.

And finally, at a point when I was ready to give up, my niece Zo read the draft in one day and told me it was "everything."

Right or wrong, the word became my mantra in rewriting.

ABOUT THE AUTHOR

MARY BLY is a *New York Times* bestselling author under the name Eloisa James, and chair of the English department at Fordham University. She lives with her family in New York City but can sometimes be found in Paris or Italy. She is the mother of two and, in a particularly delicious irony for a romance writer, is married to a genuine Italian knight.

eloisajames.com
Facebook.com/eloisajames
Instagram: @eloisajamesbooks

ABOUT THE TYPE

This book was set in Sabon, a typeface designed by the well-known German typographer Jan Tschichold (1902–74). Sabon's design is based upon the original letterforms of sixteenth-century French type designer Claude Garamond and was created specifically to be used for three sources: foundry type for hand composition, Linotype, and Monotype. Tschichold named his typeface for the famous Frankfurt typefounder Jacques Sabon (c. 1520–80).